UNDER
THE CHARCOAL SKY

BY
JOHN H. CUNNINGHAM

OTHER BOOKS BY
JOHN H. CUNNINGHAM

BUCK REILLY ADVENTURE SERIES

Red Right Return
Green to Go
Crystal Blue
Second Chance Gold
Maroon Rising
Free Fall to Black
Silver Goodbye
White Knight
Indigo Abyss
Purple Deceiver
Buried in Orange

CO-WRITTEN WORKS

Graceless
Timeless

ALTERNATIVE ENDING HISTORIC FICTION

The Last Raft

Published by Greene Street, LLC

Print ISBN: 979-8-9869200-5-4
Electronic ISBN: 979-8-9869200-4-7

The events and characters in this book are fictitious. Certain real locations and public figures are mentioned, but have been used fictitiously, and all other characters and events in the book have been invented.

www.jhcunningham.com

This book is for Bill and Linda Klipp

Thank you for introducing us to the High Arctic and for the years of friendship. We look forward to more adventures together in the future.

"Him that's born to be hanged will never be drowned." Scottish Proverb

"I have brought you to the ring, now you must dance," Robert the Bruce

"In my end is my beginning," Mary Queen of Scots

"All men die, but not all men really live," William Wallace

SECTION 1:

PROBLEM CHILD

MAP OF SCOTLAND

1

FROM THE BACKSEAT OF THE BURGUNDY ROLLS ROYCE, I gazed out at the country estate known as Hampshire Manor, home to billionaire Sir Harry Greenbaum. Percy, Harry's long-term chauffeur, placed the massive vehicle into gear and we began to creep away from the main estate. Next to me, my ex-wife, Heather waved to Sir Harry standing under the portico as a light drizzle began to drop.

Heather turned back to face me, pumped her eyebrows once, and the grin that had bent the corners of her lips since she barged into the mansion's library, interrupting Sir Harry rocking my world, had not left her face since learning why. Sir Harry, an old family friend, and initial major investor at my former for-profit treasure hunting company, e-Antiquity, had just blown my mind with this long-buried information that would change my life in ways I couldn't yet begin to imagine, and I wasn't sure I wanted to.

"Why's she all googley-eyed?" Pastor Lenny Jackson asked.

Old friend, and Blue Heaven bartender turned pastor at Key West's Church of the Redeemer, Lenny had come to Europe at Heather's request to help me with a very touchy situation at the Formula 1 Italian Grand Prix, which had just wrapped up. I hadn't understood why Harry had made me a part of his successful bid to invest in the historic Williams Racing Team and had been too involved with trying to save his life, and that of thousands of others, until the dust had settled. When we came here to Hampshire Manor, everything had been clarified in shocking fashion.

From the front seat where he sat next to Percy, Ray Floyd, my partner at Key West-based Last Resort Charter and Salvage, leaned over the plush burgundy leather seat, and stared at me, Heather and Lenny.

"I've been wondering the same thing," Ray said.

I glanced out the side window to watch as the grounds passed slowly by. Deciduous trees had begun to blossom; the grass was turning from brown to green; and stands of green conifers stood resolute like weary soldiers.

Heather elbowed me in the gut.

"Well?" she said.

I turned my gaze forward and spied Percy watching us from his rearview mirror as the car crept along the gravel drive next to the huge lake to our left. He too seemed to sense there was something newsworthy pinching my lips tight, exacerbated by the inquiries from my friends.

I cleared my throat, which caused Heather to lean closer into me.

"Harry, ah, wanted to thank us all for helping him conclude his investment into the Williams Racing team, and for, ah, helping to defuse the situation there at the end of the race."

"Defuse is right, man," Lenny said. "We would'a been liquified had that shit not worked out."

"What else did Harry have to say?" Ray asked.

His expression was serious, and there'd been enough odd unanswered questions during our week in Monza that would have his detail-oriented mind yearning for answers.

"Ah, yeah, he did have more to say," I said.

My throat was suddenly dry, and I plucked a bottle of flat water from the holder on the door next to me, unscrewed the cap and took several small swigs so I wouldn't choke on the magnitude of what I was about to share.

"Jesus Christ our Lord and Savior," Lenny said. "Can you just spit it the hell out, please?"

The last swallow of water went down hard. Heather gave my leg a squeeze, prompting me to glance toward her. She gave me a slight nod as if to reassure me that it was okay.

With another deep breath, I tried to pull the right words together.

"Harry informed me that he, ah, is my biological father."

The car suddenly swerved from the gravel into the grass.

"Watch the road, Percy," I said. "Sorry, I know that's big news to you too."

"Biological … like he's your old man?" Lenny asked.

"Apparently," I said.

Heather squeezed my leg harder. Her white teeth peeked out from her pink lips.

Now turned totally sideways to face me, Lenny asked, "What'd you do a paternity test or something?"

"No, Lenny, he told me that of his own free will. And I was far more shocked than any of you are right now, believe me."

"You're the son of British business titan and billionaire Sir Harry Greenburg?" Ray asked. His jaw hung down and rested on the top of the seat.

"He's my birth father, yes. However, I was raised by Charles and Betty Reilly, and I'll always think of them as my parents."

"They dead man!" Lenny said. "Let's turn this jalopy around and go get to know your old man. Shit, Buck, you kidding me with all this?"

I felt the car slow as if Percy was taking a cue from Lenny.

"Please continue on to Cotswold Airport, Percy," I said.

"Lenny has a point," Heather's voice cooed in my ear.

"I need to process all this, guys. There'll be plenty of opportunity in the future to spend time with Harry—in fact, that's one of his wishes, that we get to know each other on a deeper basis, even though he's known me my entire life."

"He made you, Buck. I'd say he's known you longer than anyone," Ray said.

I stared him in the eye for a couple beats.

"In the biological sense, that's correct."

"We all gonna move here or what, man? Place is huge, we could live like kings!"

"You're ready to abandon your flock, Pastor Lenny?" I said.

"Shit yeah, for this place? You kidding me?"

"If Harry's your father," Ray said. "Then who's your mother?"

Percy's eyes were wide in the rearview mirror as he stared back at me.

"Apparently, a Scottish woman named Catherine," I said.

"Catherine what?" Heather asked.

Her question caused me to sigh. I'd been so bowled over with the news, I hadn't asked her maiden name. "She was Harry's wife. They hadn't been married long when I was conceived, and, ah, she died during my childbirth."

"Dammmmmnnn," Lenny said. "That's heavy, brother."

I exhaled loudly, now wishing I'd asked Harry more questions.

"If we knew her last name, we could find out more about her and her family," Heather said.

Silence filled the voluminous car interior as I pondered that thought.

"Did you know her, Percy?" I asked.

Percy cleared his throat repeatedly for several seconds. "No, I didn't even know Sir Harry had been married." He paused. "That must've been what, thirty-some years ago?"

"More like forty," I said.

"I have been with him for nearly thirty years now, so this had all, ah, transpired long before my time."

"Do you want to turn back?" Heather asked.

I held my hand up. "No, let's get to Cotswold Airport." I paused. "It's a lot for me to digest here."

"No shit," Lenny said.

"We fly back through Scotland on our way home," Ray said.

Heather leaned forward. "We could stop for a few days and research your family—"

"Easy now, everybody," I said.

I shifted my gaze out the window and watched the bucolic countryside pass by as we drove through the Cotswolds. My friend's reactions and questions sent confused signals between my head and heart as I tried to come to grips with the new reality of my life. My initial instinct was to suppress it all out of respect and caring for my parents—my adoptive parents—the Reillys, but as Lenny had insensitively pointed out, they had been deceased for many years now, so hurting them was not a rational concern.

Maybe I should ask Harry more about my, ah, Catherine. I had no idea when I'd be back in Scotland again, so if we wanted to spend a day researching her heritage, and mine, then this would be the best opportunity. I knew myself, and if I blew this chance, the unanswered questions would fester when I was back in Key West, and I'd regret not having learned more now.

Percy pulled the Rolls into the small and now-private Cotswold Airport. Big Mama, our 1951 Grumman Albatross, loomed over smaller single- and double-engine aircraft out on the tarmac. A couple of private jets were also there, including Harry's old G450, along with his new

G650 that we'd admired when we first arrived here.

My friends had been quiet, but I felt their eyes on me and could read disappointment in them. Not for themselves, but in me. I suspected they knew I'd regret not learning more while here and the news fresh.

Maybe I should at least call Harry before we left.

2

HEATHER, LENNY AND I SAT IN THE FLIGHT LOUNGE SIPPING TEA while Ray filed our flight plan back to Edinburgh. The trip from Key West to Europe had been a grueling three-day effort with multiple stops for fuel, supplies and bio-breaks. Heather had already stated that she was flying commercial from Edinburgh and offered to pay Lenny's way, since she'd flown him over.

"Hell yeah," Lenny said. "I ain't flying for three days in that old crate."

"Hey, don't insult Big Mama," I said.

"That's what she said, man, don't get all pissy with me."

Heather smiled. She'd always made her sentiments clear about flying in antique aircraft. She'd even gone as far as to say it would invalidate the life insurance rider her modeling agency carried on her if something happened.

"Whatever. Ray and I will handle it."

A mischievous smile bent Lenny's lips. "You're a billionaire now, man. Time to up your game, get yourself a PJ."

I turned sharply toward him. "No private jets, Lenny. Nothing's changed for me. Anyway, Harry didn't offer, and I don't want anything from him."

"Yeah, well, maybe not, but you're his only kin, and he ain't in the best shape, know what I'm saying?"

Heather studied my face. She had her own money, and our romance had rekindled long after I'd lost everything—including her as my wife—which back then I believed had been because she couldn't stand the thought of being broke or stuck with a has-been. So while I knew the old Heather would be salivating at the prospect of me potentially inheriting a large sum from Harry, the Heather I knew today was less motivated by money.

Or at least that's what I believed, but I'd see how these new circumstances played out.

"Let's please not go there, okay?"

A few minutes later, Ray returned with a serious expression on his face.

"All set?" I asked.

"Yeah, but given the hour, we'll need to spend tonight in Edinburgh. Tomorrow will be twelve hours of flying to Keflavik and then Narsarsuaq and then, well, you remember the rest from when we came over."

"Makes sense," I said.

"Lenny's and my flight departs tomorrow morning from Edinburgh," Heather said. "I have a couple of rooms booked at the Glasshouse in town, so we'll get another one for you, Ray."

Ray hovered over us, the serious expression still on his face.

"So you still want to fly out of here today?" Ray asked.

All eyes turned to me.

"Yes. We need to get back to Key West."

Lenny rolled his eyes.

"We're not going back to see Harry, okay?" I said.

"You said you wanted to spend more time together after he told you," Heather said.

I was starting to feel like a cornered animal. "That's true, but not until this has all settled in, and no offense, but not with an audience."

Lenny stood up fast. "Your future, man. I mean Redeemer could use some donation money for renovations, but if you got no interest in being rich, that's your business."

"Come on, Lenny," I said.

"Just saying what everybody else's thinking, man, you know."

"If your mother was from Edinburgh," Ray said. "It'd be a shame if we don't use our time there to see what we can learn." He must've seen the scowl form on my lips because he quickly held his hands up. "For your edification, that's all."

Ray had set our departure time for an hour from now, so everybody stared at their phones, responded to emails and texts, and in my case, did some research. My birth occurred long before that of the internet, but one nice thing about the United Kingdom was that medical records were open, so I was able to find information on Catherine Greenbaum. Her date of death was the same as my birthday, which gave me goosebumps. The cause of death simply, "complications in childbirth."

I'd hoped it would list her maiden name, but all that was there was the letter "C." "Catherine C. Greenbaum."

Would the C be her middle name or maiden name? I searched other details on Catherine Greenbaum and found nothing. I felt hot breath on my neck only to realize that Lenny was reading what I was searching over my shoulder.

"You mind?" I said.

"So I guess this means you're half Jewish?" he said.

My fingertips throbbed and I balled my fists. One of the nice things about being adopted was that when people started to pry into your past, you could just play the adopted card and they usually shut up. But now, with all this fresh data, it shined a light on my life and put me in the unfamiliar position of having to speculate on my past.

"Not that I care, but I remember Harry telling me previously that only his grandfather was Jewish. His predecessors were a mixed bag of ethnicities and religions."

Ray nodded his head. "So that would make you one-eighth Jewish."

"Guys, really, is this necessary?"

"Our boy's freaking out," Lenny said.

"No, you all are pissing me off." I licked my lips and stood up. "I'm going out to get some fresh air."

I left them seated in the plush leather chairs and pushed the glass door open that led to the tarmac where Big Mama was tied down. A couple of deep breaths later, I pulled the cell phone from my pocket. I hesitated, my index finger hovering over a speed-dial key, and after a long hesitation, I finally pressed it.

The long buzz of a European phone ringing sounded in my ear. After three buzzes, Harry answered.

"My dear boy, is everything okay?"

Harry had called me that for years, but I'd always assumed it was a colloquialism of his. It now took on a deeper meaning.

"Everything's fine, Harry. We're sitting here at the airport getting ready to fly to Edinburgh. Heather and Lenny will be flying commercial back to the States tomorrow."

"I don't imagine she'd wish to endure anything less than luxury for a flight of that duration."

My pause led to silence as I struggled for the right words to my question. I cleared my throat. "After we left, I realized I never asked you Catherine's last name."

Sudden static filled the line. Had Harry exhaled loudly or gagged?

"Greenbaum, of course."

"I mean her maiden name, Harry."

It was his turn to pause.

"I'd rather we don't go backwards, Buck. While I loved her dearly, and she gave you your life, Catherine ceased to be a factor in either of our lives after you were born."

"I understand that, but since we're stopping in Edinburgh, I thought it would be fun to maybe see where she grew up or lived."

More static on the line. Then nothing.

"Harry, are you there?"

"Yes, dear boy, I am, but I will not give you that information for reasons I'd rather not get into. And, I have an appointment now, so must ring off."

Click.

"Harry? Are you there? Harry?" I lowered my cell phone and saw that the screen was blank. "Son-of-a-bitch. Harry hung up on me."

3

I DIALED THE PHONE AGAIN. It rang and rang and rang until voicemail answered.

I hung up and then dialed it again.

I was chewing the corner of my lip as if I had marbles in my mouth but felt ready to spit nails. He accepted the call, but then hung up again.

"Goddammit, Harry."

My hands shook so much, I could hardly type the text: "You can't just drop this bomb and then ghost me. I'm going to call you again in five minutes. Either answer, or this is goodbye."

The phone was moist in my sweaty palm. I walked in circles outside on the tarmac as I seethed and grumbled to myself, as my mind spun. Two minutes went by, I circled some more, now around Big Mama. I conducted the preflight check, which helped to calm my heart, but when five minutes elapsed, I hit redial.

Harry answered mid-first ring. "I am sorry, dear boy. I'm sure you are fit to be tied, and under the circumstances, I certainly understand."

"That's good because I don't understand the issue here. Tell me my mother's maiden name and why you're so reluctant to do so."

Harry's deep breath rattled through the receiver, and I waited, but also reiterated to myself that if he didn't come clean, I was done with this situation.

"What I'm going to tell you comes with both dangerous and profound circumstances."

"Was she married—"

"Let me finish." Harry's voice boomed over the phone.

I stopped in my tracks. I'd never heard Harry raise his voice before, even when my company went bankrupt, and he'd lost $30 million.

"I say dangerous because her ancestry is quite unique, in fact, so unique that there have been echelons that have guarded its secrecy for nearly 700 years."

My jaw dropped open.

"What …?"

"And profound because the truth could change the course of history in Scotland and possibly the entire United Kingdom."

My eyes fluttered as his words sunk into my head.

"And to be perfectly frank, I'm quite upset with myself for putting you in this position—and danger—but after the events that transpired in Italy with the racing team, and you saving the day, I was afraid that, ah, well, the people I'm concerned about—meaning her family—would figure out the truth."

"I'm lost here, Harry."

"Of course you are. How could you not be?"

A long silence followed as I tried to abate the dizziness that his statements had caused, while he no doubt sought the words to explain them.

"All right, well, I will share her name and some details, but I ask that you leave it there and not pursue it further."

I leaned forward onto the balls of my feet. "Why?"

"Because it will put you in danger, dear boy. Grave danger."

"Sounds like a lot of melodrama to me."

Harry cleared his throat. "Suffice it to say that our marriage was most unpopular with Catherine's family. In fact, they blamed me for her death and vowed revenge."

"It's been nearly forty years, Harry. If they wanted revenge, wouldn't they have taken it by now?"

"They vowed revenge on you if you were ever discovered."

"Still, forty years is ancient history—"

"Not in Scotland, it isn't. As I said, this issue dates back nearly 700 years, Buck, so please don't be cavalier with what I'm about to tell you."

No matter what Harry said, my gut told me it was an old concern that likely died a few years after my birth mother had passed away.

"Understood, Harry. Now, what was her maiden name?"

"Promise me you won't do anything stupid, young man."

I rolled my eyes. "Me? Never."

Harry cleared his throat again, paused and I think I heard him lick his lips. "Her maiden name was Campbell."

"Campbell? That's not exactly a unique name, Harry. I can't imagine whatever 700-year issue you are referring to impacts all the Campbells—"

"I didn't say it impacts all the Campbells. What I said was it pertains to a very narrow line of the Campbell Clan. Let's leave it at that, and again, please do not engage in any research or overturn any stones that have been safely and purposefully entrenched for a long time."

"Understood, Harry."

An internal fuse suddenly popped, and I had a momentary lapse on how to refer to Harry. I had literally known him my entire life, present circumstances aside, as he remained close to my parents and was the principal angel investor in my former company.

"I won't do anything overt or obvious, but I would like to visit my, ah, mother's grave. Please tell me where she's buried."

"Please, Buck, I implore you, keep it simple. Act like a tourist. Don't draw any attention to yourself." Pause. "She was interred in Scotland at Dunfermline Abbey, north of Edinburgh."

"Perfect. Like I said, Heather and Lenny are flying commercial out of there tomorrow, and it's Ray's and my first stop toward home, so—"

"The name on her gravestone is not Greenbaum, however," Harry said. "It's Campbell. And, well, you know the date of her death, so ..."

I'd already confirmed it was the date of my birth.

"I'm sorry, Harry, that had to be hard for you at the funeral."

"I wasn't invited, dear boy."

Oh jeez, poor Harry.

"I was allowed to provide the headstone, but only if I used her maiden name, which I agreed to. So, remember, be low-key, and do nothing stupid. Agreed?"

I cleared my throat. "That's pretty condescending of you, but given your concerns, yes, we will cruise the cemetery, look at some other headstones, and then read Catherine's without attracting any attention."

"Call me immediately after you depart from there, please."

"Will do, Harry. Thank you." I paused. "I'm sorry if this stirs up a painful past for you, but I do appreciate you sharing her name."

We disconnected and I stared off into the Cotswolds to gather my thoughts. I made my way back toward the small private terminal and considered what I'd say to the gang. Truth was stranger than fiction, so I didn't feel it was appropriate to tell them any more than Catherine's last name, otherwise Ray's spastic colon may come unglued, Lenny's paranoia unhinged, and Heather's curiosity would be piqued beyond control.

Good grief. Drama upon drama.

Why did it seem like my entire life had been one long drama?

Heather stood inside and stared out the glass door at me as I approached.

Would she have seen me circling the plane with exasperation during my call with Harry?

Would she already be on high alert?

Watching her watch me set loose inadvertent butterflies in my stomach. Our reconciliation had been on for months now. She'd helped me out of a few jams in that time, and more than that, had also been impactful in solving some puzzles that steered us clear of serious ramifications that kept me out of jail for a stupid err in judgment related to a treasure I'd found in the Bahamas. More than that, though, she'd recently told me she loved me, again. The pain I'd experienced when we divorced years ago had never fully healed, and I'd never truly opened my heart to another woman since, even though I'd parented a child with my former colleague, Scarlet Roberson. The fact that Scarlet hadn't told me about young Charlie until he was ten years old didn't help assuage my wounded trust when it came to relationships either, even though I'd left her high and dry when I first met Heather.

The fact that Heather was every bit as stunning now, albeit in a more mature manner, as she was when we first met, and continued to grace fashion magazines around the world, made me question what she saw in me, but our mutual history was far deeper than just skin deep.

I shrugged and thought back to Harry.

If what he said was true, it sounded as if the drama that surrounded my Campbell roots went back 700 years.

The only question I had now was why?

4

RAY TOOK ON THE RESPONSIBILITIES OF PILOT IN COMMAND as we departed Cotswold Airport and vectored north toward Edinburgh Airport, also known as EDI. While Ray flew, I made arrangements for tie-down, fuel and a driver with the Fixed Base Operator, or FBO, at EDI. The flight time was only ninety minutes, which was welcome news to our passengers given the turbulence over northern England.

"I'm glad this is a short flight." Heather's voice sounded in all our headsets.

"No shit," Lenny said.

I glanced back and saw that Lenny had his four-point seat belt pulled tight and his eyes closed. He'd never liked flying in any of my old Grummans, regardless of the size. The Albatross was by far the largest, and the ride much smoother than Betty, my Widgeon, or the Beast, my Goose, but given that she was seventy-plus years old, she had none of the creature comforts commonplace on commercial jetliners.

The afternoon sun had begun its slide toward the western horizon like a half-court basketball shot just dropping off its peak in slow motion. It had been a hell of a day, starting with the visit to Hampshire Manor, Harry's mansion, where he'd shared his long-buried news. He had wanted us—me—to stay longer, but Big Mama required two pilots and Ray needed to get back to Key West, as did Lenny.

"This flight, and ours going back to Key West, would be a lot smoother and faster if we had something like a Gulfstream or Falcon jet at our disposal." Ray pumped his eyebrows.

His statement was something I would've expected more from Heather than Ray, but she kept quiet, even though everyone on board could hear his statement.

"Couldn't agree more," Lenny said. "That'd be chump change for your old man—"

"Don't go there, Lenny," I said. "My father is the man who raised me. Harry is, ah, a lot of things to me, including apparently being my

18

biological father, but we have a lot of catching up to do before that means anything more."

"You could ask if we could at least borrow his G450," Ray said.

"Come on, Ray, really?"

"I didn't say the G650, I mean the 450's pretty old—"

"Take it easy on Buck, guys," Heather said. "This news poleaxed him."

Her coming to my rescue and demonstration of patience pierced my heart. If she weren't strapped into her seat ten feet away, I'd hug her.

Big Mama jumped around through the turbulent skies, which shut everyone up, but also underscored how nice it would be to be flying in a modern jet. That set my mind wandering.

Ray and I would need a Type rating on a specific jet, if we ever got one, and I hadn't piloted a jet since before e-Antiquity crashed.

I sat up suddenly.

Stop it, Buck. Don't go there.

Ray checked in with Approach Control, and we were sequenced behind a Boeing 737-800 belonging to KLM that was also on final approach toward Runway 24, which was 8,386 feet of asphalt, the sole runway at EDI. Given that over 14,000,000 passengers flew through EDI annually, it was remarkable that there was only one runway.

The airfield's history went back to World War I when it was the northernmost British air defense base used by the Royal Flying Corps, which included Aircos, Bristol Scouts, Spads, and Sopwith Camels. During World War II, Royal Air Force (RAF) Fighter Command took over and expanded the short runway to 3,900 feet to accommodate Spitfire fighter planes that were critical to home defense during the Battle of Britain. After World War II ended, the airport was opened to commercial traffic and the runway was extended multiple times to its present length. So many of the older European airports had alternated between military and commercial uses between and after the major wars, we could only hope that such rotations would not be needed in the future.

Big Mama settled down with more grace than one would think possible given her bloated shape, and Ray guided us to the taxiway that led to the FBO in the southeast corner of the airport grounds. As we ran through the postflight checklist, I realized that I still hadn't told them about my call with Harry.

Inside the FBO, Ray coordinated with the concierge to have the fuel truck brought over to Big Mama so he could supervise it's refueling, and told them that we would be departing day after tomorrow at 7:00 a.m. Once that was completed, we met our taxi and loaded our luggage—Heather's mostly. I noticed a man dressed in dark colors wearing a newsboy hat and smoking a cigarette watching us from the sidewalk near the terminal entrance. It had taken me a while to get used to traveling with Heather as people always gawked at her.

We climbed into the taxi and then headed east toward downtown Edinburgh. During the flight, I'd looked up the location of Dunfermline Abbey and saw that it was due north of the airport just over the Queensferry Crossing Bridge. It would have been faster to go straight there, but everyone was exhausted, and I still needed to share enough of what Harry had said to provide the rationale of why I intended to go there tomorrow.

We settled into the traditional London-styled Hackney Cab, which while antiquated looking with its bulbous shape and styling, had plenty of room and a large boot that handled our luggage. I was surprised to find that the car was also electric, so clearly a new version of the classic design. Heather confirmed we were headed to the Glasshouse Hotel on Leith Street. Our driver chose the fastest route on Maybury Road.

I cleared my throat.

"You got something you want to say?" Lenny asked.

"What makes you say that?"

"You always clear your throat before you say something important," Lenny said.

"Or reveal bad news," Ray said.

Heather snickered.

"Didn't realize that." I paused. "But, yes, I was going to tell you that I called Harry from the Cotswold Airport before we left—"

Lenny held his hand out toward Ray, who dug into his pocket and dropped a $20 bill onto his open palm.

"Knew you would," Lenny said.

"You guys are jerks," I said. I glanced toward the driver. "Anyway, he told me my birth mother's maiden name. It's Campbell."

Harry had urged me to keep her name secret, but Campbell was such a common one, I wasn't worried about the driver.

"Like the soup?" Lenny said.

I ignored him. "And that she's buried here in Edinburgh."

"That's exciting," Heather said. "I want to see it."

"I'm out of here tomorrow morning," Lenny said. "My congregation needs me."

I bit my tongue on that one. "Maybe we'll have time to get out there today before it gets dark."

"Is Campbell a big family here?" Heather asked. "Like a clan or something?"

"Clan?" Lenny asked. "Definitely need to get my ass out of here."

"That's clan with a 'c' not a 'k'," I said.

"No kind of clan sounds good to me, man. Call it intuition," he said.

"Is the cemetery downtown?" Heather asked. "We could go after we check in."

"No, it's northwest of town. Looks like around a thirty-minute ride."

She squeezed my arm. "I'm excited for you. What else did Harry say?"

"Not much really. He, ah, was kind of uncomfortable about the whole thing. I guess her family disliked him so much they refused to allow her married name on the monument."

"Damn, that's cold," Lenny said. "You didn't ask him about using his jet?"

"No, Lenny," I said. "Apparently they were never supportive of the marriage and blamed me for her death."

"Ice cold," Lenny said.

"Maybe you could look them up while you're here," Heather said. "It could be cathartic for them to see how well you turned out."

Lenny laughed at that but then bit his lip.

"I don't think that's a good idea." I was going to use the phrase 'let sleeping dogs lie' but stopped myself. "No need to open old wounds. We'll just go visit the cemetery, walk around and then go."

We drove on in silence, with everyone staring out at the city as we passed through it. Edinburgh Castle was on a ridge high above the downtown, and it was lit up brilliantly even though the afternoon light was bright.

"Am I the only one who's been here before?" Heather asked.

None of us responded.

"The castle is incredible and impenetrable. You should go tour it tomorrow. I did a photo shoot for Chanel there a few years ago. Truly amazing."

"How the hell you get up there?" Lenny asked.

"There are bridges that go over the railroad tracks and take you to the Royal Mile where there are numerous shops, pubs, and restaurants that line the street as it climbs up toward the castle at the end of the road."

The taxi driver leaned over and spoke over his shoulder. "The Royal Tattoo is about to start, and the town is buzzing."

Confusion bent most of our faces and Heather again smiled. "The Tattoo is a festival and military parade with international bands and performance teams along the castle's esplanade. They set up large bleachers, and last I heard, over 100,000 people attend—"

"Two hundred twenty thousand people are estimated for this year, ma'am," the taxi driver said. "Starts tonight and runs every evening through Saturday and Sunday next. Traffic will be a mess—you're arriving just in time."

"It's so exciting," Heather said. "We should go."

"Sold out, I'm afraid, ma'am."

Heather grunted. If she wanted tickets, she'd no doubt find a way to get some.

"I need to eat something before I go anywhere," I said.

"Me too," Ray said.

"Me three," Lenny piped in.

"Fine, I'll speak with the concierge when we arrive. We can have a snack at the hotel before we go to the cemetery, and then go to the Tattoo tonight if I can get us tickets," Heather said.

The taxi then stopped in front of an old gray church.

"Here we are, the Glasshouse Hotel," the driver said.

"A church?" Lenny said.

"Make you homesick?" I said.

"Don't let the exterior of the former church fool you," Heather said. "The inside was expanded and wonderfully redeveloped. Each room is a suite named after a famous single malt scotch, with a carafe of the namesake in the room."

"Perfect," Ray said. "I'm thirsty too."

The taxi driver placed our bags on the curb and while I trusted Heather's taste implicitly, my first impression was that we were going to be staying in an old monastery. She walked ahead to check in while we gathered the luggage and dragged it across the wide sidewalk toward the front door where a bellman greeted us and relieved us of the bags.

After a few minutes of working with the front desk, Heather joined us and handed Ray his key. "You're in the Glenmorangie suite."

"My favorite," Ray said.

"And Lenny, you're in the Oban suite."

"Sounds like something out of *Star Wars*," he said.

"Try some from your snifter. Super smoky tasting," Ray said.

We followed the bellman to the elevator, and all got off on the third floor.

At the Oban suite, the bellman dropped Lenny's bag.

"I'll meet you at the restaurant," Lenny said.

We dropped Ray and then walked all the way to the end of the hall and arrived at The Macallan suite. Inside, the room was spacious and contemporary. Heather did a pirouette in the middle of the room while the bellman retrieved her multiple bags.

"This is the same room I stayed in last time I was here," she said.

I glanced at the bed. Large with a thick, fluffy white duvet and a pile of pillows. "I hope you were alone."

A giggle was her reply.

"I want to go down and ask the concierge if he knows where the cemetery is and have him arrange a car to take us there," I said.

"I'll freshen up and meet you in the restaurant."

I started to walk toward the door when I felt her hand grab my arm. I swung around and she gave me a sultry look. "Tonight we break this room in right."

My half-smile didn't deter her. She knew me well enough to know my mind was elsewhere, so didn't push it. And I knew she wasn't kidding.

"It's a date."

5

THE CONCIERGE WAS IN THE BACK CORNER OF THE OPEN LOBBY. The woman behind the counter was mid-forties and dressed professionally, her salt and pepper hair cut short. She must've seen me coming as she offered a crooked smile as I approached.

"I just checked in and we're only here for a couple days."

"Here for the Tattoo?" she said.

"Not specifically, but ah, my girlfriend will come speak to you about that. I'm here to visit the grave of a relative and wanted to see if you can look up the cemetery and arrange a car for us."

"Certainly. What's the name of the cemetery?"

"It's at Dunfermline Abbey—"

The woman's shoulders sunk forward, and she spat a laugh.

"Royalty, are we?"

"Excuse me?"

"Dunfermline Palace was a favorite residence of Scottish monarchs and royalty."

"I just need the abbey."

"Pretty much one and the same. The abbey was attached to the palace, which is now a ruin. The cemetery surrounds the abbey and is also the eternal resting place of Scottish kings, queens, noblemen and ladies, as well as other important people from history. It's the most important cemetery in Scotland." She paused. "What did you same your name was?"

My heart double-clutched, Harry's admonition ringing in my ears. Nobody would know my name though.

"Buck Reilly. I'm in The Macallan suite."

"Irish then. Not too many Irishmen buried at Dunfermline." She pulled out a tourist map and ran her finger along the route to cross a body of water and then to the north where the town of Dunfermline was located. "Will take about thirty minutes."

I told her we were going to have lunch at the hotel and then head over. She said lunch consisted of afternoon tea offered at the Snug or on the rooftop bar, and that she'd have a car waiting for us. I tipped her twenty euros, and realized I needed to convert some cash to Scottish pounds. I walked to the elevator with my head spinning.

Why was my birth mother buried with Scottish royalty at the most important cemetery in the country?

The elevator opened to the third-floor corridor flanked with mirrors, and I walked forward to a maître d' standing at a podium at the centrally located equivalent to an upstairs lobby bar. I saw Ray and Lenny at a table so nodded to the maître d' and walked past her. Ray had a beer in front of him, and Lenny a Coke.

"This place is fancy," Lenny said. "Afternoon tea." He lifted his Coke with his pinkie finger extended.

"Would you expect any less from Heather?"

She entered the Snug with a flourish, and like every other time I'd ever met her anywhere, I watched as several conversations stopped and heads turned to watch her enter. Men and women alike whispered to their dining companions and nodded her way. As a successful model who had repeatedly graced every top fashion magazine cover for a couple of decades now, it was impossible for Heather to go anywhere without being recognized. She, however, focused on us and the smile in her eyes matched the one on her lips.

I cringed because I knew the news of where Catherine was buried would fan the fire of excitement that had begun when everyone learned my birth father was billionaire Harry Greenbaum, and now that my mother must have some high-level family connection to Scottish nobility. But I had to share some information before we got to the cemetery, so they didn't make a scene once there.

Lovely.

We ordered food from a waitress, which came quickly. Everyone was starving, so other than describing their rooms, the focus was on devouring our fish and chips, biscuits and skinny little sandwiches.

"I called the concierge and she's working on getting us tickets to the Royal Tattoo tonight," Heather said. "Was she helpful? Did she know the cemetery?"

I cleared my throat and Lenny raised his eyebrows.

"Yes, she was, and there's a car waiting for us."

Heather glanced at me over her teacup as she was about to take a sip. "I've done a fair amount of traveling around Scotland in the past," Heather said. "What's it called? Maybe I'll recognize it."

I concentrated on *not* clearing my throat. "Dunfermline Abbey—"

Heather gagged and spat her tea across the table—

"Goddamn!" Lenny jumped up.

I held my breath and dabbed my shirt with the white napkin.

"Did I miss something?" Ray said.

"Did you say Dunfermline Abbey? Buck, really?"

I nodded my head slowly. "Don't go crazy here, Heather."

"Crazy? That's where Robert the Bruce is buried. Along with—"

"Who's the guy with two first names?" Lenny asked.

"Sorry, that would be Robert I, the King of Scotland back in the twelfth century." Heather said. "If you ever saw the movie *Braveheart*, he was the guy who coordinated the overthrow of the British monarchy with William Wallace."

"Mel Gibson?" Ray asked.

"He was William Wallace. I forget who played Robert the Bruce," Heather said.

I'd looked up the abbey before lunch. "According to Find A Grave, 700 people are interred there, so don't let your minds run wild."

"I don't know, Buck, but last time I was at Dunfermline, I don't think there'd been anyone buried there for seventy-plus years," Heather said.

"Whatever. Let's just go there and see what we find. Okay?" I cleared my throat. "I don't want to attract any attention, so no matter what we find, please just act like tourists, all right?"

Heather stood abruptly. "Got it, let's go. I'm dying to see what we find."

Lenny stuffed his mouth with the remaining fish and chips, and we all set off for the elevator. Our car waited out front, as promised, and as the others got in, I had a sensation of being watched, so I glanced around. Nothing was—wait—there was a man dressed in dark clothing wearing a newsboy hat walking up the sidewalk across the street. I had a feeling I'd seen him before, but couldn't place where, so erased it as jitters caused by the pending trip to visit my natural mother's grave.

That thought ricocheted around my skull as we drove through Edinburgh and until the Firth train bridge was visible crossing the water.

"Cool-looking bridge," Ray said. "What body of water is that?"

"That's the Firth of Forth, which goes out to the North Sea," the driver said.

Lenny's eyes narrowed and he whispered to Heather, "Dude got a lisp?"

Heather smiled. "Firth is a Scottish word for estuary or bay, and the river itself is the river Forth."

"Fifth or Forth, forth or fifth, firth or *thecond*," Lenny said. "Can't say that shit three times fast."

We turned onto the car bridge that ran parallel to the Forth Bridge, and I felt my chest tighten. Anxiety had me rubbing my knuckles into my sweaty palm. I'd never spent a lot of time thinking about my birth parents, primarily because I was raised by my wonderful adoptive parents. My brother, however, turned out to be psychopath, but I didn't know that until many years after the death of my parents. When Harry dropped the bomb on me, it blew my disinterest to smithereens, and his caution over sharing even my birth mother's maiden name had only heightened my curiosity.

I would have been fine never knowing the identities of my birth parents, and doubt whether I would have ever sought them out, but with the information thrust into my face, and given the circumstances of knowing Harry my entire life and him having been the principal investor behind my company, I had to know more.

Here and now, approaching one of the most important cemeteries in Scotland, the burial place of kings and queens and other people important to history here, along with my mother, added a weight to the discovery. Was it a weight, or was it pure dread? Either way, my gut told me I was on the brink of a monumental discovery that would change my life forever.

The question was, would it change my life for the good, or the bad?

Ray held up his phone. "Okay, guys, I've been doing some research on the cemetery. The palace is long gone, and the abbey dates back to the early 1100s, but part of it—the great tower—was sacked in 1560 during the Scottish Reformation. It was rebuilt in the early 1800s. That's where they found the bones belonging to Robert the Bruce. He's now buried inside the newer part of the abbey in a bronze sarcophagus."

"Shit's old, man," Lenny said. "Bones? Ugh."

"The whole property looks pretty small, really," Ray said. "On the north side of the abbey is the old cemetery that was closed to additional burials in 1896. The cemetery on the south side came into use in 1823 and was used until the mid-20th century." Ray looked up at us. "That's more than fifty years ago."

"Damn, Buck. How could your momma be buried here?" Lenny said. "You don't look a day older than forty."

"Hell if I know. She should have been buried here in 1984 or 1985 if they waited for some reason," I said.

"Unless she was cremated," Heather said.

"We'll find the sexton. They usually have a map showing where all the graves are located," I said.

Our driver took us along Queensferry Road, through several traffic circles, past a golf course, and when we crossed over the train tracks, we turned left on Nethertown Broad Road, now inside the town of Dunfermline. Several brown signs indicated that the abbey was just ahead. We took a few more turns and the ride became a bit rougher. The streets here were made of brick. To our left was a vast wooded area that led steeply downward.

"What's this green space here?" I asked.

"That is the Tower Burn, which among other things contains Pittencrieff Park," the driver said. "The whole area was dedicated to Dunfermline by Andrew Carnegie in 1903. He was from here, if you didn't know."

"Too bad *he* wasn't your daddy," Lenny said.

I ignored his wisecrack.

Moments later, the abbey rose over the trees, and I felt the air rush from my lungs. It was a sensation I hadn't experienced since the last time I'd made a significant archeological find, but this was clearly different. The driver pulled up to a wrought iron gate, that was open. It was the newest part of the abbey, which as Ray had reported, was 200 years old. It looked older.

The stone was faded, had eroded in several areas, and was discolored.

A dozen steps led up to the knoll where a massive pair of wood doors were framed by five layers of soldier-course stone that formed an arch over top of Dunfermline Abbey's entrance. Three large arched window openings, one on each side of the doors, and one above it, included multiple smaller windows within them, and all were protected by steel mesh. The overall architecture was choppy and disproportionate, which surprised me given the historical significance of the site.

We climbed out, thanked the driver, and I followed Heather up the steps.

My heart rate accelerated, and my breathing was labored.

It was time to finally meet my mother, or at least pay her respects.

6

"THE SIGN SAYS THAT THE ABBEY CLOSES IN AN HOUR," Heather said.

I shook my head to try and break out of the funk I'd fallen into. I breathed deeply and glanced around to center myself. The sun peeked out intermittently from gray clouds, the grass around the abbey was a bright green, a small number of people strolled the grounds, stopping occasionally to glance at headstones, and my friends stood in front of the abbey doors watching me and waiting.

"You all right, man?" Lenny asked. "Want me to say a prayer here about all this?"

I bit my lip. Lenny's transition from being a troubled youth, to Blue Heaven bartender, to political protégé of his uncle, Pastor Willy Peebles, had been derailed when Willy died of COVID a few years ago. His dying wish—command, really—was that Lenny abandon politics and take his place as the pastor of the Church of the Redeemer in Bahama Village. I still hadn't gotten used to his new role, even though the transition was long past. Maybe it was because his vocabulary was more Kevin Hart than Billy Graham, but I did respect the efforts Lenny had made to fulfill Willy's dying wishes.

"I'm okay, Lenny. Thanks, though. Let's go inside and find the sexton."

I took the lead through the open door and was surprised at what I found. Unlike so many old churches that were too often relatively dark inside, this one was bright with white walls, columns and brilliant light pouring through the colorful stained glass. It was also clearly an active church as there were bibles and hymnbooks in the pews, with fresh flowers on the altar. There was a simplicity to it that provided an immediate sense of scale and comfort compared to the large cathedrals throughout Europe. Several people milled around the transept up on the right side of the altar.

"That must be where Robert the Bruce is buried," I said.

30

"His heart was removed after his death, per his wishes to have it transported to the Holy Land," Ray said. "Didn't make it though as the man he charged with that responsibility was killed in a skirmish with the Moors."

"Nasty. Nothing but bones," Lenny said.

I spotted an official-looking gentleman who was wearing a red vest and carrying a clipboard. "You all wait here," I said.

I walked up the center of the nave and then turned left at the transept, away from what I confirmed was Robert the Bruce's altar and sarcophagus built into the floor. I went straight to the man riffling through pages on his clipboard.

"Excuse me, are you the sexton?"

His frown turned to a smile as he lifted his eyebrows wide. "Yes, yes, I am. How may I be of service?"

"My friends and I are touring the area and have been blown away by the beauty of the abbey and grounds," I said.

The man nodded proudly.

"I was wondering if you had a list of all the gravesites here, and who was buried where?"

His smile slid back toward a frown. "No, no, sorry. Several of the graves are so old that any markings have long ago vanished. We do have signs and information on many of the Royals who are interred here—"

"Not a problem, we can look around and read all of those." I paused. "I am curious about any newer burials that have occurred here though."

"Yes, well, the North Cemetery was closed in the 1800s once the southern portion opened. That's where the most recent burials have occurred, until the Halbe Road Cemetery opened in 1863, that is. After that, community burials were directed there."

I bit the side of my lip. I wanted to keep this as conversational as possible.

"I studied the Find a Grave website and saw that there had been some more recent burials in the 1950s and into the mid-1980s."

His expression became more inscrutable. "Yes, yes, there were a few." He paused. "Is there one in particular you're seeking?"

I took in a slow breath. "As a matter of fact, yes. A woman named Catherine Campbell was buried here, should have been around 1984 or

'85."

I held my breath and kept my eyes on his. He didn't flinch but hesitated a few seconds.

"Ahh, yes, yes, Catherine Campbell." He cleared his throat—was that a similar tell to my habit of doing that? "I don't recall that anyone has ever come to visit her grave before." He licked his lips. "She was the very last person buried here at the abbey. Ever."

"Last one, huh. Wonder why the family placed her here instead of the other cemetery you mentioned."

"Special circumstances, I believe."

"Can you direct me to where her grave is?"

He again licked his lips. "I could. It's in the North Cemetery—"

"I thought you said that the North Cemetery was closed in the 1800s? Why was she buried there?"

He again cleared his throat. "As I said, special circumstances. Come, I'll show you."

I followed the man down the nave toward the front door. Heather and the guys watched me, and I crooked my finger for her to follow me but held my palm up to the others.

The sexton walked a steady pace, and we were quickly back out the front door. He turned to the left and followed a gravel path that abutted the abbey. Many old gravestones poked up from the green grass. Most were flat, but several were low-slung with some information etched into the top—the majority of which were weathered and illegible, and some markers were taller and composed of rectangular, triangular, or cross shapes.

Heather caught up to me, but the sexton had yet to turn back around until we arrived at what I assumed was the older part of the church, given the different and even more decayed architecture. The foliage of several mature trees provided a colorful canopy over this area of the cemetery, and the sexton turned and walked over the grass to the trees. He was careful to walk in front of headstones to not trample over the graves themselves.

Almost exactly in the middle, was a newer-looking stone, compared to the others around it. My heart fluttered when I saw the name Catherine Campbell etched into marble. There was no date of birth or death, only small figurines in relief or carved into the stone.

"Here you—oh—I didn't see you join us, young lady."

His smile returned upon seeing Heather.

"I was admiring the stained glass when I saw you walking Bu—back out the door."

I'd turned my head to face her so the sexton couldn't see my expression, and she spotted me bugging my eyes just as she was about to blurt my name out.

"That looks like it." My loud voice made him wince. "No dates or other information though, I see."

"That's not unusual," he said.

Now that we'd come this far, I felt emboldened. "You'd mentioned special circumstances before. Can you share what they were?"

The man cleared his throat again, but now shuffled his feet and glanced around as if he was worried someone might be listening. "Um, well, you see, Ms. Campbell is situated here amongst several of the Stewart clan—she's surrounded, in fact."

"Stewart? Is there something special about them, or why she's in the middle of them?"

The man exhaled hard and puckered his lips a moment, before he shrugged. "Robert I, or Robert the Bruce, as you may know him, was the king of Scotland. He had a daughter named Marjorie. She married Walter Stewart, and their son, Robert II was later king as well."

My mouth had run dry, and I could think of nothing to say, so just waited.

A pedantic look now twisted his lips, no doubt from the rube American's lack of Scottish history.

"Robert II marked the beginning of the S-t-e-w-a-r-t and S-t-u-a-r-t kings. Who even today represent the greatest number of monarchs throughout Europe. How Ms. Campbell was related to the Stewarts, I cannot say, but the special circumstances must have come very high up for her to have been placed here."

Silence fell between us. The sound of dry leaves rustled in the wind that blew over the cemetery. Heather poked me in the back.

"Wow," I said.

The man offered a sanguine smile. "Wow, indeed."

Heather stepped around me. "Thank you so much for showing us her grave, and for the history lesson. So fascinating."

He studied us for a moment and then nodded back toward the abbey. "If you'll excuse me then, we'll be closing soon. I must tend to my duties."

I cleared my throat. "Of course, thank you again."

The man hurried back over the grass to the path, and without looking back, turned the corner around the front of the church.

"Holy shit," Heather said.

"Yeah," I managed.

I bent down on my knee, drew in a deep breath and hovered over my birth mother's grave. I never thought I'd even know the identity of my birth parents, so to be here now was beyond surreal. The fact that she was buried amidst royalty swirled in my head and—I dropped a hand onto her stone—dizzy and light-headed. Memories of my adoptive parents caused my eyes to flutter, and I suddenly felt untethered, like a balloon that slipped from a young boy's grasp and floated skyward.

The stone was cold to the touch. I ran my fingers along the letters that comprised her name, cut sharply into the rock. There were flowers—what kind I wasn't sure—carved into the stone, and in the lower right corner, was a skull with what appeared like a four-leaf clover above it. The skull was the only detail on the stone that was in relief, and it stood maybe a quarter inch above the surface. Must be some kind of *memento mori.*

I felt Heather's hand on my shoulder. "Are you okay?"

A moment passed as I continued to study the stone. I pulled my phone out of my pocket and took a photo of it, and then stood up.

"Yeah, pretty weird feeling though."

"I'm sure," she said. "Not to mention the circumstances. Why didn't you want me to mention your name?"

"Glad you picked up on my cue. Harry would only tell me her name if I promised not to bring attention to myself."

"What's Harry concerned about?"

I shook my head. "He said the family had blamed me for her death and vowed revenge. They'd opposed him marrying Catherine in the first place, and as I said before, when she died, refused to allow her married name on the stone."

"How awful for him." She wrapped her arm around my waist. "I'm sorry."

"Yeah, it's all pretty strange."

We stood for another moment gazing down at her grave, and then glanced at the Stewart graves around her. One was Robert Stewart who had died in 1420. Others appeared more recent, and a couple were dated in the early 1880s.

A chill ran through me, and I turned back toward the abbey.

"Let's get out of—"

What I saw back at the front of the abbey stopped me in my tracks. Lenny and Ray were outside talking to a man and then pointed toward me and Heather. The man, who was dressed in dark clothing and wearing a newsboy hat, turned toward us and waved.

My gut tightened.

What the hell?

The man walked over with urgency, a smile on his face. I stood, frozen, questions spun through my head about where else I had seen him. The airport? Near the hotel?

He spoke before he reached us. "You're Buck Reilly, the bloke who saved the Formula 1 race in Monza, right? Saw you on the telly, was sure it was you—and the other man, the black one." He nodded back toward Lenny, who along with Ray had followed him. "He was there too."

"Yeah, that was, ah, quite an event," I said.

"Oh, and you're Heather Drake, the model," he said.

She smiled at him but could obviously sense my apprehension because she squeezed my hand. "And you are?"

"I'm nobody, really. Name's Roger. You here on holiday?"

"Something like that," I said. "Just taking in some local sights."

"None more important to Scottish heritage than Dunfermline Abbey," he said. "Some would say it's the cradle of our independence. A lot of critical history here."

The man's eyes were also dark, and even though his mouth smiled when he spoke, his posture was almost a fighting stance with his shoulders back and his feet set perpendicular to one another.

"You find your mother's grave?" Lenny said.

My heart dropped when I saw Roger's eyes narrow.

"Your mother's buried here?"

"No, she's at, ah, the other cemetery here in Dunfermline. We're just sightseeing here."

"Scottish lad then, huh? Reilly's typically Irish," he said.

"Okay, well, nice to meet you," I said. I turned to others. "Let's get back to town."

The man leaned closer. "Can I give you a lift? Least I could do for you saving all those lives at the race."

I held my palm up. "No, thank you, but we have a couple of stops to make along the way."

"Right, well, I imagine you'll be off to America soon. Key West, isn't it? Remember hearing that on the news."

I swallowed.

"That's right. You take care now. Let's go, guys."

I walked across the grass toward the front of the Abbey. The others followed. When I reached the front, I glanced back and saw Roger, or whatever his name really was, standing at the gravesite watching us. He held a cellphone to his ear and his expression reminded me of a cheetah circling for a kill.

I just hoped I wasn't the prey.

7

THE TRIP BACK TO THE GLASSHOUSE HOTEL WAS QUIET, largely because I wasn't in the mood to talk. I told Ray and Lenny about my mother's grave, whom she was surrounded by, and showed them the picture of the headstone.

"So it turns out you really may be King Buck after all," Lenny said.

"Hardly," I said. "And regardless of Catherine's family line, which I intend to research more fully, some of the Stewarts she was buried around date back 700 years. I'm so far removed from them, I can't imagine there would be but a fraction of shared DNA at this point."

"You could always do one of those genealogy tests that shows where you're from and connects you with any other blood relatives who had also signed up," Heather said.

"Based on Harry's admonitions, that might not be such a good idea."

"What do you mean, 'Harry's admonitions'?" Ray asked.

Without getting into too much detail, I again explained the Campbells had blamed me for Catherine's death and Harry for marrying her, and that they had apparently vowed revenge.

"Say what?" Lenny said.

"It was forty years ago, guys. Don't get your panties in a bunch."

"You think that guy, Roger, is associated with any of that?" Heather asked.

"Something was fishy about that guy," I said. "But maybe he really did just recognize us from the Monza race. Lenny and I were broadcast all over the world and referred to as heroes."

The taxi turned on Leith Road and then pulled to a stop in front of the Glasshouse.

"I'm going to do some research," I said. "Let's meet for cocktails and dinner in an hour."

"I'll check on the tickets for the Tattoo if you're still interested," Heather said.

Nobody responded, but I thought it could be as good of a place as any to avoid Roger if he showed up again. We entered the elevator, and on the third floor, all headed to our rooms. Once inside ours, I lay face-up on the bed, my head still spinning over the day's events.

Heather had poured us each a dram of The Macallan single malt scotch from the decanter. She handed me one and sat next to me on the bed. We clinked glasses and I took a sip of the brown liquor and thought it tasted like raisins and rose water.

"Quite the day," she said. "How are you feeling?"

"Overwhelmed." I paused but knew I should share my greatest concern with her. "There's something about that guy at the cemetery, Roger."

"Aside from being creepy?"

"I saw him at the airport here, and pretty sure I saw him outside the hotel, too."

"If he's watching us, how could he have known we were flying into Edinburgh today?" Heather asked. "We didn't have to go through customs, so even if your name was on a watch list, how would they know we were here?"

"Maybe they know about Last Resort and our planes? Based on what the sexton said, the Campbells are super connected throughout the continent. If they really were intent on some kind of strange vengeance, then they'd have the resources to monitor all sorts of things."

She took another sip of her scotch, put the glass on the nightstand, and then rubbed her hand across my chest and down to my waist where she took hold of my belt buckle.

"What are you doing?" I asked.

"Taking your mind off your worries."

I grabbed her hand as she took hold of my zipper. While some of her lusty therapy could be useful right now, I wanted to research more about the Campbell clan before dinner.

"Raincheck until later, okay?"

She pulled her hand away with a brief pout before retrieving her iPad from her mammoth-sized Prada bag. "Fine. I'll do research then."

I used the browser on my phone and searched Campbell + Scotland.

The first thing I saw was the clan crest, which was a boar's head with long tusks.

"Says here that Clan Campbell is a Highland Scottish clan and is historically one of the largest and most powerful of the clans," I said.

"I'm seeing the same thing."

"Not sure what that matters though."

"Says here that during the wars of Scottish independence that the family of Colin Campbell was a staunch supporter of King Robert the Bruce and that they fought beside him at the Battle of Bannockburn," Heather said.

"Again, that was over 700 years ago," I said. "Is it a coincidence that Catherine and Robert the Bruce are both buried at Dunfermline Abbey? It's not like the cemetery's huge."

"I didn't see any other Campbells there either, did you?"

"I searched Find a Grave and there's only one other Campbell buried there—Helen Erskine Campbell. She was buried in 1855."

"What about the Stewarts? Why would Catherine be buried amongst them?" Heather asked.

I searched the two clans and found an interesting article in *The National.*

"The opening line of this article says there can be no doubt that after the Stewarts, the mightiest and most influential of the Highland clans for centuries past has been Clan Campbell."

"I'll bet there's been inter-marriage between the two clans," Heather said. "The best way to mitigate a competitor is to make them part of your family."

I pointed to my phone. "Descendants of Sir Duncan Campbell, and his wife Lady Marjorie Stewart, are descendants of Robert the Bruce, the King of Scots, and Robert II Stewart, a later King of Scots"

"I knew it," Heather said. "So that at least partially explains why Catherine is surrounded by Stewarts, but not why they would be seeking revenge for her dying during childbirth."

Heather refilled our glasses with more scotch.

"I don't know which is more exciting, that you may be related to Scottish and British royalty through the Campbell/Stewart connection, or that you're the biological son of a billionaire."

I sniffed the scotch, then lowered the glass. "Neither matter, Heather. In fact, per Harry's request, the Campbell/Stewart information needs to stay buried, and I have no interest in his billions."

"But you're his sole heir—"

"I've been rich before, it didn't suit me. In fact, it caused me to lose everything, including you. Been there, done that."

"I've earned my own wealth," she said. "The trick is to maintain a balance."

I climbed off the bed. "I'm not having this discussion. I'm going to take a shower before dinner."

I pulled my shirt off and dropped my pants.

Heather glanced at her Cartier watch. "We still have thirty minutes. I'll shower with you."

"Shower, Heather, okay?"

"We're going to be all wet." She swung her hair away from her face. "I'll call in that raincheck early." She then pulled her top off over her head, snapped her bra with one deft move and kicked off her pants.

I couldn't help but smile. She reciprocated and followed me into the bathroom, her hands already grabbing me from behind ...

8

THE RESTAURANT WAS FULL, BUT LENNY AND RAY HAD A TABLE in the center of the room. Heather and I were late, as usual, and as she walked ahead of me, I could see people turn to check her out. Recognition led to several smiles. The reality was that I liked Heather getting attention because it kept people's focus off me. I'd had more attention than I had ever wanted between the rise and fall of e-Antiquity, subsequent news stories related to the various investigations, some of my salvage and rescue operations, and most recently the issues around the Formula 1 race in Monza. Heather loved the attention, I loathed it.

Lenny pumped his eyebrows when he saw us walk in, and Ray, on the other hand, had on a very serious expression.

"Everybody get some rest?" I asked.

"Shit, I walked up to that Royal Mile," Lenny said. "Crazy up there with this "tattoo" thing."

"The concierge emailed me and got us tickets for tonight, if you guys are interested."

"What's up, Ray? You look concerned."

He shuffled in his seat. "I'm not concerned, but I did some research on the Campbells, Stewarts, and Robert the Bruce while in my room."

"And?" I said.

"Like the sexton said, the collective families were and still are very influential in Scotland and throughout Europe. Nearly every royal family is connected to one or more of those families, in some form or another."

"King Buck," Lenny said. "Sure does have a nice ring to it."

Heather grimaced after seeing the look on my face.

"I'd say your days of slumming in the La Concha are numbered," Lenny said.

The waiter arrived, read us some specials, and we ordered drinks. I'd spotted the restroom down the hall on the way in, so I stood up and excused myself. My mind was still bent around the day's discoveries, which Lenny had taken great joy in reminding me of.

41

Out of the corner of my eye, I saw someone come from the opposite direction down the corridor, and then follow me into the bathroom. I didn't pay him any attention as I squared off in front of the urinal, but before I could lower my fly, I felt something sharp against my back—

An arm suddenly swung around my neck and pulled me back to what I was sure was a knife pressed into my ribcage.

"You should've stayed away from here," a husky voice whispered in my ear.

"Wait, what—?"

"Forget not," the man said.

He pulled back on my neck—I jammed an elbow backward just as the knife penetrated my skin—the man's arm swung wide—the knife clattered across the tile floor.

I spun around expecting Roger, but it was another man, younger, unshaven and six inches shorter than me. His eyes had gone wide at the loss of his weapon and my spin—I kicked him hard in the knee, further catching him off guard—he took a step back and I lunged toward him with balled fists ready to strike—

The door opened and an elderly man walked in with what must've been his young grandson. My assailant dashed out the now-open door as the man and the boy hesitated in front of me, startled, but blocking my way.

I scurried around them and ran into the hall, but the assailant was gone. Stairs, two elevators and multiple other doors were to the left and the restaurant was to the right. I turned to the restaurant and hurried inside to make sure Heather and the guys were okay.

"Sir!" the maître d' yelled after me as I ran past her.

My friends were sipping drinks and looked oblivious, so I stopped and turned to the maître-d. My heart pounded, and my expression must've been on attack mode, because she took a step back.

"Yes?" I said.

"Ah, your back's bleeding." She frowned. "Quite a bit, actually."

I felt backward and when I looked at my palm, sure enough, it was smeared in blood.

"Damn, ah, thank you. I, ah, slipped in the bathroom."

When I turned to my friends, their mouths all hung open. Heather jumped up.

"Are you all right?!"

She took her napkin and held it up to my back. All conversation had stopped in the restaurant, and all eyes were on us.

"We need to get out of here," I said.

I turned toward the door, and the others followed me.

Son-of-a-bitch!

Once in the corridor, Heather caught up and again applied pressure to my wound.

"The hell happened, man?" Lenny said.

"Let's get to my room."

Ray pointed up to the right. "The stairs are there."

We hurried up the three flights of stairs, me in the lead and Heather, in heels, struggled to keep up.

"You're dripping blood everywhere," she said. "Can you slow down?"

I ignored her and took the stairs two at a time.

At the third floor, we exited into the corridor that was thankfully close to my suite. Heather hurried ahead with her card key, and we dashed inside. The door closed with a slam.

"Lock it," I said.

Ray did so and then they turned to me as I pulled my shirt over my head.

"Oh my," Heather said. "You need stitches—what happened?"

"No doctors," I said.

"What the hell, man?" Lenny said.

"I have some Band-Aids in my bag," Heather said. "I'll try to butterfly it closed."

She zipped open her bag and I caught my breath.

"I was jumped in the men's room."

"That'll go in my Trip Advisor review," Ray said.

"Guy had a knife in my back and tried to stab me, but I got away. Someone came in and startled him so he bolted."

"Did he try to rob you?" Ray asked. "You think it was random?"

"No, he knew who I was. Said I should have stayed away."

"That's it?" Heather asked.

"There was something else he said, 'afraid not', or something like that."

Heather was busy wiping blood off my back with one hand and

applying pressure to the wound with the other.

"'Afraid not' about what?" Ray asked.

"Nothing, it was just some random statement." I paused. "Maybe it wasn't 'afraid not.' Could've been 'forget not'."

"I'm calling the police," Heather said.

"No!" I said.

She jumped at the volume of my voice.

"No police. Whatever the hell's going on, we need to get our arms around it to determine who we can trust," I said. "How bad's the cut?"

"About three quarters of an inch deep and nearly an inch across," Heather said.

"Lucky I was able to repel the bastard. My kidney was only another inch away."

"Was it that guy Roger from back at the Abbey?" Lenny asked.

"No, someone I'd never seen before."

"This is crazy," Heather said. "Scotland doesn't have high crime—"

"I found something," Ray said. He was staring at his phone. "I searched Campbell and 'forget not,' and you won't believe what I found.

He turned his phone around to face us and there was the crest of the Campbell Clan. The boar's head with big tusks I'd seen before. Underneath it was a family motto in Latin, but below that it was translated: "Forget not."

"What the hell's that supposed to mean?" I said.

We all stared at each until Lenny broke the ice.

"Guess forty years wasn't enough to forget that vow of revenge, was it?" he said.

Ray was still reading on his phone and his expression soured further. "A lot of crazy history with the Campbells. They were one of the most successful clans, but there's a thing called the Massacre of Glencoe where they slaughtered thirty-eight members of the MacDonald clan in 1692."

"Ancient history," I said. "I've done archeological analysis all over the world in the e-Antiquity days, and whether it's the Mayans, Sumerians, Indians, you name it, cultures who have faded away, generally do so with grace."

Ray shrugged. "Those in the Middle East may beg to differ."

"Or Native Americans," Heather said.

"Or former slaves," Lenny said.

I held up my hands. "Of course there are exceptions, my point is that it's unlikely the Campbell Clan is still engaged in some kind of feud over a massacre that happened 350 years ago."

"I never said they were," Ray said. "My point is that they've been at the sharp edge of the sword, literally, throughout Scottish history. Somebody tried to murder you and stated the Campbell motto as he did so. Whether it's the revenge that Harry mentioned, or something else, someone seems determined to kill you."

We all stared at each other.

"Glad we're getting the hell out of here tomorrow," Lenny said.

I bit my lip. My gut told me I needed to get to the bottom of why these people wanted me dead, or they'd just come after me back home when I wasn't expecting it.

"If I leave now, then I'll be watching over my shoulder all the time in Key West," I said.

"That's our home turf, man," Lenny said. "We have help there."

Ray vigorously nodded his head.

"Sorry guys, but I need to stay and dig deeper." I paused. "Ray, since we need two pilots to fly Big Mama, are you okay with that?"

"Like I have a choice?"

"Just another day, two max."

Heather crossed her arms. "If you're staying, I'm staying."

"You all are crazy, man," Lenny said. "When people try to kill you, it's time to get the hell out."

"That guy Roger mentioned Key West. They know where I—we—live."

Lenny rolled his eyes. "Ain't this some shit. Here we are in another Buck Reilly trainwreck. Goddamn."

I held my hands up. "Get on your flight tomorrow, Lenny. I don't blame you one bit. You have a church to run. We won't be far behind."

"Damned straight, man," Lenny said. "Heather called me over here in an emergency situation anyway thanks to that mess at the Formula 1 race, and with everything that's happened since, I'm still freaking here."

I patted him on the shoulder. "I get it, my friend. No worries."

Ray was chewing on the side of his mouth, and I knew he had to be falling dangerously behind with his other clients in Key West, but unless he found another pilot to accompany him home, he'd be stuck with me. I didn't want to abuse that, but given the attack tonight, I needed to figure out what the hell was going on and how to defuse it. Plus, I've never had any luck running from a fight.

"Sorry, Ray," I said. "I promise we'll get out of here ASAP."

He grunted in response and looked away.

The days of me running roughshod over Ray were long over, and he was an essential partner to me at Last Resort Charter and Salvage, plus one of my closest friends. I had to do something …

I cleared my throat. "Once this is all said and done, how about I talk to Harry about our using one of his jets?"

Ray's eyes immediately lit up. "Yeah? That would be amazing."

"Jet?" Lenny said? "Damn, boy, you guys gonna be living high on the hog at Last Resort. May have to change the name to Luxury Resort, or First Resort, or Diamond Platinum fucking Resort, or something."

I shook my head. These new circumstances with Harry were going to be a nightmare. In my experience, access to money always complicates relationships, families, everything. And billions of dollars? Nuts.

Out of the corner of my eye, I saw Heather smiling.

Jesus.

"Anyway, my flight's at 10:00 a.m., so I'm going to bed," Lenny said.

"We'll see you in the morning," I said.

"Since I'm staying, I need to change my flight," Heather said. "Unless I won't need to fly home commercial …"

I rolled my eyes. "Come on, Heather."

"I'm going to read more on the history of the Campbell Clan," Ray said.

"We need to track Catherine's family down and try to understand what the issues are here," I said.

"Forget not," Ray said.

"That too."

Ray and Lenny left our room, and Heather sat down in front of her laptop and started to search for information on Catherine Campbell. For once we were alone in a swanky hotel room, and she was focused on something other than romance.

I, on the other hand, poured some of The Macallan and paced the room trying to get my bearings on what we were up against.

SECTION 2:

DIRTY DEEDS DONE DIRT CHEAP

9

HEATHER WAS BUSY MAKING NOTES AS SHE RESEARCHED CATHERINE, but I couldn't sit still. The wound in my back was aching and I'd already bled through the butterfly stitches and Band-Aids. Concerned about being a sitting duck here in the hotel had me thinking about how we could enhance our safety.

"I'm going to rent a car," I said. "I don't want us to be standing on street corners hailing taxis or waiting for Ubers."

Heather barely looked up from her computer. "Good idea."

I peeled back the curtain to peer out to the main street that our room looked over. It was dark and there was steady traffic but not many pedestrians—

I leaned closer to the window and stared at someone I saw across the street leaning against a bus stop enclosure. It was a man wearing a newsboy cap.

Son-of-a-bitch.

Roger.

I glanced around the room but saw nothing I could use as a weapon to defend us, other than the decanter of scotch. I didn't want to alarm Heather, but waiting around in our room made no sense as a strategy for defense, but what choice did we have?

An idea popped into my head. Perhaps a foolish one, but we needed to turn the tables on whoever was behind this incomprehensible grudge. Would someone really blame the death of my birth mother on the infant son she gave life to? I had to find out.

I pulled a dark shirt from my bag and pulled it on. "I'll see if they can have a car delivered here in the morning."

Heather glanced up, her eyes blinked rapidly. "I'm finding some interesting stuff here."

I studied the hotel floorplan on the back of the room's entry door and noted the locations of the stairwells. The one near our room emptied by the main lobby, but another one on the back of the floor led to what

I deduced to be the rear service area. There looked to be an exit door to the outside from there too.

"I'll be back."

She blew me a kiss and turned her attention back to her laptop.

I took the stairs down one level and cut through the Snug where there were a few patrons sitting in leather chairs and imbibing brown beverages from glasses. My pace was intentionally casual, and nobody paid me any attention. I found the rear stair and took it down another level. The sign on the exit door said, "no re-entry from this door." I pushed it open, and as I hoped, it was a service corridor with boxes stacked, vacuum cleaners lined up, trash cans in a row, and doors marked with "locker room" and another for "loading dock."

After glancing both ways down the corridor, I held my breath as I walked up to the loading dock entry and pushed down on the lever handle—it wasn't locked. The loading dock consisted of two bays, one of which had a large recycling compactor with a stack of cardboard next to it, and another that had a load leveler on the lip of the dock, and a mop in a bucket in the corner.

I grabbed the wooden mop handle and unscrewed the damp mop attachment. I tapped the wood pole on the ground, and it was solid. There was an exit door next to the closed garage door that I assumed would lead to the street. I pushed it open and stepped out into the darkness of the alley behind the hotel. I walked past the backs of the neighboring retail center and movie theater that also had loading dock entrances off the alley. The alley was short and led to the main street up from the hotel. I hesitated at the corner of the building and peered around the corner. The bus enclosure was on the other side of the road, and I couldn't tell if Roger was still there or not but didn't see him anywhere else.

A group of teenagers walked out of the movie theater entrance and stopped at the crosswalk that led across the street. I used the mop handle as if it were a cane and ambled up behind them to blend in. The light changed and I followed them across. Once to the sidewalk, I glanced over to the glass bus enclosure and could see through it to where a man stood on the other side. He faced the hotel.

I placed the end of the mop pole on the ground to continue the charade of it being a cane in case anyone saw me, and slowly continued down toward the bus enclosure. Ideas of what to do when I got there rattled through my head, and while the more popular ones included violence, it would depend on Roger's reaction when I confronted him.

My heart raced as a I got closer to the glass box, and I gritted my teeth to ready for—

CLANK!

My attention was so focused on Roger, I failed to see an empty soda can on the sidewalk that I inadvertently kicked. It clattered toward the enclosure and Roger stepped back to inspect what had happened and spotted me there, fifteen feet away. I took a fast step toward him as he reached inside his jacket and quickly pulled out a gun.

I froze as he stepped toward me, the gun extended.

"Reilly. Kind of you to solve my problem of how to get inside the hotel."

Past him I saw a bus coming up the slight hill.

"Bus is coming," I said.

His eyes were fixed on mine, and his expression was serious. Deadly serious.

"Bullshit."

The bus slowed and its brakes let out a shrill screech—Roger turned his head to see the bus over his shoulder—I swung the mop handle in a circle and whipped it down toward his arm with all the strength I could muster.

As if possessing a sixth sense, he moved his arm slightly before the pole struck, and the result was just a graze. He still held the gun firmly, but with the bus nearing, he pulled it back toward his side to hide it. Unfortunately, once the driver must have seen there was nobody waiting in the enclosure, the bus accelerated past us.

"Drop the stick, Reilly."

I held it out as if I was going to do a mic drop, but then jabbed it hard into his chest and rushed him—we collided and thankfully the gun didn't go off. I hit him with an uppercut in the stomach, which he must've anticipated and dodged.

He countered by swinging the gun around and connecting on the side of my head—

Stars erupted momentarily behind my eyes.

When they cleared, Roger had taken a step back and had the gun aimed at my chest.

"Say goodbye, Greenbaum-Reilly—" He cocked the trigger.

"What have I done to you, or the Campbell family that merits you murdering me?"

"You're the evil spawn that killed Catherine—"

"I was a baby!"

"Your father, Greenbaum, pulled the wool over her eyes. The family forbade their union, but he conned her into marrying him and persuaded her to take something of incredible importance to us. We demanded it back, but Greenbaum claimed he didn't have it, even though we suspect he used the contents for his own benefit after Catherine died."

He raised the gun toward my heart.

"What are you talking about?" I asked.

"He robbed us of our legacy, and then profited from it. Since you're *his* legacy, we'll rob *him* of you."

"How could he have profited from—"

"Your blood will be on his hands—"

I raised my arms. "Wait! I just found out he was my natural father, and I didn't even know Catherine's name until this morning."

"Not my problem. History ignores the ignorant."

"What did he steal? Maybe I can help you get it back."

Roger had tensed, clearly about to pull the trigger, but he suddenly hesitated.

"We've studied you closely since the word got out that you were the one. Archeologist nicknamed King Buck, you live in the La Concha Hotel in Key West, Florida, and Greenbaum was one of your original investors, which makes you duplicitous to his evil."

"Let me try and help you," I said.

"You said you knew nothing about it, which given your reaction, I tend to believe." Roger paused. "We'd wondered if you had it hidden away yourself, but since I don't think you did, my orders are to eliminate you."

"I'll get Harry to tell me the details behind whatever it is you're talking about. If he still has it, I'll get it back."

His eyes were in the shadow of his cap, but his face contorted in a way that made me believe he was considering the options. I had a second, maybe two, where I either had to run or attack him, but in either case, I'd be adding getting shot to being stabbed tonight, and at this range, likely killed.

Roger suddenly lowered the gun and pocketed it in his dark pea coat.

"I'll give you three days. If you fail, I'll kill you and your little band of oddballs."

"Tell me what's missing? I mean, what am I looking for?"

"Talk to your father. We would've already killed him, but we want him to suffer the same sense of loss we've endured. Plus, if he was killed before we found you, we'd have no way to recover the missing material." He paused. "I'll be watching you."

With that, Roger turned on his heel and hurried down the street. I thought of tackling him and beating more information out of him but given the knife attack earlier and his use of the word, 'we', it was clear there were other people involved, several other people.

Fucking Harry.

What had he done?

10

MY HANDS WERE CLAMMY FROM NEARLY GETTING SHOT. I re-entered the hotel through the main lobby, and the last thing I wanted to do was make arrangements for tomorrow, but I stopped to speak with the concierge as a matter of importance. There was now a clock ticking on my solving whatever the mystery associated with Harry and Catherine was, and recovering whatever they'd taken from her family, or Roger and his people would kill me and my friends.

The concierge was friendly and efficient and promised to have a rental car here at the hotel in the morning. I requested an SUV. The discussion helped me to calm my nerves and think more clearly, which was important before I went up and filled Heather in.

Should I alert Ray and Lenny too?

Not until Heather and I brainstormed the situation. I had a strong inclination on what to do next but needed her to calm me down and think this through. Once out of the elevator, I hurried down the third-floor corridor, past Ray's room, past Lenny's room and with our room key in my fingers, I had difficulty inserting it into the lock since my fingers were still aflutter.

I pushed the door open, and Heather jumped up from the bed.

"Where have you been? That took forever."

"I, ah, had a little meeting with our friend, Roger."

"The creep from Dunfermline Abbey?"

"One and the same."

"Was he in the lobby?"

"I saw him loitering outside watching the hotel, so I snuck around and confronted him."

"Are you crazy? After already getting stabbed tonight?"

"He pulled a gun on me—"

"A gun?!"

"He smashed me over the head with it—so it's been a grand slam of getting my ass kicked today."

Heather placed her hand on my head—I winced at her touch.

"That's quite a lump you have under your hair. How'd you get away?"

"After learning what their issue is based on, I negotiated."

"What *is* the issue?"

I explained that Harry had supposedly persuaded Catherine to take something of great value from her family, but Roger wouldn't tell me what it was, other than that Harry may have used it to enrich himself after Catherine's death, and that they were going to kill me for revenge.

Heather crossed her arms. "Why wouldn't he tell you what it was?"

"I don't know."

"So how are we going to find it?"

The fact that she said "we" gave me a small boost of encouragement.

"He told me to talk to my father. Harry, that is, who is quickly climbing up the ranks of my shitlist."

"Okay, let's call him."

I bit my lip a second. "One other thing." I cleared my throat. "Roger only gave me three days to find whatever it is that they took."

"And if we're not successful?"

"Then he'll kill me, you, Ray, and Lenny."

Heather sat suddenly on the bed. Her mouth fell open, and the color drained from her cheeks. I sat down next to her and put my arm around her waist.

"So, we have our work cut out for us," I said. "But I did get a car rented. It'll be here in the morning."

"Let's call Harry," she said.

"That's my inclination as well, but I wanted to speak with you first. I'll need to play hardball if he doesn't fess up."

"Absolutely. Harry's a damned billionaire. Whatever he took he can certainly afford to give back, or at least reimburse them for the cost."

I exhaled hard and pulled the cell phone from my pocket. My finger hovered over the speed-dial button as I contemplated how to finesse this situation. I pushed my finger down on the button.

After two rings, Harry answered. I put the call on speaker.

"Buck, I'm so glad to hear from you. How did it go at the cemetery?"

"We found Catherine's grave—you might have told me that Dunfermline Abbey was one of the most important cultural sites in the country, and that she was a descendent of European royalty—"

"How have you deduced all that from her grave site? The stone says practically nothing."

"Nor have you, Harry—"

Heather waved her hands in a downward motion at me.

"I'm sorry, dear boy?"

"I learned some of that from the abbey sexton who showed us the grave—"

"I told you to speak to no one—"

"But I learned a lot more from this guy named Roger who has been following us from the moment we landed in Edinburgh."

Silence followed.

"You still there, Harry?"

The sound of him trying to clear his throat was my answer.

"I confronted him tonight after I was stabbed in the hotel restroom—"

"Stabbed, you say? Dear God—"

"In the back while I was taking a leak. Fortunately I foiled the assassin's effort before he finished me off—"

"I'm so sorry—"

"Then Roger nearly shot me, but, hey, I'm still ahead of the game."

Again, silence.

"When you said they wanted revenge, you weren't kidding," I said. "But I bought a stay of execution, Harry, and I have three days to perform."

I could hear him smacking his lips together, but he said nothing.

"Aren't you going to ask how?" I said.

"Of course, how?"

"I told him I'd recover whatever it was that you and Catherine stole from their family—that's why they want revenge, not because of me. You defied them by getting married, but what you took from them seems to be of even greater importance." I paused. "What was it you and Catherine took, Harry?"

A high-pitched sound came through the phone, and I glanced at it for a moment. Was that a whimper?

"Look, I don't really care what it was Harry, I'm sure you had your reasons, but if I don't return it in three days, they'll kill me, Heather, Ray and Lenny. I can't run because they know where we all live, and as you said before, they do want revenge—on you—which they will extract by killing us."

It was as if Harry was a balloon that had a leak and was losing all its air. His response was a whisper. "I'm so sorry, dear boy. I should have never confided in you or given you equity in the racing team. It exposed you and was pure selfishness on my part."

My exhale caused static on the line. "It's okay, Harry, let's just give them what they want, and we can all move on."

"I'm afraid that's not possible," he said.

Heather and I locked eyes. "Why's that?"

"I can't tell you," Harry said.

Heather held both hands palms up.

"Can't or won't?" I said.

Click.

Silence followed.

"Harry? Are you there? Harry?" I said.

Nothing.

"Did he hang up?" Heather said.

"Maybe we lost our connection," I said.

I dialed his number again. It rang and rang and rang until a recorded female voice with a British accent answered.

"Sir Harry is indisposed currently. Please leave a message and someone will return the call …"

BEEP.

"Harry, call me back. This is life or death here …"

I hung up and lowered the phone. Heather had turned pale.

"The son-of-a-bitch must've hung up on me … again."

11

HEATHER AND I WERE ALREADY SEATED IN THE RESTAURANT when Ray and Lenny entered. It was early, but Lenny had to get to the airport to catch his plane soon. He had a look of relief on his face, which my news would soon obliterate.

"How's the wound on your back feel?" Ray asked.

"It's fine, but, ah, I have some new information to share."

My description of seeing Roger, sneaking up on him, fighting and nearly getting shot had both of their mouths hanging open, along with Heather squirming in her seat. I didn't embellish, but I didn't hold back either. Ray had long ago grown tired of partial briefings, which I usually did to spare him overreacting or worrying, but today I laid it all out for them.

"So what happened?" Lenny said.

"Apparently, Harry and Catherine took something of value that they want back. Their desire to kill me is revenge for him marrying her against her parents' wishes, for persuading her to swipe something from them, and for her dying in childbirth."

"What the hell did they steal?" Lenny asked.

"No idea. Roger said to ask Harry." Anticipating their next question, I said, "I called Harry afterward and he basically said he couldn't help me and hung up."

"What the hell's his problem?" Lenny asked.

Ray was chewing on his lip, and I could see in his eyes that he'd already fast-forwarded to where this might be going. "What will Roger do if you can't retrieve whatever it is they stole?" he asked.

"He gave me three days to find it and bring it back."

"Or?" Lenny asked.

I cleared my throat. "He and his goons threatened to kill all four of us if we don't get it back in three days."

"Kill us? Including me?" Lenny asked. "And we got three days to find something we don't even know what it is?"

"Well, it's more like two and a half now—"

"Man," Lenny said. "Let's all get on my flight and go home—"

"Unfortunately, they know where we all live, and he said they'd come after us."

Ray leaned back in his chair, a blank expression on his face. Lenny jumped up and paced the room, totally ignoring the breakfast buffet.

Heather had already dealt with the fear and emotion of the situation last night, so she sat calmly as our friends absorbed the news. Lenny sat back down after a few minutes of circling the room mumbling to himself.

"No point in my leaving today if they're going to hunt me down in Key West anyway," Lenny said. "I need to help you all find the mystery-whatever-the-fuck-it-is they stole."

"I did some research on Catherine's family before Buck dropped the bomb on me," Heather said.

"And I was doing research on the history of the Campbell Clan," Ray said.

"I rented a car to get us out of here and on the trail of whatever it is we're looking for," I said. "Which given that we don't know, perhaps we start with Catherine's family to see if they'll tell us anything."

"Other than they want to kill us all," Lenny said.

"I have an address for the Campbells," Heather said. "They live in an apartment within Inveraray Castle in the county of Argyll in western Scotland." She glanced from face to face. "The castle sits on 60,000 acres."

"Goddamn," Lenny said. "Kings, castles, and killers. What a legacy you were born into, man."

Ray was already on his phone checking the location. "Looks like a two-and-a-half-hour drive."

"Should we fly Big Mama?" I asked.

"Inveraray is right on the edge of Loch Fyne. Water landings are allowed here, so we could—"

"But what if that leads us somewhere else and we need a car?" Heather asked.

Everyone looked at me. "By the time we go to the airport and deal with all that, it'll be faster to drive," I said. "Eat something and let's get on the road."

The vehicle that the rental agency delivered was a brand-new Range Rover Sport that fit the four of us comfortably. Ray drove so I could concentrate on Catherine's family and how we could approach them. Even though they clearly knew we were here, I'm hoping that crashing in on them at home will loosen their tongues. Neither Roger nor Harry had given me any specific details to work with, so if the Campbells really wanted me to recover the item of value, I needed to know what the heck it was.

We headed west on M9 and passed by the turn at Queensferry that led to the bridge and Dunfermline. The gray cityscape turned to green countryside, with rolling hills and farms on both sides of the highway. The sky was overcast, and rain appeared likely, but that describes most days in Scotland. Small villages that consisted of more farms, small homes with smoke rising from chimneys, and businesses set in what we would refer to as strip centers, but in this case, were ancient buildings that lined the road, was the norm until we reached Stirling, which was a larger town.

"The Duke of Argyll is the Chief of Clan Campbell," Heather said. "Looks like Inveraray castle has been used in the TV show, *Downton Abbey* and also recently on *The Diplomat*."

"What are Catherine's parents' names?" I said.

Heather licked her lips. "Her father is Colin, and her mother is Rosemary. They're both in their eighties." She paused and looked up. "No other children."

The news pressed my lips tightly shut. I had only fantasized about my birth family a few times over my life because I never really cared, aside from maybe learning some health information. As an adoptee, every time you go to the doctor, you have to claim ignorance on family health history. I'd never done one of the DNA tests that connects you with family, because I loved my adoptive parents and didn't want to do anything to tarnish the memory of our relationship and all they'd done for me. Maybe that's silly now where so much information is at our fingertips, but given that my birth family wanted me dead, it was a good thing I hadn't.

Conversation fell away as we drove west. I felt nothing but dread since this was far from a happy reunion in the making. At the town of

Balloch, we turned north onto A82 and followed the western shore of Loch Lomond. The rolling hills grew more steep to our left, and broad, gray rock peered out intermittently between the spring foliage. The two-lane road had no shoulder, aside from thick green grass and abundant ferns along the edge of the forest. The road weaved in and out from the shoreline the further north we drove, and at Tarbet, we turned west, away from the lake. Traffic was minimal, and the speed limit slowed until we reached Arrochar, where we passed through the tiny village at the top of Loch Long.

"I gotta pee," Lenny said.

The green and gold hills through here were spare of trees. A bus and other vehicles were parked ahead to our right where a green sign noted the area as Argyll Forest Park, and the parking area was dubbed, "Rest and Be Thankful." Ray drove into the small parking lot, which contained a few picnic tables, benches, and a catering vehicle.

"Don't see any bathrooms," Lenny said.

Ray parked in the spot farthest from the road. "No, but there's a nice stand of pine trees over here. That's where I'm headed."

Heather and I got out to stretch our legs while they relieved themselves. She studied a map on her phone. "So remote and beautiful," she said. "The mountain pass here is at the divide between Glen Kinglas and Glencoe."

She spread her fingers apart on the surface of her phone and on the next loch over was the town of Inveraray where the Duke of Argyll's home was situated. My heart double-clutched at our proximity to where my grandparents lived.

Had Catherine grown up here?

Had she driven these same roads to escape to the bigger cities as a teenager and in her early twenties? Or did she love small-town life?

Where did she meet Harry?

I realized he hadn't told me where they'd met. He really hadn't told me much at all, and then refused to tell me more when I pleaded for information about whatever he and Catherine had stolen from her family.

"How are you feeling?" Heather asked.

She rubbed her hand along my back, which combined with the cool temperature, caused a shiver to run through me.

"Just want to get this over with. Time is clicking by, and we haven't learned squat."

"You're about to meet real family members. Your grandparents."

"I'm sure they'll be thrilled. Good thing the castle is a public place. They won't be able to kill us there."

The thought caused me to look around at the half-dozen other cars parked here. Would Roger have followed us? Ray hadn't mentioned seeing anything suspicious in the rearview mirror, but we were more focused on our destination than the path behind us.

They emerged from the woods, and I opened the back door on the Rover.

"Let's roll, daylight's burning."

We continued a short distance and arrived at the top of Loch Fyne, where we continued over to the western shore. The lochs, or lakes to the rest of us, all looked the same to me now. Gray water surrounded by colorful trees, and round barren buttes that climbed toward the cloudy sky. Signs for the town of Inveraray and the castle gave me another jolt of adrenalin. Ahead, we could see a long line of white buildings facing the water.

"That's the town up ahead," Ray said. "The castle's off to the right."

"The inn looks cute." Heather's voice was wistful.

After all we'd been through these past several months, I owed her a real vacation to a romantic destination. To her credit, she hadn't whined about our hectic pace, or canceled plans caused by one distraction or another, and when our eyes met, she offered me a gentle smile. It struck me as pity, which rankled me.

As we reached the town, we saw a sign for the castle to the right.

"Bet they got some decent food at that inn, too," Lenny said.

"No time for food. Turn right and let's get this over with," I said.

Ray followed the sign for the castle, and the road followed a sinewy course through the trees until it opened onto a beautiful, heavily landscaped formal garden with wide stone paths cutting straight through it. A parking area was off to our left, where Ray turned in, found a spot and killed the power to the Rover.

We climbed out and saw that there were a dozen or so people, spread out around the grounds, so we walked toward them. My attention was focused ahead, anxious to spy the castle. When we rounded a wooded corner, the castle appeared ahead.

"Goddamn," Lenny said. "It really is a freaking castle."

The gray stone edifice was about the same size as Harry's place, Hampshire Manor, but Inveraray had large round turrets on each end, with pointed spires on top. The Georgian architecture was simple yet bold, and the three-level structure rose up from the flat plateau like a massive stone outcrop. Only the knob of a tree-covered hill behind it provided any scale to the castle. I could feel my heart pounding in my neck and concentrated on my breathing.

"From what Heather found, the family lives on the top floor, but the grounds and first floor are open to tourists. Let's go inside and look around before we announce ourselves."

My friends exchanged glances as we walked forward, our feet crunching in the brown gravel. We came to a ticket office, and I paid for the tickets with my credit card. The vendor handed me four copies of a tour map that listed the different rooms, had a brief history on the castle, the duke's family and that of Clan Campbell. I handed them out.

"Just can't see you living in the La Concha anymore, man. First Harry's mansion and now this place?" Lenny said.

"Let's not mention Harry here, okay? I want to control when we identify ourselves."

We entered the building through the main door and stepped into a rather modest entrance hall. "Says here that the castle was started in 1746 and completed in 1789," Heather said.

Ancient paintings of men and women in formal clothing, portraits, landscapes and ones of royalty were framed in gilt and stared down at us from all angles. French-inspired tapestries and an impressive collection of rifles and other weapons graced the yellow walls framed in hand-carved, white wooden molding.

"Where can we find information on the history of the Campbells?" I asked.

Heather scanned through the brochure until her eyes lit up. "The Saloon has a large collection of Campbell portraits dating back to the 1780s." she paused. "It's up ahead past the State Dining Room and Tapestry Drawing Room."

I trudged forward and the sounds of my friend's oohs and ahhs echoed behind me. Inside the green-walled Saloon were games, a grand piano, a billiard table, and countless portraits. On top of the piano I spotted photographs and headed in that direction, more interested in recent rather than ancient history.

"Says here that songwriters Lerner and Loewe composed some of the songs for their musical *My Fair Lady* here," Heather said.

"Ain't nothing fair about this place," Lenny said. "Imagine all the workers it must've taken to build it. Where'd they live?"

The photos were of the Duke of Argyll and his wife, Rosemary. One was a black and white photo of them years ago, and Rosemary was holding a baby. My heart stopped when I saw a picture of a young, blond-haired beauty with bright blue eyes and a confident smile. She looked to be between late teens or early twenties.

Could that be my mother?

A lump formed in my throat, and my breathing turned shallow. An older couple entered the room, and I turned away as I fought to compose myself.

"Mr. Reilly?"

The male voice caught me by total surprise.

I turned to find a tall, dapper, elderly gentleman in a tweed sport coat and French blue shirt, with his hands behind his back. Just to his left, and a step behind him was a tall woman in a gray skirt with a lemon-yellow blouse, long hair and nervous eyes. She bit her lip.

"Yes, that's me," I said.

He stepped forward and extended his right hand.

"Colin Campbell, the Duke of Argyll, and my wife, Rosemary."

"Oh shit," Lenny said.

Oh shit, indeed.

12

I STUDIED THE DUKE AND DUCHESS AS THE OTHERS INTRODUCED THEMSELVES. They didn't seem to recognize Heather, which was a first. They also didn't glance at me with any obvious malice. Finally, after the introductions, I needed to press the conversation forward as time was running out.

"Very nice to meet you and thanks for coming out to see us," I said. "But, if you don't mind me asking, how did you know we were here?"

"The sales office let me know you were here," Colin said.

I'd paid with my credit card on purpose to see if anyone was paying attention. Obviously, they were. I needed more of an explanation though.

"I figured Roger let you know we might stop by," I said.

"I'm sorry, who is Roger?" Colin asked.

I paused. "Roger who has been following us all over Scotland? Newsboy hat?"

"Doesn't ring a bell," he said.

"You do know who I am, right?"

Colin shuffled his feet and Rosemary took his arm, her face very serious. "From all we've seen in the press the last week, we believe you're, ah, Harry Greenbaum's son," Rosemary said.

"And Catherine, your daughter, was my birth mother."

Colin licked his lips and a moan from deep inside Rosemary's chest passed her lips.

She nodded fast.

"We never thought we'd meet you," Colin said. He stood tall and stepped closer to me. "You have the Campbell height—"

"And Catherine's eyes," Rosemary said.

"The only picture I've ever seen of her was this one on your piano."

Rosemary's eyes lit up. "We have dozens of pictures of her."

Heather glanced at me with a smile, which I read to mean she felt the meeting was going well, which I'd agree with if I was simply looking for a distant blood relative. But I wasn't.

A group of four old women wandered into the Saloon and were speaking loudly about each item they walked up to.

"Please, you and your friends join us upstairs for tea," Rosemary said.

I glanced at the duke, and he nodded his head in the affirmative. He turned to lead us out, with Rosemary falling in next to me and we walked back into the great hall, and to a door that was locked. Once open, it was a private stairwell upstairs. We climbed to the top and found the next floor to be far homier and not museum-like at all. Colin led us to a large living room where two large leather couches faced each other, and several large armchairs were spread about the room. Rosemary sat next to me, and Colin in a chair to my left.

"Once we learned your identity, we searched and read everything we could about you," Rosemary said. "Quite impressive, King Buck."

A laugh sounded behind me. "King is right," Lenny said. "Working on emperor now."

"Oh, well, thanks. It hasn't all been great, as I'm sure you saw, but we made some important discoveries at e-Antiquity."

"And Harry was an investor from early on? So you knew he was your biological father?"

"No, I just found out literally a few days ago. We were in Italy for the Formula 1 race—"

"We saw," Colin said. "Very heroic."

I felt blood rush to my face and the warmth of a blush.

"Buck and Lenny were very heroic," Heather said. "They saved thousands of lives."

"So Harry told you after that?" Colin asked.

"Soon after," I said. "But literally nothing about Catherine, er, my birth mother, aside from the family being highly opposed to their marriage, and when she died giving me life, that you had sworn revenge against him ... and me."

The pedantic smile on the Duke's face turned instantly into a frown.

"Revenge? That's hardly the case." He paused. "No, we didn't approve of the marriage—he was twenty years her senior and was just an ambitious chap we believed had taken an interest in her due to her lineage. She got pregnant—"

"Which led to the hurry-up wedding," Rosemary said.

"And then she died before we'd ever had the chance to come to terms with it all," Colin said.

A maid in a uniform brought out a tea set on a silver tray.

I glanced around at my friends and could never have imagined we'd be sitting in a Scottish castle with a duke and duchess, who happened to be my natural grandparents, discussing the shaky ground that my long-term investor, Harry Greenbaum, and their daughter, Catherine, had rushed their wedding, because she was already pregnant with me.

I took a sip of tea to gather my thoughts, and when I looked over the top of my cup to see Lenny sipping his tea, pinkie finger extended, I nearly spit mine out. Ray slurped his, and Heather, her legs crossed daintily, held her teacup with both hands as if it were a Fabergé egg.

What a scene.

"We did, and frankly still do, have an issue with Mr. Greenbaum," Colin said.

"You mean Sir Harry?"

He grimaced. "Quite."

I placed my teacup back in its saucer, and with fresh resolve, sat forward.

"As much as I'd like to take the time to get to know you better—and let me say, I have no interest in pushing my way into your family—we are on a deadline imposed by this man Roger, who along with at least one other man who stabbed me in Edinburgh—"

"Stabbed!" Rosemary said. "Oh my."

Heather nodded her head quickly.

"Which expires at the end of the day after tomorrow." I continued. "So, I'm afraid I need to ask more pointed questions so we can find whatever this group is looking for, or we will literally be on the run for our lives."

The momentarily friendly expressions on our hosts' faces slid to serious masks.

"This man, Roger, told me that Catherine had taken something of historic value, some type of heirloom, perhaps, when she ran off with Harry to get married in London. If we can't find this and return it to Roger by tomorrow night, then we're up shit's creek without a paddle."

Rosemary sat back abruptly in her chair.

Colin exhaled hard and looked past me into space as if he were reliving that situation for the first time in a very long time. He cleared his throat, which I instantly hoped was not a family trait, or tell of deception.

"Let me repeat, neither Rosemary nor I, or Clan Campbell, for that matter, has ever stated or sought revenge against Harry for marrying our daughter." He paused. "We were not happy about it then, and when she passed during childbirth, we were destroyed—"

"Which was made even worse when Harry put the baby—you—up for adoption," Rosemary said.

"Did you offer to take me?" I asked.

Rosemary pursed her lips and glanced toward her husband, whose expression remained serious. A moment passed, and the answer was clear. No, they had not.

"We're convinced that Catherine, under Harry's guidance, took a very old relic of great importance to Clan Campbell that vanished with her death."

"What exactly is the relic?" I asked.

"It was a sealed metal canister with papers inside, important papers, mind you, but nothing we would have wanted our daughter to die over, nor for revenge to befall you," Colin said.

I sat back in my chair, and my eyes met Heather's. Hers were narrow as if she wasn't buying what they were selling.

"So who would this Roger be?" she asked.

"I don't know," he said.

Colin hesitated, and glanced at Rosemary, who with an extra blink seemed to communicate something to him. Colin glanced around—we're in his living room—who was he concerned about, the maid?

"It's very likely to be the Sect."

"The Sect?" I asked.

He shuffled in his seat, crossed his legs, uncrossed them, and then crossed them the other way. He exhaled a deep breath.

"The Sect is an ancient group that was established to protect the monarchy and the historic continuity of Scotland."

His revelation left me speechless. Heather's brow furrowed, Ray's eyes opened wide, and Lenny's squint preceded him sitting forward.

"They some kind of Secret Service or something?" Lenny asked.

"No," Colin said. "If they're still in existence, they operate outside the law with a mysterious purview. Legend has it that they are impossible to reason with."

Lenny sat back hard. "Shhiiit, man."

"How long has this Sect been in existence?" I asked.

Colin took on a professorial flair now, clutched his hands together, and spoke calmly as if discussing current events. "It dates back to King Robert I, or Robert the Bruce as you may know him. There have been multiple deaths, assassinations even, attributed to them throughout the millennia, but nobody has ever been caught or prosecuted, so it's hard to be certain."

"Pretty murky," I said.

"Sounds like any murder could be attributed to this Sect and the killer could get off scot-free," Ray said.

"Of course, even though the existence of the organization is largely unknown, it has achieved some level of urban legend and there have been cases where blame was directed toward the Sect, but when the suspect was apprehended, it proved to be a case of deflection," Colin said. "But I have never heard of any case where a deadline was established, and a party was given the opportunity to atone for whatever their perceived sins were."

I grunted. "Until you mentioned this metal container, we didn't know what we're looking for," I said.

The group fell silent for a moment.

"Interesting that Catherine is buried at Dunfermline Abbey, along with Robert the Bruce, given that that this Sect was established during his reign," Heather said.

Bingo.

"Good point," I said. "She's buried amongst several from the Stewart Clan. Why's that?"

Colin cleared his throat and did the same leg-cross shuffle he'd done a few moments ago. "At the time of Robert I, Clan Campbell was closely associated with him, and very instrumental in maintaining order in the High...lands..."

Colin 's voice cracked, and Rosemary reached over and placed her hand on his knee and gave it a squeeze. "It's all right, dear."

He licked his lips and continued. "Given the close relationship between the Stewarts and the Campbells, for literally close to a thousand years, the House of Stewart offered to have Catherine buried at Dunfermline, which was a tremendous honor."

I absorbed his statement, but it fell short in my mind.

"Surely there've been thousands of Campbells who have perished since Robert I, so why the special dispensation for Catherine?"

The duke dropped his foot to the floor and now leaned toward me. "Because she was the last of the line of Campbells who were directly related to those close to Robert I, and those who followed him. *Our* line of Campbells."

His eyes became keenly intense as he spoke.

Silence followed.

"Until Buck came along," Lenny said.

Rosemary sucked in a breath and Colin squirmed again.

"My understanding is that as part of your adoption, your British citizenship was relinquished and you went to America where you have lived your entire life," Colin said.

The memory of my brother, Ben, and I going to claim the contents of the Swiss bank account where my parents had deposited the maps and clues to unfound treasures that I'd taken from e-Antiquity before the government shut us down came to mind. The most shocking contents my parents had placed in the vault there were my adoption papers—since until then I thought I was 100% Reilly—and a letter from the British government confirming that my citizenship had been revoked. I'd never understood why that was necessary. Even after learning that Harry was my birth father, it didn't seem like a necessity associated with my being adopted by Americans, but sitting here now, the dime dropped.

My mouth fell open for a moment as I processed that revelation.

"You required that, didn't you?" I said.

Colin licked his lips again, sat back and crossed his arms.

"It was a complicated time of high emotion and incredible disappointment."

Even though I'd only known these people for an hour, that I was of Scottish descent and that Harry and Catherine were my natural parents for a few days, the recognition still caused a jolt of emotion to curl my hands into fists. Neither the duke or duchess betrayed any emotion, so I breathed in deeply to control my own.

Back to business.

"So, all that being said, and whatever the Sect is, if Roger is indeed a henchman for them, we still need to know the contents of whatever Catherine stole, so we can try and determine what happened to it."

Colin's eyes were sharp.

"As I said, it was a sealed metal canister. It had been handed down through the generations, but we never paid much attention to it," Colin said.

"You said earlier that it contained important papers, what were they?"

Colin waved a hand as if to brush away the question. "Yes, they were important papers to Clan Campbell, but just for historic reference. Nothing one could monetize."

"So their importance must have had something to do with history itself, of the clan and, what, certain events, like details the Massacre at Glencoe maybe?"

"Certainly not!"

"Something to do with Robert the Bruce then? Given her burial at Dunfermline, or the origin of the Sect?"

Now Rosemary furiously licked her lips, then stood up.

"Well—"

"Our lives are on the line here," I said. "I told you I'm not looking for anything from you, or even Harry, for that matter, but people are threatening to kill me and my friends, and the clock is ticking, so I need answers, and now."

A moment passed. Rosemary stood behind Colin and was wringing her hands, but he maintained a cool demeanor. "Sit down, dear," he said.

She picked up a bell off a side table and wrung it loudly. The maid appeared a moment later. "Bring us water, please, Gretchen," she said.

"Quite simply, the papers detailed an agreement between the Campbells and the Stewarts for a peaceful coexistence following the death of Robert I."

I absorbed that information.

"Why was such an agreement necessary?" Ray asked.

Good question.

"At the time of Robert I's death, his son became King David II. He was five years old and an arranged marriage to Joan of the Tower, the daughter of Edward II of England and Isabella of France, occurred to establish strategic alliances going forward."

"Dude got married at five?" Lenny asked. "That shit's crazy."

"Later, David II was imprisoned in England for a decade at an important time in his life, and when set free and returned to the throne in Scotland, he was without heirs. Upon his passing, Robert I's daughter, Marjorie, and her husband Walter Stewart's son, became King Robert II, which began the House of Stewart that led the monarchy for 300 years, not only in England, but much of Europe."

"Robert the Bruce died in 1329," I said. "So this agreement with the Stewarts was some kind of pact to work together and maintain power after that?"

Colin cleared his throat and nodded quickly. "Basically, that's correct."

"And those papers were what's inside this sealed metal container that Catherine took? That's it?"

Colin looked at Rosemary and again received some kind of veiled sign, because he turned back to me with a smile.

"There was also a rudimentary map of some sort, believed to be from Robert I himself."

"A map?" I said. "Like a treasure map?"

"We have no way of knowing the answer to that," Colin said. "But it too was in the canister."

I tilted my head back. A sickening feeling stirred in my gut. Why, exactly, I wasn't sure, but the longer our discussion went, the more uncomfortable I became. I had the urge to get the hell out of here, but still needed more information.

"So who would want the contents of the canister?" I asked. "And where might we find it?"

"As to the second part of your question, you would need to ask your father—"

"Birth father—"

"—And as for who would want it, the Sect to be sure, would seek it as it relates to an important moment and agreement in Scotland's history, and aside from that, every Tom, Dick, or Harry who ever dreamt of finding something for nothing may seek that map in the hopes of it leading to instant wealth, fame, or at least recognition for finding something that dates back to Robert the Bruce."

It was instantly clear to me that my dear grandparents would be no help at all in finding what they referred to as the canister. I stood up, which surprised everyone.

"We won't take up any more of your time," I said.

The duke stood, relief on his face. Did I see sadness in Rosemary's eyes?

It gave me a thought.

"Do you happen to have any other photos of Catherine we could see?"

"Oh, that would be lovely," Heather said.

Colin looked to Rosemary, who paused a moment, then offered what I read as an artificial smile. "Of course," she said.

She hurried from the room, which left us in an awkward silence, but returned quickly with a shoebox—dukes and duchesses must keep valuables in the same kinds of boxes as the rest of us.

She opened the lid and produced a couple of dozen pictures, both black and white and color. There were pictures of Catherine as a child, sitting in a highchair, and others playing outside with the castle in the background. Then came some as a teen, and then in her twenties.

"You look just like her," Heather said.

It was true. She was tall, had dirty blond hair and blue eyes, and a facial bone structure that matched my own. I took out my phone.

"Do you mind if I take pictures of these?"

"Be my guest, dear," Rosemary said.

I snapped pictures of several of them and then returned them to the box.

"Thank you."

"Do keep in touch," Colin said.

There was no familial warmth in his statement, and I suspected he was more interested in the fate of the canister than my well-being.

"If we get lucky and find the canister, should I return it to you, or Roger?"

He paused to consider that, which unto itself told me something, but what exactly, I wasn't sure.

"Do let me know, but of course I'll understand if you must appease the Sect."

"Right."

No hugs or handshakes marked our exit down the private staircase and back into the great hall. I walked quickly to get outside before any of my friends spoke anything further of our meeting. The late morning air outside refreshed me instantly as I'd felt increasingly claustrophobic, even inside the massive castle.

"Damn boy, you was on his shit," Lenny said.

"They were so dry," I said. "No emotion at all."

"Your grandmother got a bit choked up, I'd say," Heather said. "Now what?"

"We need to confront Harry, but I want to go back to the abbey first."

13

EVERYONE CLIMBED INSIDE THE ROVER, AND I TOOK THE WHEEL.

"Another two and a half hours back to Dunfermline Abbey," I said. "I'll find a place near the airport to drop you, Ray, so you can get Big Mama ready to fly back to Cotswold Airport."

"I'm starving," Lenny said.

"We don't have time for a restaurant, but I'll look for a drive-thru in Inveraray," I said.

"I bet that inn has some good food," Heather said.

"We need something fast," I said. "So what did you think of my dear grandparents?"

"Insincere would be the word I would use to describe them," Heather said. "But from my experience, titled people in the UK are bred to exude a distant flair."

"I don't know about that," Lenny said. "I'd say they were conniving."

"Both are applicable," Ray said. "But more than that, they were holding back on us. I think they know more than they alluded to."

"I agree," I said.

We drove down the serpentine entry road from the castle to town, and even though I wanted to drive as fast as possible to the abbey, the troops were restless, so we needed to find some snacks for the ride. At the intersection on A83, I turned right toward town—

A van came roaring up behind us and almost rear-ended me—

"Son-of-a-bitch nearly rammed us," I said.

Everyone craned back to see the van inches from our bumper. From the backseat, Ray spoke up.

"Ah, Buck? That looks like our friend Roger driving the van. He's pointing to the side of the road telling us to pull over."

"What the hell?" I said. "Has he been following us all day?"

"I never saw him when I was driving," Ray said. "Ahh, he just held a gun up and waved to the side of the road with it."

Seated next to me, Heather turned pale. "I'm scared," she said.

"Okay, guys, let's drive into town and see if we can either lose him or get him to back off."

The van was still on our ass, so once past the Inveraray Inn, I took a hard right into the cute little town composed of white two- and three-story buildings and stomped on the accelerator.

"Stay on the left side!" Heather shrieked.

Yikes—I swerved to the left to avoid oncoming traffic—Roger bumped his van into the back of the Rover, which caused me to swerve again.

The road was short and led straight toward a building in the middle of a traffic circle—I flew blindly around it—a pedestrian jumped out of the way—

BANG!

Roger rammed us again—

"Buck, do something!" Heather said.

There were more white buildings on both sides of us, but up a little farther, the road opened up and Loch Fyne was on our left. There'd be no place to lose or avoid Roger up ahead—I turned sharply to the left—the water was dead ahead.

Roger stuck to our tail, and I turned hard left again, and the loch was now on the edge of the road to the right—

"I've got the map up on my phone and this road's a dead-end," Ray said.

"Shit!" I said.

Potted plants and the backside of the white building was close to our left side, and there was a stone wall up ahead. An idea struck me. "Everybody buckle up!"

Roger was literally tailgating me so closely, I didn't think he could see around us, so I floored the accelerator—

"What are you doing." Heather's voice was shrill. "There's a wall straight ahead!"

"Hang on tight!"

We were doing nearly 100 kph and were approaching the wall fast—with Roger still on my bumper. I pumped the brakes once hard—he backed off a few feet—I locked the brakes and our tires screeched and black smoke erupted—

Roger braked the van, which was impossible—the white wall of a building was to our left, so he had no choice but to turn his wheel hard right to miss us—

BANG!

The van clipped our right rear quarter panel, which launched him further to the right—he hit a white bench on the lakeshore, spun in the strip of grass there and then took off over the edge of the low seawall and corkscrewed over the water and crashed hard, which sent an explosion of water in all directions.

My brakes squealed until I was a foot away from two liquid propane bottles in front of the stone wall where we screeched to a stop.

"Goddamn!" Lenny said. "Motherfucker's crazy!"

I jumped out of the Rover, ran around behind it and saw that the nose of the van was underwater and starting to sink. I waded out into the water, reached the side door of the van, pulled the handle—it was locked.

Damn!

The vehicle now rested on the muddy bottom, and as I slogged through the cold water and slop toward the driver's side door, I could see Roger slumped over the steering wheel. I grabbed the handle—his door opened very slowly as water poured inside.

Roger turned toward me, his right arm bent at an unnatural angle and the gun in his left hand.

"Damn you, Reilly!"

I punched him hard on his right cheek—his eyes crossed—the gun fell from his hand. He wasn't buckled in, so I grabbed him by his jacket and pulled him out of the vehicle and into the water. Dazed, he didn't struggle. I dragged him to shore and laid him down on the gravel there.

"My bloody arm's broken!" he said.

He swung at me with his left hand, but I pushed him down and put my knees on his shoulders—

"Agghh! My arm!"

"What the hell are you doing, Roger?"

"Why'd you go see the duke?" he asked.

"What choice did I have? You wouldn't tell me what I was looking for and we're running out of time."

"Cut the shit, Reilly!"

"Why are you following us?"

"Something happens to me, your timetable fast-forwards straight to your execution."

I shifted my weight onto his right arm—he screeched in agony.

Nothing I'd rather do than torture him, but to what end? Plus, I needed information from him. I dropped my right knee to the ground, which lessened my weight on top of him.

"How long have you been a part of the Sect?" I asked.

Roger growled, exposing his brown crooked teeth. "The duke must've been talkative. Unless you bushwhacked him too."

"We had a jolly reunion," I said. "He told me about the canister."

Roger grimaced. "What exactly did he tell you?"

"The canister contains some kind of cooperation agreement between the Campbells and the Stewarts."

"What about the map?"

"He said something about a diagram belonging to Robert the Bruce, too. It's a map, you say?"

Roger gritted his teeth and foam was caked in the corners of his mouth. His hand was bent in an impossible direction and his arm or wrist had to be broken, at least. I slid off him and stood up with my foot on his chest.

"Tell me about the Sect," I said.

"You're going to learn all about it now, laddie." His words hissed out between gritted teeth. "What else did the duke tell you?"

"That the Sect was established to protect the Scottish monarchy and history," I said. "Sounds like a rewarding career, good for you. I have no interest in either, so what the hell do you want from me?"

"My job was to kill you." He paused to grit his teeth. "But I gave you a break and caught plenty of shit over it from the Council. My mistake."

"What's the Council?"

Roger bit his lip and narrowed his eyes. "No more questions."

"Sorry, Roger, but I still have more I need to know." I slid the foot from his chest onto his right shoulder and then down his arm—his eyes bugged open, and he bit his lip to stem a scream.

"There's another document missing too, we believe it was with the canister," Roger said.

"What's so special about that other document?"

"I can't—"

I stepped down harder.

"Agghh!"

"Buck?" Heather's voice sounded behind me. "What are you doing?"

I ignored her.

"What's the other document?" I said.

"An ancient document … that belonged to … King Robert …"

"Back to Robert the Bruce? That's when the Sect started, right? During his time?"

"Just …" Roger winced, and I saw tears on his cheeks. "After his time."

"What kind of document is it?"

Roger pressed his eyelids closed tight as he fought through the pain of his broken limb. "A Codicil."

"That's like an appendix, or an amendment to something," I said. "To what?"

"That's all … I know."

"What about the map?" I asked. "What's it to?"

"I … don't know—they don't tell me … everything!"

"The Council, you mean. So you're just a soldier for the cause." I paused. "But you must have some sense of the map. The Council wouldn't kill us all for a cooperation agreement, I presume."

"The map … supposedly leads … to a cache of … precious … items."

I stood up straight. "So this is some kind of treasure hunt?"

"No … not at all." Roger sat up slowly and clutched his arm.

The sound of a siren was getting closer.

"Did the duke … offer any other suggestions on where … to find it?" Roger asked.

"He said I needed to speak with Harry. Just like you did. Only problem is, when I called and asked Harry for details, he hung up on me."

Roger's eyes narrowed, and then went wide. He started to laugh.

"The old bastard's buggering you just like he did your mother."

"What the hell's that supposed to mean?"

A calm passed over Roger's face. He'd adjusted to the pain and probably heard the siren too, so knew my time was running out.

"The Sect's been in existence for centuries. We operate with impunity here. I gave you three days, and half of that's up. No matter what happens to me, there are dozens of others who will pick up where I leave off."

Roger smiled, but there was evil, not joy in his eyes.

Another nagging question bothered me. "Why did the Duke of Argyll have the agreement, Codicil and map in his possession?"

Roger nursed his broken arm. "He's the head of Clan Campbell, the latest in a long line of Campbells to hold that role. Who else would hold the agreement?"

"What about the map?"

"No idea, but you'd better convince your old man to tell you the truth, or you'll suffer the same fate as his old mate."

"What old mate? What's that supposed to mean?"

"Frederick Lassiter. See if that name loosens Greenbaum's tongue."

The siren was now very loud, just on the other side of the building. I glanced over my shoulder and Ray had turned the Rover toward the left where a small alley led out between the buildings and back toward the center of town. Heather waved frantically for me to get in the vehicle.

"Better scoot, boy," Roger said. "The police don't take kindly to the torture of their citizens."

"Leave us the hell alone. I'll try to find out what happened to the damned canister and its contents, but if I see you again, I'm going straight to the American Consulate."

Roger began to laugh, so much that he shook as he stared back at me. "Don't think the Sect is only on our soil here, laddie. Plenty of Scots have emigrated to the States and throughout Europe. I'll leave it at that."

I started toward the Rover. "Leave us alone!"

"The Council won't roll over, Reilly." Roger shouted over the wail of the siren. "You got a day and a half left, that's it. And I'll be counting down the hours, believe me."

Roger spat at me when I looked back at him. Flashing lights rounded the corner now from the direction we'd turned off the main road and would be here any second.

I dove into the back of the Rover and Ray hit the gas, which pitched gravel back behind us as we fish-tailed away. I just got the door closed before we entered the narrow alley.

"Holy moly," Lenny said. "The shit show's getting worse and worse."

Once I was sitting upright, I pulled on my seat belt.

"Let's get to Dunfermline Abbey, ASAP," I said. "The sexton must know more than he told us the other day."

"You still want me to go to the airport and get Big Mama ready?" Ray asked.

"No," I said. "We don't have time for backtracking. After that run-in with Roger, we need to move fast and efficiently."

Ray drove through the town and then stomped on the gas pedal as we headed north around Loch Fyne. Time was of the essence.

14

THE DRIVE WAS LONGER BECAUSE WE TOOK A DIFFERENT ROUTE THAN when we came, just in case any of Roger's associates had followed us this morning. I don't recall if I even looked out the window at all on the ride to Dunfermline, focused instead on using my phone for research as we went in and out of cell coverage.

I found no information or even references on "The Sect."

I found no information on Robert the Bruce's Codicil.

I found no information on Frederick Lassiter.

All in all, the two-plus hours was wasted on the supposed information that Colin Campbell and Roger had given me.

Had it all been lies?

I pondered that for the balance of the ride and concluded that no, it would not make sense for them to give me bad information. There was less love than ever between us, but it would be a win for Roger and whatever the Sect's Council is if I found the missing information, so it would be silly for them to deceive me.

Ray pulled into the parking lot for Dunfermline Abbey, and I checked my old stainless steel Rolex Submariner. It was only 1:15 but felt more like two days had passed since we left Edinburgh this morning.

"You guys look around Catherine's grave. Now that we know about this cooperation agreement with the Stewart family, there must be more to her being surrounded by Stewarts here than we were told before."

"Want me to come with you?" Heather asked.

"No, better not."

She gave me a long look and I saw something in her eyes I'd never seen before.

Fear.

Not *for* me, but *of* me.

"It'll be fine," I said. "Just don't want to crowd him when I press for answers."

I climbed out and walked purposefully toward the abbey. Time was our most precious commodity right now and the trip to Inveraray used

84

more than we could afford but did provide some critical data. I only hoped the sexton would be as forthcoming.

Inside the abbey, there were a couple of small groups of tourists perusing the stained glass and Robert the Bruce's tomb. I walked up to see the tomb, which I hadn't focused on before. It was a seven-foot gold relief sculpture of him dressed in armor and carrying his sword and shield, with his hands together as if in prayer. A lion was curled around his feet and the entire golden relief was embedded in a dark red field of composite with a brass inscription that ran around the entire exterior edge. The inscription was in Latin, a language I didn't read, but on top was, "Roberti de Brus."

"What mysteries do you hold, old man?" I said.

No inspiration came to me, so I scanned the room and saw an office off to the right. The door was closed, but when I knocked, someone said, "Be right there."

A moment later the door opened, and the sexton stood in front of me with a fake smile and curious eyes. "Can I help you?"

"I was here yesterday, and you showed me to the grave of Catherine Campbell."

His smile faded and was replaced by a serious expression. Maybe even a worried one.

"Why are you back?"

"Can I come in?"

"I was just about to—"

I pushed him backward and cut off whatever excuse he was about to make. I closed the door behind me.

The sexton's eyes widened. "Excuse me, sir, but—"

"This will just take a minute, okay?"

The man backed away from me, and then circled around his desk where he stood as if to shield himself. He glanced at his phone.

"I need to better understand why Catherine was interred here amongst the Stewarts."

"I don't appreciate being cornered here—"

"Just answer my questions and I'll be on my way," I said.

"You have to understand, this is a sensitive subject—"

"Because of the Sect? Not to worry. My interests are aligned with theirs and I have no interest or intent to undermine Scottish history."

His mouth clamped shut for a moment as he studied my face. I smiled to try and keep the discussion light but given the circumstances of cornering him in his office, that wasn't likely. Since this was an important cultural site to Scotland, it made sense that the sexton had a role in the Sect, or at least reported to the Council.

"Why are you so interested in the details around Catherine Campbell?"

I'd anticipated this question, and while I wavered on my response, I banked on the truth being the best approach.

"Catherine Campbell Greenbaum was my natural mother."

His jaw fell open, and his eyes bugged. "She died giving birth to a ..."

"Son, that's right. Me. My birth father put me up for adoption and I was taken to America. I only recently learned of my heritage and that's why I'm here."

The sexton sat down at his desk. Had his face turned pale?

"To be totally honest, I don't know why she was buried here, but I can tell you the decision was made within the government—or at least by members of the government—and I was told to make it happen." He paused. "I'd be lying if I didn't say I'd been curious about it myself."

I sat in the lone chair facing him. I glanced around the small, but orderly office. There were no family photographs or mementoes here, only a simple wood desk with neat stacks of paper, an old computer and printer, a landline telephone, and some old photos of the abbey on the walls. No information to help me assess the man's personality or his nature.

"Any speculation?" I asked.

He licked his lips and sat back in the old leather chair that squeaked as it angled back.

"The Campbells have been a major clan in Scotland all the way back to the 1200s. My research upon being told to fit your, ah, Catherine in here, noted that the Campbells were important supporters of Robert I prior to Bannockburn and later." He paused. "But frankly, that didn't seem sufficient to explain the importance placed on her being here amidst the Stewarts, who of course are the descendants of Scottish and English kings and queens."

"So …?"

"So, nothing. I never found sufficient information to determine the rationale."

I decided to share some information myself to see how he responded.

"Are you familiar with a cooperation agreement between Clan Campbell and Clan Stewart that dates back to the time of Robert the Bruce?"

His expression was sincere as he shook his head side to side. "No, never heard of that. There're lots of Campbells in Scotland, and around the world for that matter, so even if that existed, I'm not sure why in Catherine's case it would have mattered."

"Understood," I said. "The Sect is interested in her case though, which must mean there is something unusual about her. I met with Colin Campbell, the Duke of Argyll, her father—"

"He would be your grandfather then."

"By birth, yes." I cleared my throat. "Would him being the head of Clan Campbell be sufficient to merit her burial here?"

"It is noteworthy, but again, why her and why that very specific location? We literally had to relocate another grave to accommodate the demand to place her there."

"That's what I'm trying to figure out too," I said.

The sexton rubbed his chin between his index finger and thumb. "The kings' names get confusing, so let's refer to Robert I as Robert the Bruce to make it easier. So, when Robert the Bruce died, his five-year-old son became King David II until he died. David had no male heirs, so protocol reverted to Robert the Bruce's daughter, Marjorie, who had married Walter Stewart, and had a son who became King Robert II. He was the first of the Stewart Kings and they controlled the monarchy for centuries."

"But what does that have to do with the Campbells?" I asked. "Or the rationale behind this cooperation agreement."

The sexton rubbed his hands together. "Since we're delving into the obscure, there was another theory amongst academics who had focused on Catherine's burial here," he said.

"What's that?"

"Colin is the 10th Duke of Argyll, but back in the mid-1500s, the

5th Earl of Argyll was Archibald Campbell. He was quite close to Mary Queen of Scots, who was a Stewart—and by the way—the Stewart monarchy includes both spellings of the name, S-T-U-A-R-T and S-T-E-W-A-R-T, so don't be thrown off if you see both."

"What was the obscure theory?"

"Just that the Campbell–Stewart relationship began with Robert the Bruce due to the Campbells' involvement and support in the fight against the English, particularly in Bannockburn, but continued and was also notable over two-hundred years later. We guessed that since Catherine was the 10th Duke's daughter, that the Stewart's thought it appropriate to have her buried with nobility from their past here at Dunfermline."

"Are there Stewarts that are buried here from that era?"

"We have Stewarts here dating back to Robert the Bruce, and as recent as the late 1800s, so, yes, but again, there are no definitive connections." A smile bent the sexton's cheeks. "However, the cooperation agreement you mentioned may shine a light on the specifics, which would be most interesting."

With no definitive connection between the Stewarts and Campbells as it relates to Catherine, his rationale at least provided a starting point to search for the purpose of the cooperation agreement. But there was also Robert the Bruce's map and this document referred to as a Codicil. The sexton was knowledgeable about the chronology of kings and when the Stewarts came to power and why, but these other elements may be too much of a tangent for me to raise. I didn't need to create more attention on the situation unless it would help me find the canister. Plus, since a Codicil was a type of amendment, maybe it changed the cooperation agreement somehow, and he had no knowledge about that anyway.

The sexton must've read my internal deliberation as confusion, because he then said, "The Campbells have always been a powerful clan, but back in the medieval times, they commanded armies, vast amounts of strategic land holdings and had the close ear of kings and queens. They had the power to topple kingdoms and change the course of history, which is exactly what the Sect's mission is designed to prevent."

It was the first time he acknowledged the existence of the Sect.

"How well known is the Sect?" I asked.

"It is known to exist but unclear as to how their mission evolved into modern times."

I grunted, which raised his eyebrows. I could elaborate on the Sect's threats against me, but again, didn't think it wise.

"So no idea who would be on the Council?" I asked.

"If it even still exists. There have been cases throughout the centuries of people being murdered or disappearing who were deemed a threat to the monarchy, and in some cases, of people who had challenged the chronology of recorded history due to secret alliances, agreements, or birth rights, but since the Sect operated outside the law, they always sought to stay out of the spotlight."

"It must consist, or consisted of, influential people though."

"Absolutely. The true movers and shakers who had no compunction against taking the law into their own hands for the greater good," he said.

"Or their own self-interests."

"As you say."

With that, I glanced at my watch. An hour had passed, and every minute counted. I stood up. "Thank you for taking the time, and sorry for forcing my way in."

"It's a pleasure to meet you, Mr. Campbell," he said. "Please let me know what you learn as we like to understand the details of those interred here under our care."

I hurried from his office and from the abbey itself. Americans are not accustomed to thinking about history that's nearly a thousand years old. As an archeologist, however, I found it fascinating, albeit a serious challenge to analyze the complicated relationships of all the parties. Since my life, and those of Heather and my friends, is on the line, this was far more than an intellectual challenge though. It was a matter of life and death.

Outside, I found Heather, Ray and Lenny sitting on a bench. Ray and Heather had their laptops out and Lenny was looking at his phone. Heather looked up when I walked toward them.

"Anything?" she asked.

"Lots, but not sure what any of it means yet. What are you all doing?"

"Researching the dozen Stewarts buried here. All are nobility, or closely related to members of the monarchy. Some have histories that mention Campbells, but nothing specific," she said.

"I'm going to take another look at Catherine's grave," I said.

"I'll come with you," Lenny said. "All this research bullshit's making me sleepy."

We walked along the perimeter of the abbey, like I'd done originally when the sexton first showed me the grave, and then cut under the trees to get there. Lenny grumbled about needing to get home, but my mind still swirled around the discussion with the sexton as my eyes focused on Catherine's headstone up ahead.

We stood in front of the simple yet intriguing block of granite. Simple due to the lack of information beyond her name, sans Greenbaum, and intriguing due to the symbols on the stone itself, particularly the skull. I got down on one knee to inspect the stone more closely.

While there was no date, it had been here nearly forty years and there had been some mild deterioration, along with moss and lichens that had attached themselves to the stone. I peeled those away and used my palm to clean the stone as much as possible. In doing this, I felt my throat begin to constrict with unexpected emotion.

What would my life had been like if she hadn't died?

Would Catherine have been a good mother?

How would Harry have been for a father?

I exhaled hard and tried to clear these thoughts. I loved my family and was proud to be a Reilly. None of this changes that, but still, I couldn't help but wonder.

The green and black lichens on the stone were more difficult to brush off, especially around the carved flowers and the skull, which protruded outward. I took the hotel room key from my pocket and scraped the fungus out of the flowers and turned to the skull last. It was the only detail in relief, and an odd ornament for a grave. A *memento mori* seemed unnecessary since there was no greater reminder of death than a tombstone.

The key was effective in scraping off the lichen, but there was a groove around the entire skull that was more difficult to penetrate as it was very fine and narrow. I pushed the key into the crack to dig—the skull moved in slightly.

"What the hell?" I said.

"What's the matter, man?" Lenny asked.

I dug some more around the groove and then pressed on the skull with my thumb—it pressed in more.

"The skull moves."

"What are you talking about?"

"You have anything sharper than my room key?" I asked.

Lenny pulled a steak knife from the hotel out of his pocket. "Don't look at me that way, man. People been trying to kill us."

I smiled. Can't blame Lenny for being prepared. The sharp knife was able to dig a fraction deeper, and once I'd scraped everything from the channel around the skull, I repositioned myself so I could assert maximum pressure on the relief. My thumb turned red from pressing so hard, but the skull sunk a half-inch into the stone, and I heard a scraping sound.

"You hear that?" I asked.

"Sounds like something's stuck."

I glanced around the face of the stone and saw nothing. I checked the right side as Lenny checked the left, and still nothing. In the back, near the bottom, there was an anomaly. I repositioned myself and scraped the moss and green/black fungus, which was thicker on this side of the stone. There was a slight bulge near the base, and when the organisms were scraped away, I noticed there was another fine groove that was rectilinear and two inches long. I dug furiously at that to scrape away the four decades of growth.

"Keep an eye out for anybody coming," I said.

"You can add grave-robbing to your résumé."

Once the groove was clean, I tried to force the knife into it, but the space was too fine.

"Try pressing the skull again," I said.

Lenny bent down and grunted when he pushed.

His eyes lit up. "It went in further."

The rectangle of stone in back popped out an inch. I was able to grab the sides and pull on what turned out to be a small tray that was spring operated. It didn't pull out all the way, but it didn't need to. Lenny must have been watching my face, because he bent down and looked around to the bottom.

"The hell's in there?"

My breathing had stopped when I saw the contents. I reached down and retrieved the small item and held it up to study.

"That another skull?" Lenny asked.

I placed it in my flat palm and we both scrutinized it. It was heavy for its size.

It matched the skull on the front of the tombstone, but it had a long, thin piece of metal extending from it with teeth carved into both sides.

"It's a key," I said. "A skeleton key."

"To what?"

"That, my friend, is what we need to figure out, and fast."

15

THE RIDE TO THE AIRPORT WAS FAST as it was just across the Queensferry bridge from Dunfermline, west of downtown Edinburgh. We exited the M9 highway at the Newbridge roundabout and followed signs to the airport. Once the terminal was in sight, we turned right into a long-term parking lot. If we didn't make it back to Edinburgh, I'd alert the rental company where it was—

A black van turned ahead of us into the parking area and stopped in the street to block our path—the rear doors flew open, and two men jumped out with guns. They were dressed in dark clothes, wore beards and hats. They walked toward us with their guns, some type of automatic weapons, pointed at the windshield.

"Ah, Buck?" Ray said.

"Back up!" I said.

The guns had long suppressors on the ends of their barrels. The men took positions on each side of our Rover.

Ray dropped the Rover into reverse and looked back over his shoulder—

THUMP, THUMP!

The Rover suddenly listed to the right. One of the men had shot our front right tire, which deflated immediately.

"What's happening?" Heather said.

"I don't want to die here, man," Lenny said.

"I'll handle it," I said.

I opened my door, raised my hands and climbed out. The man on my side of the vehicle walked up to me quickly, his gun aimed right at my head.

Is this it?

Are they here to kill us?

"Roger gave me three days," I said.

"Shut up, Reilly." The man's Scottish accent was strong. "Roger is in the hospital getting his broken arm set, thanks to you."

"It was an accident—"

The man was a few inches shorter than me, but handled the gun expertly, and alertly kept his eyes on me and the others in the Rover, as well as any other cars moving around the parking area near us.

"He told me to take the woman as insurance."

"No freaking way!" I said.

He jammed the gun in my gut and pain shot through my side doubling me over.

"He also said if you resist to shoot all of you here and now."

The door I'd climbed out of was still open and I glanced inside. Heather's mouth hung open and her eyelids were fluttering.

"Buck?" Her voice was brittle.

"You! Heather Drake, get out of the vehicle, now!" the man said.

The other man was positioned between the driver's door and passenger door on the other side, with his gun pointed at Ray's head.

"Take me," I said.

"We take you, who's going to find the missing canister?"

Shit. I glanced at Ray and Lenny.

"I'll go," Lenny said. "Goddammit."

"No," the man said. "Roger was very specific to take the woman."

Heather was breathing quickly in shallow gasps, until a sudden expression of resolution tightened her mouth. "It's okay," she said. "Ray and Buck need to fly the plane, and Lenny, I got you into this, I'll go."

I stepped toward the man with the gun, who had shifted the aim of the barrel toward Ray—I dove at him and wrapped my arm around his neck—

THUMP, THUMP, THUMP!

I'd caught him by surprise, and he fired straight up into the air—

Lenny popped the other rear door open near the other shooter—

The man stepped forward and jammed the end of his gun barrel into the side of Lenny's skull. "Let him go!" he yelled.

On my side, I still had the shooter's neck in the crook of my arm and was squeezing tight trying to make him pass out. He struggled but had the presence of mind to raise his gun and point it at Heather.

"Buck!" Her voice was a shriek.

"Now, Reilly!" the other shooter said.

I shoved the man forward and he slammed into the side of the Rover—he swung around and tried to slap me in the head with the gun—I leaned back and he missed.

"Stop!" Heather said. "I'll go with them."

I stepped back to the open door and leaned inside. "Heather, no ..."

"What choice do we have?" she said. "Just get back to Harry's and force him to cooperate."

She stepped down out of the Rover, visibly nervous, but miraculously calm too.

I spun around toward the gunman, who I guessed had to be in his mid-thirties. "You hurt one hair on her head—"

"If I hurt a hair on her head, that'll mean you're dead too. Clock is ticking, boy. The Council isn't happy about this, so don't give them an excuse to punch your ticket early."

Heather grabbed me by the arm. I could feel her hand shaking as she held onto me. I took her into my arms and pulled her tight.

"I'm sorry, Heather. We'll go straight to Harry's and get to the bottom of this immediately."

She held on tight, and my neck was suddenly wet with her tears. I squeezed her harder.

"Let's go, now!" the man next to me said.

Heather pushed out of my grasp. She had her phone and we shared locations, so as long as they kept it, I'd know where she was. The man grabbed her arm and led her quickly toward the back of the van while the other gunman covered us with his weapon. He helped Heather inside, slammed the door and then hurried back to me standing there, my mouth hung open and my jaw was trembling.

"Tick-tock, tick-tock, Reilly." He reached into his pocket and removed a cheap-looking cell phone. "Keep this on you. It has a tracker and Roger's number saved. Keep him informed on your progress and he'll establish a place to meet tomorrow."

I stepped toward the man. "You take good care of her, asshole, or so help me, God, I'll rip you apart, limb from limb."

He smiled.

"Such talk, it's like foreplay, to me, laddie." The smile faded. "Now get the hell out of here."

The two men backed away toward the van, their weapons still trained on us. They climbed inside and before I could do anything, had already spun the van around and drove past us out of the parking area.

"Un-fucking-believable," I said.

I ripped open the passenger door and jumped inside. Ray and Lenny were both pale and looked as if they were in shock.

"Let's move it, guys! Get us to Big Mama, ASAP."

Ray shook his head and exhaled hard. The private terminal was a good hike from here, which he must've realized we had no time to wait for a shuttle, so he backed the Rover into the grass, spun the wheel and turned back out toward the road.

CLUNK, CLUNK, CLUNK!

The flat tire bumped hard against the road as we drove, but we didn't care. Ray drove faster, the front end shook and turning was mush, but he drove like a champ toward the front of the private terminal.

"Should I park it?" he asked.

"Leave it out front. I'll text the concierge at the hotel and have them arrange for the rental company to pick it up."

"What the hell we gonna do now?" Lenny said.

"Beat the truth out of Harry, if necessary."

"What if he's gone?" Ray asked.

Damn, good point. I texted him that we were on our way and would be there within an hour or so and asked him to have Percy at the airport to pick us up. I ended the text by stating: "It's an emergency."

"He better damned well be there."

SECTION 3:

BEATING AROUND THE BUSH

16

I SET BIG MAMA DOWN HARD ON THE RUNWAY AT
COTSWOLD AIRPORT. Ray had wanted to fly, recognizing how
distraught I was, but I needed to concentrate on something other than
Heather's fate in their custody. Plus, even while flying, I was able to think
about my plan from here, which depended on Harry's cooperation.

With any luck, we'd retrieve the damned canister and get back to
Edinburgh tonight.

I taxied Big Mama to the same location we'd left her at a couple of
days ago. To think we'd gone to Scotland excited to learn about my birth
mother and her family, only to return in a race for our lives, was beyond
comprehension. Harry had warned me to stay under the radar, which
we'd done, but somehow, Roger knew we were coming and tracked us
from the minute we'd landed. I wish Harry had been more convincing.

Harry's dark burgundy Rolls Royce rolled slowly around a hangar
and onto the tarmac where it drove unhurriedly toward Big Mama.

"I'll do the postflight check," Ray said.

"Forget it. If we're not successful in the next twenty-four hours, we
won't be flying her again," I said.

Both Ray's and Lenny's jaws dropped open.

"Sorry, guys. I don't want to sugarcoat the circumstances here. We're
up to our eyeballs in a deadly situation and hold very few cards."

I shut down both engines, turned off the batteries, and then
unbuckled my harness.

I took my cell phone out of the pocket next to my seat. No calls, no
texts. I pulled up Heather's name to check her location, but her phone
was no longer sharing that information with me. Bastards must've shut
it down.

"I hope that damned skeleton key leads to something," Lenny said.

I touched the breast pocket on my shirt where it was placed.

"Me too, now let's go."

I led the way through the fuselage, popped open the rear hatch and
swung it open. Percy was there waiting. I'd wondered whether Harry

would come, but he hadn't. A sudden jolt of anxiety hit me—what if Harry was away but got the message and sent Percy?

When the ladder was in place, I climbed down and walked straight to Percy.

"Where's Harry?"

"At Hampshire Manor awaiting your arrival."

Whew.

"Where's Ms. Heather?" Percy asked.

"Being held hostage by the Sect," I said.

His brow wrinkled as if I'd responded in an alien language. He studied my face, and with no humor visible, he climbed back in the Rolls and started the engine. We followed him in and Percy set off down the taxiway much faster than when he'd arrived.

The drive to Hampshire Manor was quick. Without having been told, Percy had picked up on the urgency of the situation and drove accordingly. The rest of us weren't much in the mood for conversation, so I ran through the circumstantial facts we'd amassed to date. There wasn't much, and I had no idea where it would lead, but if Harry were obstinate, then I'd at least have some facts to press him on. I used the notes app on my phone to make a list of what seemed to be the most pertinent items:

1. Catherine was the daughter of the Duke of Argyll, who was also head of Clan Campbell.

2. The canister that Catherine and Harry took from the duke was considered a family heirloom and contained some type of cooperation agreement between the Campbells and Stewarts, dating back to the 1300s and possibly the time of Robert the Bruce.

3. There was also some type of map that belonged to Robert the Bruce, but nobody knows what it leads to, aside from some mention of "riches."

4. There was some other historic document referred to as "the Codicil" either in the canister, or with it.

5. The Sect is an ancient organization run by something called "the Council" and is tasked with protecting the monarchy and Scottish history.

6. The Sect wants me dead—why?

7. We found a secret drawer in Catherine's headstone, and it contained a skeleton key—to what?

8. Who is Frederick Lassiter, an old friend of Harry's?

I read over the list again and there were more questions than answers, but several were ones Harry could shine a light on. Percy turned off the main road, entered a code on the keypad to open the gates and then proceeded down the long gravel road to the lake in front of Hampshire Manor.

"Wonder which is worth more, this place or the castle at Inveraray?" Lenny said.

"Both are insane," Ray said.

"A lot of former 'summer homes,' which is what the Brits call a place like this, can be purchased on the cheap," I said. "If they're not well maintained, you can imagine the cost to get them up to snuff would be extraordinary. Most families can't afford to keep them."

"Except yours," Lenny said.

"Not my family, Lenny. In either case…" I paused. "The Campbells have no interest in me, and Harry's been great to me as both an investor and a friend, but our future relationship hinges on what happens next."

Percy peeked in the mirror for a second and shuffled in his seat but kept driving. Part of me hoped he'd report my statements to Harry. The situation was bad enough before Heather got taken, but now, well, it was scorched earth.

Either Harry cooperated or our relationship was over.

The Rolls pulled to a stop in front of Hampshire Manor's main entrance. Harry was not there waiting with open arms, which I took as a bad sign. I jumped out and hurried toward the front door without waiting for anyone else. My adrenalin pumped harder with each step. The door opened as I jumped up the steps two at a time. It was a butler in full uniform.

"Master Buck," he said. "Sir Harry is waiting for you in the library."

Master? Please.

I continued forward, stopped suddenly and turned on the ball of my foot back to face the man. "My friends are hungry. Can you have someone feed them?"

"Of course, sir."

What's this Master bullshit? Harry must have told his staff I was his son. Since he's knighted, the term Master would fit his son. I remembered my way to the library and walked there directly. The door was closed, and I didn't bother knocking or asking permission to enter. I pushed it open and walked inside.

Harry was seated in the same leather chair by the fire where he was when he blew my mind about being my birth father. That was only a few days ago but felt like a lifetime. The news had commenced a domino effect of escalating events that would change my life and the lives of my closest friends forever. Harry didn't bother trying to stand. I saw he was wearing his silk smoking jacket, but thankfully, didn't have a cigar burning.

"Buck, welcome back—"

"Spare me the bullshit hospitality, Harry." I stood in front of his chair and looked down upon him. "I wouldn't be here if you hadn't ghosted me. The Sect took Heather as collateral, and I have a day and a half left to find and return the canister you and Catherine took from the Duke of Argyll, or we all get killed."

"The Sect," he said. "I see. You have been busy."

"I've been stabbed in the back, gun-whipped, treated with disdain by my biological grandparents, and nearly killed in a car chase. But more importantly, as I said, Heather's been kidnapped."

Harry repositioned himself in his well-worn leather chair. His face betrayed no emotion, regret, or repentance, but what did I expect from a billionaire who had bought, built, and sold multimillion-dollar companies for sport.

"And you hung up on me and ignored my plea for help," I said.

"I am truly sorry for all that you have been through." He paused. "I hung up on you because I was trying to keep you out of danger, not send you into it ..." His voice trailed off and he cleared his throat. "It's been forty years. I'd hoped that the ghosts of the past had settled into oblivion by now. I should have never made it known that you were my son—"

"Biological son," I said.

Harry winced.

"How did the duke and duchess respond to you?"

"With total indifference. I might have been any tourist ogling their castle were it not for the missing canister, which they clearly want back very badly."

Harry grunted. "I'm sorry to hear that."

"Some things in life are better left buried," I said.

I hoped Harry recognized the innuendo in my statement—that he should have left our biological connection unspoken—but it was too late now.

"Quite."

"Tell me about the canister, Harry. What's inside it?"

Harry forced his massive girth upright in his chair. "It's been a very long time since I—"

"Don't bullshit me, Harry. Heather's life—all our lives for that matter—are on the line."

"As I recall, there were a couple of historic documents that she— your mother—was fascinated in researching."

"Biological mother."

I already knew what was in the canister but wanted to see what Harry shared with me.

"Do sit down, won't you? Would you like a sandwich, or something to—"

"I just want answers."

Harry reached for his beverage on the small table next to him—was it water? Wine? Something stronger? Right now I didn't care.

"First of all, the canister was aptly named. It was a silver, waterproof tube with an elaborate locking system. There were two documents in the canister, but Catherine guarded them quite closely, even from me. One, she'd said, was some type of accord between Clan Campbell and Clan Stewart that dated back very far."

"Like a cooperation agreement?" I asked.

"Something like that."

"Why would two families need that?"

"I do recall asking her that exact question, and she dismissed me stating that these things were not uncommon in those days as strategic relationships changed frequently based on who was king, whether there was war with England, feuds with other clans or during transitional times between kings or queens."

I kept quiet. Harry was talking and I wanted to give him as much rope as possible.

"I don't think I ever read it in detail," Harry said. "The other document was referred to as a Codicil and dated back to Robert I, but frankly, I wasn't much interested in an ancient document of that nature so never read it."

"Was that it?"

"What do you mean?"

"The total contents of the canister."

More rope … Harry studied my face. I suspected he was searching for any sign or change of expression that might give him a clue what else I'd learned. I concentrated on maintaining my poker face.

His lips puckered and unpuckered a few times as he clearly wrestled with how much to tell me. Was that to protect me, or something else?

"There was another item." He paused and again studied my eyes.

"And?"

He clasped his hands in front of him and wrung them together. My tone indicated greater knowledge, even to me, which for the sake of our relationship in the future, I was giving him a clue not to lie or omit important details—like Robert the Bruce's map.

"The other item was one that Catherine cared little for, but I was enamored with."

"What was it?" I asked.

"There was a crude map that dated back to Robert I himself."

"What kind of map?"

"It was a simple sketch with a few landmarks. Virtually impossible to deduce."

"I didn't mean what it looked like, what do you think it was of?"

"Oh, I see." He sipped his drink again. "Legend had it that it led to a cache of valuables that Robert I had hidden during his reign."

"How did the Campbells attain this canister with these historically important documents?"

"You were raised in America where the duration of history is a mere footnote compared to that of the British Isles. Clan Campbell is, and for the last thousand years, has been highly influential here, all the way back to Robert I and prior. In fact, the Campbells played critical roles in the success of not only Robert the Bruce at Bannockburn, but even William Wallace before him. So, while I don't know how exactly the duke came into possession of what you refer to as the canister, his ancestors were extremely close with the monarchy, especially Robert I."

"That's not really an answer."

"I can't tell you with any certainty how the contents were appropriated, aside from speculating that members of Clan Campbell were close to Robert I. Perhaps he gave it to them for safekeeping, or they stole it from him. The truth lies somewhere in between." He paused. "The only certainty was that the canister that housed the documents was very old."

I let silence play out as I absorbed what Harry had said and thought of what else I hoped to learn before demanding the canister back.

"Now that I've been to Dunfermline Abbey, where Robert the Bruce and several other members of royal families were buried, I realize the significance of Catherine being placed there is considerable." I paused to let that sink in. "How did that happen?"

"As I told you previously, I had no say in the matter."

"You said you provided the headstone though, sans your last name, which they prohibited."

"Correct."

"Is there anything special about the headstone?"

Like a secret compartment!

"Hardly. The instructions were specific on what was allowed."

"Where did you have it fabricated?"

Harry paused, pursed his lips and fidgeted in the chair. "Actually, since I was not allowed to attend, and frankly, feared for my life, I had an associate arrange for it in Edinburgh."

"So you never saw it?"

"Not initially. I snuck to Dunfermline some years later to ... pay my respects ... and ... mourn."

"What instructions did you provide to your associate for the headstone?"

"Why the fascination with the headstone? Am I missing something?"

Interesting.

"There are some odd details that I didn't understand."

His face lit with recognition. "Ahh, the skull. Yes, I have to say I was surprised by that feature as well. It was not included in my instructions. I assumed her family had requested it, or my, ah, colleague added it as an editorial feature given the estrangement between the parties."

Did Harry not know about the secret compartment?

Unsure how to proceed, I crossed my arms and felt the lump in my shirt pocket. I undid the button and removed the skeleton key and held it out to him.

Harry took it from my hand and rolled it around in his palm studying it. His face was of complete confusion. "What's this?"

"You don't recognize it?"

"Looks like a prop out of *Pirates of the Caribbean*," he said. "Did Johnny Depp give it to you?"

"Take a close look at the skull."

Harry donned his reading glasses and spun it around slowly close to his face. His eyebrows suddenly arched, and a higher-pitched tone sounded from his open mouth. He grabbed both sides of his chair and pulled himself up and out.

"Where are you going?" I asked.

He ambled over to the massive executive desk next to the glass French doors that led outside. From where I sat, the desk appeared to be a mountain of paperwork, bound reports, a humidor, and a pitcher of water.

Harry reached down to the back corner and plucked up a small picture frame. He glanced from the frame to the key, let out another grunt, and walked back to the fire where I watched him.

"It appears to be the same skull we were just discussing on Catherine's gravestone."

He handed me back the key and the frame which contained a 4- by 6-inch color photo of Catherine's headstone. It was taken on a fall day, with the sun shining and the foliage red and orange on the tree that shaded her grave, and that of the Stewarts around her.

"You have a picture of her grave?"

Harry sat abruptly in his chair, which let out a woof of air from the seat cushion as his girth compressed it. His eyes suddenly fluttered and his jaw quivered.

"She was the one love of my life, Buck. Of course I do. Not a day goes by that I don't think of her."

Harry's flush of emotion made me pause. I'd been so focused on the details of the canister, the Sect's efforts to kill us and my concerns over Harry's lack of transparency, I'd completely overlooked the fact that he'd lost his wife in a brutal fashion—so brutal that he'd given their son—me—up for adoption.

"I'm sorry, Harry. It had to be terrible for you."

Now he squirmed in his seat. Harry was old school. The discussion of loss and emotion were frowned upon in his generation. A man was meant to power through, not dwell on sadness, but that didn't mean it hadn't been soul-crushing.

Harry stared into the fire. The recognition of his—our—loss took the edge off my posture, my gut told me he was still holding out on me. I bit the side of my mouth and pulled my cell phone from my pocket. I'd taken a photo of the secret compartment on the stone before closing it again. I handed my phone to Harry, who studied it closely, but when he peered up over his reading glasses, he wore a look of total bewilderment.

"I don't understand," he said.

"There's a secret compartment in the headstone. Once cleaned up from moss and dirt, the skull turned out to be a button that once pressed, opened a small compartment on the back bottom of the stone. The key was inside."

"Well, I'll be buggered."

That was the raciest thing I'd ever heard Harry say before.

I handed him his photo back. "You didn't know about it?"

"Absolutely not."

Harry may be a master negotiator and business titan, but I'd always considered him honest and relatively straight forward. I took his shock at face value and mulled over the remaining few pertinent facts I'd learned but not yet raised. One now seemed timely.

"Who is Frederick Lassiter?"

Harry exhaled deeply and closed his eyes.

17

HARRY'S EYES GOT WIDE AND HE SAT BACK IN HIS CHAIR. "Your resourcefulness never ceases to amaze me." Harry paused to sip his drink. "Frederick, among other things, was the man who had Catherine's headstone made for me in Scotland. Where did you hear his name mentioned?"

"From Roger, the guy from the Sect who is counting down the hours to kill us if I don't return the canister to him."

"I can't believe this is still so relevant that this so-called Sect will kill over it."

"Take my word for it, they're serious." I studied his face. "You said, 'among other things,' what else did Frederick do?"

Harry shook his head. "Frederick was what you might call a fixer. He was quite handy and helped me to, well, solve some issues early in my business career. When Catherine died, I gave Frederick the canister and told him it contained important historic information and to place it somewhere that would not be discovered until far in the future, and only at a time when the world had bigger problems to sort than aspects of ancient history."

"Why'd you do that?"

"Because the bloody Campbells were threatening my life at the time. My home was broken into, rifled to shreds, and demands were made by intermediaries—perhaps from this Sect—that if the information from the canister was ever made public, they would kill me and hunt you down as well. I needed it in a safe place without knowledge of its whereabouts so they couldn't torture the truth out of me—which their henchmen tried to do."

"You were tortured?"

"Indeed I was. They gave me no grace period after your mother's death, and it was bloody fortunate that Charles and Betty adopted you when they did, or the Sect may have taken you hostage, or worse."

A shiver passed through me, and I had to fight back tears. I jumped up from my chair, walked over to Harry's desk, and poured water from the pitcher into a glass. I closed my eyes for a moment and pictured Heather being whisked away by her kidnappers, which strengthened my resolve.

"Back to the contents, Harry. You didn't make copies for yourself before entrusting them to Frederick Lassiter?"

"Whether copies or originals, the outcome would've been the same—me getting killed and them hunting you down. When their men did come for me, it was fortunate I'd had that foresight as they asked that same question, under extreme duress, I might add."

I paced around his massive office, glancing at paintings, sculpture, business awards, and other mementoes of Harry's life.

"Did you tell them you gave the canister to Frederick?"

"Alas, I gave them Frederick's name—I had no choice—but he was of royal lineage himself, so a protected class from the Sect, or so I thought."

"What's that mean?"

"Frederick died under mysterious circumstances some ten years ago. I hadn't spoken to him in decades, and per our agreement, he never told me what became of the canister."

"That's a big gap in between," I said. "What do you think took them so long?"

"I suspect Frederick had another royal hold the canister for him or help to hide it. My guess is that Frederick was either running his mouth, or the Sect believed the contents may come to light, so they may have killed him."

"Great. Heather's their captive now, and I have thirty-five hours to produce the canister, or she dies."

Harry exhaled hard. "Is there any means for a counter-offensive?"

"No way, Harry. We just don't have enough time and I have no idea who is on the Sect's Council, which is who I'd go after to gain her release."

"I'll work on that," he said. "In the meantime, last I heard, Frederick's widow is still alive and living in Amsterdam. Maybe she has some knowledge of what Frederick did with the canister."

"Sounds like another wild goose chase," I said. Then, under my breath, "But what choice do I have?"

"I'll find her address."

I glanced at my ancient Rolex Submariner. The gunman's phrase, "tick-tock, tick-tock," came to mind. I jumped up. "Can Percy take us back to the airport?"

"Of course."

"Is there anything else of relevance you can remember about the canister or Catherine that might be helpful in understanding the big picture here?"

Harry licked his lips and then fiddled his fingers for a moment.

"There is one other detail you should be aware of," he said.

Already headed to the door, his statement stopped me in my tracks. I spun around to face him.

"Catherine was under the impression that she was a direct descendant of King Robert the Bruce—an illegitimate one, that is."

"Robert I died nearly 700 years ago, Harry. Why on earth would another bastard child matter?"

There was no answer to that question, and I couldn't imagine why it could matter either, but our ignorance was irrelevant as it might be of greater importance to the Sect.

Harry and I said our goodbyes, I gathered up Ray and Lenny from their impromptu feast, and Percy was waiting for us out front to return us to the airport. We again made the trip in record time, and I filled the guys in on what I'd learned from Harry along the way. Percy couldn't help but hear the discussion and glanced repeatedly in his rearview mirror as I shared the new information.

Ray filed our flight plan to Amsterdam via an app on his phone, so when we arrived at Cotswold Airport, we were able to get going right away. Harry texted me Frederick Lassiter's widow's address, which was in downtown Amsterdam, so by the time we took off, we had a plan. It may have been a flimsy plan, but at least we were moving forward.

Anxiety for Heather's safety wrenched my gut as Ray flew us to Schiphol Airport, where we landed and taxied to the VIP terminal with all the other private planes. As we taxied toward our designated ramp, Ray spoke with the team at the FBO to arrange for Big Mama to be fueled up, and for a car to town. When they asked if we were staying the night, Ray turned to me.

"Arrange for one night in case the damned canister is still here in Amsterdam."

"Always wanted to visit Amsterdam and check out the red-light district," Lenny said.

"Hoping to save some souls there, Pastor?" I said.

"Something like that."

The FBO also arranged a driver for us, and I provided the address that Harry had sent me: Prinsengracht 343, 1016 GZ Amsterdam. I checked the map app on my phone and saw that this was an apartment downtown, on the outer ring of canals, near the Pulitzer Hotel where I'd stayed previously while on business here back in the e-Antiquity days.

The ride to town didn't take long, and next thing we knew, we were dropped off in front of the red brick, four-story building. It faced a broad canal of brown water, with a bridge to the right and more three- and four-story, narrow buildings on the other side. There were five buttons by the door, and the Lassiter apartment comprised the third floor.

"Think we should all go up?" Ray asked.

"I think so. Our numbers highlight the importance of the situation."

With that, I pressed the button marked "Lassiter."

The speaker popped to life and a female voice asked a question in Dutch.

"*Wie is daar?*"

"Oh shit, man, what if she don't speak English?" Lenny said.

I pushed the button again. "Hi, my name's Buck Reilly. I'm here from England and have a couple questions about your husband, Frederick."

The microphone again popped back on. "Freddy's been dead forever."

"I know, ma'am. My, ah, father, used to do business with Freder—er—Freddy, and we just want to see if you recall anything about one thing they worked on together."

A long pause ensued.

A buzzer finally sounded, and I grabbed the door handle and pulled it open. Inside there was a small, bright lobby with a half-dozen mailboxes built into the wall, a stairwell, and a small elevator. I pushed the button to the lift and the door opened right up. It was so small, we could barely all three fit inside.

"Keep your hands off my ass, Ray," Lenny said.

Ray rolled his eyes as he fidgeted in the tight space. The elevator crept its way up to the third floor and opened to another smaller lobby.

There were doors on both sides, and the one on the left popped open. A woman, I'd guess in her seventies, wearing a knee-length floral skirt in muted colors, stood there inspecting the three of us. I stepped between Ray and Lenny and extended my hand to her.

"Ms. Lassiter, my name's Buck Reilly and these are my colleagues, Ray and Lenny."

"You don't sound British."

"Ah, that's right, ma'am, I'm—we're American, but my father lives in the Cotswolds."

"Fancy," she said.

She looked at each of us again, and then waved for us to follow her. Inside, the apartment was full of antiques and area rugs that may have once produced an aura of wealth and sophistication but were now just dusty and old. She led us to a small living room with a couch and a chair that faced an old television. She lowered herself into the chair, which left us to squeeze shoulder-to-shoulder on the paisley couch.

She took a sip of tea but didn't offer us any.

"You say your father did business with Freddy?"

She glanced toward an old photograph on a buffet. It was of her and a man I assumed to be her husband. He had dark beady eyes that reminded me of a crow.

"That's right, ma'am. Back in the mid-eighties, or so."

"Yes, well, we lived in London in those days. Freddy was always in the middle of crazy schemes back then. Who did you say was your father?"

"His name is Harry Greenbaum. Now, Sir Harry, in fact."

"Freddy was not a nice man, nor were most of the people he did business with."

"My father is considered quite nice, I think. He was just knighted recently for his success in business. The matter I'm here to inquire about was of a personal nature that Freddy helped him with."

"He must be a shit if he was knighted for business. Nice people are not as successful as shits."

She sipped her tea as she studied us closely. She focused on Lenny.

"Who are you, young man?"

Lenny sat forward. "I'm Lenny Jackson from Key West, Florida. Pastor Lenny Jackson, that is."

"Man of the cloth, eh? Wouldn't have guessed it looking at you," she said.

Lenny was wearing jeans, white tennis shoes, and a bright yellow polo shirt, so it was a fair point. I just hoped she wasn't going to say something that would insult him as Lenny isn't one to hold his tongue. I intervened.

"We came to ask you about a silver canister my father had given to Freddy for safekeeping—"

"Who's the quiet one with the fancy moustache?" she asked.

Ray held a finger up. "Ray Floyd. I'm a pilot. I flew these gentlemen here."

"Private plane, eh? You must have money, Mr. Reilly. And a man of God, too. Do you always travel with your pastor?"

I bit my lip. The zigging and zagging of the conversation was wasting precious time that we didn't have to spare, but this was a critical connection, so I had to play along.

"My plane was built in 1951, so it's not exactly luxurious." I paused. "And yes, Pastor Lenny travels with me frequently."

She scowled. "Religion is hogwash."

Crap.

She narrowed her eyes and focused on me. "Private planes, Cotswolds, and all, sounds like you can afford to help a destitute old woman if I'm able to help you."

"Of course, I'd be happy to. If you can recall anything useful. Did my father's name, Harry Greenbaum, sound familiar to you?" I asked.

"From the 1980s?" She said something else in Dutch, which based on her expression, seemed to be derogatory. "Harry, you say?"

I nodded my head.

Her eyebrows lifted. "I remember someone Freddy called Hank who he ran around with in those days." Her eyes lit up. "He had a beautiful Scottish wife. Tall, blond hair, quite enchanting as I recall. She was pregnant, I think."

I swallowed my surprise. "That would have been Catherine, my mother. She was pregnant with me around that time."

"She died, as I recall."

My smile slid to a frown. "That's correct. In fact, that's when my father gave Freddy the silver canister."

"We left England for here not long after that." She grimaced. "Freddy got into some kind of trouble—he wouldn't tell me what—but he felt it would be better for us to come back here, where I grew up."

"Do you recall the canister? I can't really describe it, but it wasn't large. It contained a few small items," I said.

"Some kind of documents, maybe?" she said.

"That's right." I sat forward unable to contain my excitement. "Do you have any idea what he did with the canister, or the documents that were inside it?"

"That was forty years ago! How would I remember that?"

I sat back into the couch and ran through my conversation with Harry in my head.

"Was there a British nobleman who Freddy consulted with around that time? Harry thought maybe he gave the canister to someone like that."

Madame Lassiter blew out of her mouth so hard her lips flapped. "That would have been James Conway, Duke of something or other. Freddy was so thrilled to be hobnobbing with royalty—even though he was a baronet—he was blind to the fact that Conway was a total ass."

"Do you know if the duke is still alive?" I asked.

"He was twenty or so years younger than Freddy, so I would think so."

"My father said Freddy had died ten years ago. I'm so sorry—"

"Don't be. He was a bastard in every sense of the word."

"What was his cause of death?" I asked.

"Impact." She raised an eyebrow. "He fell off a building."

"Fell, or pushed?" I asked.

"Likely thrown. Bloody well deserved it, but the local police deemed it to be suicide even though there was no note."

"Did that happen here in Amsterdam?"

"No, Oslo. Business trip." Her eyes lit up again. "James, the Duke of arrogance, was there too."

I mulled this information over. Harry speculated that the Sect may have thought the info in the canister was going to come to light, or that Freddy had been running his mouth as rationale behind his death. He also thought Freddy gave the canister to a noble to protect himself and provide some level of immunity from the Sect. Given that she said James Conway was on the business trip too, maybe there's some validity to his speculation.

"Do you know where James Conway lives?" I asked.

"I believe he's in London with a summer house out in the countryside somewhere, but he's one of those mover-and-shaker types that tries to be in the middle of everything to peddle influence." She paused. "Just like Freddy used to."

"You've been very helpful, Madame Lassiter," I said.

I dug in my pocket and pulled out my money clip. It was a hodgepodge of currencies but only added up to a hundred dollars. I spied a frown on widow Lassiter, so turned to Ray and Lenny and nodded toward the cash in my hand.

"Pass the hat, boys," she said. "Just like at church, Mr. Pastor."

Lenny groaned and made a dramatic show of pulling out his wallet. He removed a $100 bill and dropped it in my palm with my cash. Ray contributed eighty euros, and I handed it to the woman who may have been more like her deceased husband than we realized.

"You said the police had investigated Freddy's death. Do you recall the name of the detective?" I asked.

"Her name was Pedersen." She smiled. "That's my maiden name, so I never forgot it." Her eyes lit up. "In fact, I still have the detective's business card."

She stood up, went to the buffet and opened a drawer below where the picture of she and Freddy was, shuffled some papers around and then lifted up a business card.

"Do you mind if I take a picture of that?"

"Suit yourself."

She handed me the card, and I took a picture with my phone. I'd call her when we left here and arrange a meeting.

"Can I get your phone number if I think of any other questions? And maybe you can look around for any information from back in the mid-80s when my dad gave Freddy the canister."

She took a pen and a pad of yellow sticky notes off her side table and wrote her number on it. "I'm available and happy to provide wiring instructions for additional assistance."

We all three stood simultaneously, took turns shaking her hand and then left her flat and waited for the elevator.

115

"What a hustler," Lenny said.

"Gave me the creeps," Ray said.

"Let's see what we can find on Duke James Conway," I said. "Hopefully it made this use of precious time worthwhile."

18

"WE CAME ALL THE WAY HERE FOR THAT ONE MEETING?"
LENNY ASKED.

We stood in front of Madame Lassiter's building while we waited for
a taxi.

"I didn't expect the canister to be sitting on her coffee table, but at
least she was home, she let us in and gave us some valuable information."

"You mean *sold* us some information," Ray said.

Lenny held his fist up and Ray bumped his knuckles.

"I owe you guys, not only for the cash, but for sticking around to
help me out," I said.

"We gotta get Heather back, man," Lenny said. "What if we can't find
this damned can of worms? You think of a way to go after this Sect yet?"

"Possibly, but we need to find out more about Duke Conway first."

"Duke, Duke, Duke, Duke of Earl, Earl, Earl, Duke of Earl …" Ray
sang.

"Spare us the oldies, Ray," I said.

The taxi pulled up and we climbed in.

"Schiphol Airport, please," I said.

"Which terminal?" the driver asked.

"Private aviation."

"How we gonna find out about the Duke of Earl?" Lenny asked.

"First of all, that's not his name. That's an old song from the 1960s,"
I said. "Second, I'm hoping that Harry will know the guy. If he's really a
mover and shaker, then Harry should, especially now that's he's so
devoted to king and country."

"Sir Harry, Sir Harry—"

"Ray, please. I'm not in the mood for this," I said.

I held up my phone and hit the speed-dial button for Harry. It rang
a few times before he answered.

"Hello, Buck. Any luck in Amsterdam?"

"Yes, we met the widow Lassiter. She suggested we find a duke named
James Conway."

"James Conway," Harry said. "The Duke of Oxford. Slippery old coot, that one."

"Well, it sounds like he may be the one that Frederick, or Freddy the frontman, entrusted the canister to." I paused but Harry didn't respond. "You know him?"

Harry exhaled into the phone. "Yes, I have done business with him in the past—unsuccessfully, I might add."

"How so?"

"He claimed to be authorized to sell a company I was interested in acquiring, but that turned out to be false and it created a mess at the closing table when the firm's real representative demanded to be paid. Cost me double the transaction fees because right or wrong, I couldn't stiff the duke," Harry said.

"Sounds like a real upstanding gentleman," I said.

"Quick lesson on peerage, young man. In Britain, dukes and duchesses are the highest form of title below the monarchy. Then come marquesses, earls, viscounts, barons, and baronets," Harry said.

Ray started humming *Duke of Earl* again and I waved my hand at him to stop.

"I wouldn't say that dukes are above the law, but they do have a lot of latitude." Harry hesitated. "Given my interest in attaining a title myself, I wasn't going to create a stir over his six-figure impropriety."

"Whatever, Harry. Sounds like maybe he owes you one. I need you to call him and set up a meeting for later today."

"That's very short notice—"

"You do remember that we're up against a clock here, right? Tick tock, tick tock, and all that?" I hesitated, but then said, "And I need you to be at the meeting."

"I'm afraid that's not ..." Harry stopped himself. He cleared his throat. "I will call him as soon as we hang up."

"Thanks, Harry. Madame Lassiter speculated that the duke may have a country estate, which I presume would be in Oxford, but otherwise he spends his time hustling people in London."

"I will let you know what I find out."

"We're on our way to the airport now, so timing is important, so we know where to go. Call me back ASAP."

Harry hung up and my friends stared at me. I didn't have it on speakerphone as I didn't want the driver to listen to the details.

"Duke of Oxford," I said. "Oxford is between Harry's place and London, as I recall."

"I'll search for airports," Ray said.

"File a flight plan to whatever's the closest airport to Oxford and another one to London, so we can get airborne," I said.

"You're not supposed to file two separate flight plans for the same time," Ray said.

"Really, Ray?"

Ray rolled his eyes. He knew me well enough to know that I wouldn't let formalities get in the way of what I was after, especially in this case since all I really cared about was Heather's safety, and ultimately our own. I checked her location again and her phone was still off. Roger's burner phone was in my pocket, so I assumed he'd been tracking our travels. I could only hope that would prove our desire to be helpful if in the end we failed to find the canister.

The cab ride to Schiphol's VIP terminal was quick and given the simplicity of the flight plan to Oxford, Ray completed that quickly. The plan to London was more challenging.

"Let's hope he's in Oxford because we can't get into London Heathrow for a few hours," Ray said. "I can change our flight plan en route, if need be."

"Fine, just be ready to file a plan to another private airport just outside of London if necessary. We need to be ready to go when Harry—"

My phone rang. It was Harry.

"I spoke with the duke. He's a bigger boor than I even recalled. He smells money, of course."

"Where is he?"

"Waddesdon Manor, which is northeast of central Oxford."

I put the phone on mute and turned to Ray.

"We're heading to Oxford, some place called Waddesdon Manor."

"On it," Ray said.

Harry continued. "It's a spectacular French Renaissance-style chateau that Baron Ferdinand de Rothschild built in the late 1800s. It's been open to the public for decades, but James has been squatting in an adjacent residence for some time. He likes to pretend he owns it, but that's not the case."

"Looks like it's about thirty minutes from Oxford Airport," Ray said.

"When are we meeting?" I asked.

"I explained it was an urgent matter and he agreed to see us in three hours. Can you make that?"

"It's going to be tight, but Big Mama's fueled up and ready to go, so we're on our way."

"Percy and I will leave immediately. The A44 will take us directly by Oxford Airport. Fly there and we can collect you and ride together to Waddesdon."

"Perfect. See you there."

I ended the call.

"Another duke in another palace, no doubt. Nothing but rich English people here, man," Lenny said. "I'm going to need a serious shower when I get back to Key West. I feel dirty from all these greedy bastards."

We were delayed leaving Schiphol by thirty minutes due to sequencing delays from inbound traffic. Ray was pilot in command, so I called and left a message for Detective Pedersen in Oslo that I'd like to meet to talk about the death of Frederick Lassiter. After that, I accessed the internet to search more deeply into Duke Conway.

Once in the air, it took us nearly two hours to get to Oxford Airport where we were given clearance to land on runway 19. Big Mama touched down smoothly on the asphalt strip, and we used two-thirds of the 5,092-foot runway. The asphalt was grooved to channel water, and it caused Big Mama to vibrate as we slowed. Built in 1938, the airport was known as RAF Kidlington during World War II, and like so many older airfields in Europe, it had a fascinating history of evolution since that time, and now was one of the busiest private airports in the UK.

Ray coordinated with the FBO, which guided us to a specific location in front of the voluminous gray hangars with curved rooflines. I would have said the airport was austere and had no personality were it not for the main terminal, which had the look of an old, two-story schoolhouse. The tan concrete structure was framed with blue trim and had reflective silver windows. It wasn't handsome, but it was memorable.

Several private jets were parked nose to nose in one area on the apron, but they were outnumbered by single-engine planes, particularly

Diamond Twin Star DA42s emblazoned with Leading Edge Aviation, which I presumed to be the local flight school.

"Hey, Lenny, if you want to stay here in the UK, you could learn to fly," I said.

"Funny, man. All I want is to get back to Key West, ASAP."

"I know, and I'm sorry this has all happened, believe me."

"Been here for over two weeks now." Lenny shook his head. "That damned race seems like a lifetime ago, man."

"We're down to it now, one way or the other. Hopefully Duke Conway will either still have the canister or can point us in the right direction. We have twenty-four hours left until we turn into pumpkins."

"Trick or freaking treat," he said.

Ray finalized the logistics, which did not include an overnight stay as I hoped we'd be on our way sooner than later. He pulled off his headset and turned to me with a big smile.

"They have warbirds here that you can catch a ride in." His eyes were wide. "A Mustang, Spitfire, Hawker, and even an ME109 Messerschmitt."

"Very cool," I said. "Next time ..."

His smile faded.

"I have a text from Percy, they're waiting outside and we're running late for the duke."

I helped Ray run through the postflight checklist, and within fifteen minutes from touchdown, we walked through the terminal, which was as nondescript inside as it was out. My pace was fast, and the guys hurried to keep up with me. I burst through the double doors out to the parking area and found Harry's burgundy Rolls Royce parked directly in front.

Percy jumped out and opened the rear door to where Harry sat on the far side. I climbed in and slid over next to him. Lenny sat next to me, and Ray walked around the outside of the car and climbed in the front with Percy.

"We may be a few minutes late, but the duke will wait," Harry said. "He mentioned twice on the call that his services were always available for a fee. Nauseating, really."

Percy wove the land yacht through a maze of airport buildings and once clear, we merged onto the A34 to Bicester.

"It's a thirty-nine-minute drive, but we can make it in thirty," Percy said.

"Giddyap," Lenny said.

Harry's eyebrows rose. Harry had come to know both Ray and Lenny in Italy when we were there for the Formula1 race at Monza, and then afterward at his Hampshire Manor estate.

"What else did the duke say?" I asked.

"I didn't want to provide too many details in case there's more to his involvement than we know. I just told him it was an urgent matter."

I exhaled loudly.

"Have you heard from Heather?" Harry asked.

I pulled my phone out and checked for messages—none, and tried her location, but it was still dark. "Nothing."

There were no voicemails or texts on the burner phone either.

"What do you intend to say to the duke?" Harry asked.

"I don't know yet, Harry. We'll play it by ear after he knows who I am."

"He did congratulate me for my—our—investment into Williams Racing, so he must have seen the news from Monza," Harry said. "He'll know who you are."

"I'm more worried about ancient history than recent events."

"Indeed."

We drove on in silence. I hadn't found much on the duke on the internet. A distant relative achieved some fame as an explorer who later became a member of the House of Commons. He had been a baron, which per Harry's description of peerage in Britain, was the lowest of all titles.

"How did Conway become a duke?"

"Through marriage. His Grace's wife died twenty or so years ago, and he's been milking the title ever since."

"I hope you brought your checkbook," I said.

Harry turned his considerable bulk to face me but didn't say a word.

The road led through rural countryside with green fields and stands of trees alternating on both sides. Once we reached Bicester, which appeared to be a dense village, we turned abruptly to the east onto the A41, which again led through farm country.

We arrived on the outskirts of Waddesdon, but again, didn't enter the town, which at a glance, looked smaller than Bicester. We turned off the A41 onto Silk Street, passed the Waddesdon Cricket Club and then through a beautiful pastoral area until the narrow road took us into a forested and curving route.

"Is this a road or the driveway?" I asked.

"Both. We're almost there."

Percy pulled into a small circle that had a round fountain in the center with three statues of nude men and women wrestling with different serpents. More white statues of what appeared to be mythological characters stood erect outside the circle. Three quarters of the way around, Percy turned left onto a long straightaway with broad swaths of manicured green grass on both sides and the most ornate palace we'd seen yet, dead ahead.

"Holy shit," Lenny said.

"As I had mentioned, the estate was built by the Rothschild family and is now open to the public. His Grace lives in the building to the left of the main estate," Harry said.

That building was of the same architecture and three stories but lacked Waddesdon's ornate roof spires that were typical in French Renaissance architecture.

"Is everybody rich in this country?" Lenny asked.

"Ah, no," Harry said. "But many of my contemporaries come from long lines of influential families."

We drove straight up to the front of the main building where there was a large gravel parking area. It was after hours so there were no other vehicles here. Percy pulled up to a walkway that led to the duke's residence and turned the car off.

"Are we supposed to call him 'His Grace'?" I asked.

"That is how one addresses a duke in Britain."

"We didn't refer to the Duke of Argyll that way," I said.

"He's your grandfather."

"Shit," I said. "Hardly."

We climbed out of the Rolls and Harry led us down a garden path toward the residence flanked with mature trees. I glanced at my Submariner. We were fifteen minutes late.

The residence was larger than any house I'd ever visited, and I could certainly understand why the duke squatted here. There was a small café attached to the building, but it too was closed. We continued down the heavily wooded and landscaped path, with the ornate building looming on our right side, until we reached an open area with a large porte-cochère that led to an impenetrable wood door.

We stepped inside, and I pressed a button that I assumed was a doorbell.

A moment passed before the door opened. A tall, skinny man dressed in a gray suit stood before us. He was bald on top, and his cranium looked buffed with turtle wax, but the hair on the sides was silver and plastered to his head. He had a small, pencil-thin silver moustache and bright, watery blue eyes.

"Sir Harry, what a pleasure to see you again."

"Your Grace." Harry bowed.

The duke looked from Harry to me, then Ray and Lenny, and his smile turned to a sneer.

"And who do have we here?" he asked.

A sudden lump filled my chest. How would Harry introduce me?

Harry cleared his throat. "I'd like you to meet, Buck Reilly, a world-renowned archeologist—"

"Bloody hell, you're the one who saved the day in Monza," he said.

His smile was back. He looked past me, and he pointed to Lenny.

"You were there as well. I saw you on the telly."

"We were all there," Harry said. He introduced Ray and Lenny too. The duke didn't offer to shake hands with anyone.

"Do come inside."

He led us into the stately entry, which like the road coming in had gaudy statues of mythological characters in each corner of the room. We followed him into a seating area that had a two-story coffered ceiling, and the walls were covered with massive oil paintings of scenes from centuries gone by. Whether real or reproductions, the paintings were in the style of—

"You have a good eye, Mr. Reilly," the duke said. "That's a Gains-borough. We have over 300 original pieces of art at Waddesdon, including paintings by greats like Reynolds, Romney, Guardi, and sculpture by several French masters."

124

He led us to a large room with a combination of couches and chairs. Once the duke sat, I chose a seat close to and facing him. I wanted to make sure I could read his expression as well as hear him clearly.

"My time is limited due to an engagement this evening, but you said it was urgent, and given our past, I wanted to make my services available to you, Sir Harry."

"Kind of you to see us on short notice, your Grace," I said.

The corners of the man's lips perked upward. He probably wasn't expecting an American to address him properly. I wanted him feeling confident at the outset, because I was going to challenge him for the truth. I'd already decided that if I felt he wasn't being straightforward, I'd push him harder than he's likely ever been pushed.

Heather's life depended on it, as did all of ours.

"My pleasure, really, but as I said, my time is—"

"We need some information about Frederick Lassiter," I said.

His smirk faded.

"And the Sect that was established in the 1300s to protect the monarchy and Scottish history."

Harry groaned.

Duke Conway's lips now dropped decidedly into a frown.

19

"THE SECT IS NOT SOMETHING TO BE TAKEN LIGHTLY," THE DUKE SAID. "Or bandied about."

"Have you had issues with them?" Harry asked.

"Consider yourself lucky, Sir Harry. Most titled families, from baron up, are charged an annual stipend by the Sect, even though they don't use that name publicly."

"Why the stipend?" I asked.

"For the purposes you stated. To help defray the costs of maintaining our way of life, protect the monarchy, and to mitigate any challenges to the established history within the British Isles."

"The British Isles are still a thing?" I asked.

Both the Duke and Harry looked upon me with dark eyes.

"Learn your heritage, young man," the Duke said. "There remain nearly 190 inhabited islands that comprise our territories."

His statement caused me to pause. Finally, I said, "My heritage, you say?"

The Duke adopted a pedantic smile and canted his head to the side. "Your celebrity due to the Formula 1 race in Italy, along with Sir Harry making you a partner in his share of the Williams Racing Team, has…how would you Americans state it? *Outed* your relationship with Sir Harry."

My throat was suddenly dry as I glanced from the duke to Harry, who was now smiling. Great. Fresh gossip amongst the aristocracy was no doubt what kept their gilded wheels turning. If he knew that, then he must know who my grandparents were.

"If you're referring to the heritage of my birth family, you must also be referring to the Duke of Argyll?"

"Of course," Conway said. "It is him you should be inquiring to about the Sect."

That caught me off guard.

"Why's that?"

Conway laughed out loud. "Because he's a member of the ruling body."

"The Council?" I asked.

Conway bowed his head in a deep nod. "Precisely."

I glanced to Harry, who looked every bit as shocked as I was.

"Surely you're mistaken, your Grace?" Harry said.

The dapper man shook his head slowly from side to side. "I'm afraid not, Sir Harry. In fact, Colin Campbell is one of the leading advocates who collect the annual tax amongst our class and believe me when I say they do not tolerate tardiness with the levy."

Acid reflux suddenly burned my throat, and I swallowed it back, but the taste of bile lingered on my pallet.

"Knew that guy was full of shit," Lenny said.

Duke Conway's forehead wrinkled when his eyebrows arched up.

"How much is the annual toll?" Harry asked.

"It's different for each family depending on their holdings, title, and proximity to power."

"How involved is the Stewart family now?" I asked.

"The House of Stewart became extinct upon the death of Cardinal Henry Benedict Stuart in 1807, but most of the European monarchies still have distant connections."

"Including King Charles III?" I asked.

"You have some work to do here, Sir Harry." Duke Conway leered at me. "Charles III is the head of the House of Windsor, as well as the King of the United Kingdom—not to mention fourteen additional Commonwealth titles and realms—and whilst there were seven Stewart monarchs that ruled the combined thrones of Scotland and England, he is related to only one of them, James I's sister, Elizabeth Stuart."

The monarchy and aristocracy was like a Rubik's Cube of variations that had my head spinning. Frankly, I didn't much give a damn aside from how it might impact my mission to recover the canister and get the Sect off our asses. I crossed my arms and felt the skeleton key in my breast pocket. I sat forward.

"Are the Stewarts still relevant in today's society?" I asked.

"Indeed." His eyes narrowed. "In fact, even though they're no longer in power, certain Stewart heirs of distinction remain heavily involved in the leadership of the Sect."

Figures. His epiphanies on my charming grandfather, the Duke of Argyll, and the Stewarts shed some light on my birth mother's eternal resting place. Harry appeared as confused and astonished as I felt. But still, was Harry also obligated to pay annual fees to the Sect?

"Is your being knighted still too new to have been added to the Sect's rent roll, Harry?"

"I'm not—"

"Knights are not royalty," Duke Conway said. "In fact, they're not even considered nobility—no offense, Sir Harry."

"Knighthood is bestowed upon citizens for several reasons, but primarily for achievements or service to the country," Harry said.

"Does knighthood get passed down?" Lenny asked.

I glared at him, knowing why he asked the question.

"I'm afraid not," Harry said.

Duke Conway focused on me. "Sorry, lad, you'll need to earn your own title."

I glanced at my watch. Beyond what the Duke had shared about the Sect, including Colin Campbell being a part of the Council, the discussion about nobility and titles was a waste of time. I needed to move the conversation to more immediate concerns.

"The other thing we wanted to ask you about was Frederick Lassiter," I said.

The Duke's naturally snotty demeanor cooled at the mention of Freddy's name. He sat back in his chair, and he licked his lips. "What about him?"

"Allow me, Buck," Harry interjected. "After my wife, Catherine, passed, I charged Freddy with placing a Campbell family heirloom in a safe place that wouldn't be discovered until well into the future, if ever at all. There were documents in an ancient metal canister that the widow Lassiter told us he passed along to you for safekeeping."

Duke Conway nodded slowly, then rubbed his index finger and thumb over his narrow mustache. "Yes, I recall that."

I sat up straight. Finally.

"Where is it?"

My question was indelicate, at best, and the duke frowned. Harry's eyelids fluttered a moment as he clutched his hands together. "The reason Buck is inquiring about both the Sect and the canister is because of heightened interest in the fact that my wife took the vessel and contents from her family when we were married, and the Duke of Argyll, under the guise of the Sect, wants it back."

Duke Conway's eyes popped open as if he'd just stumbled onto an opportunity. I recognized the greed brewing in the faraway gaze that had clouded over his cerulean, blue eyes.

"I see ..."

I slid closer to him and could feel my nostrils flare due to the injection of adrenalin into my system. "There's also a treasure map we believe dates back to Robert the Bruce inside the canister, which if you're familiar with my background, you'll appreciate my expertise in recovering such things."

Harry clutched his hands together and cleared his throat. "I don't think that's what the Sect is interested in—"

"We'd be happy to cut you in on anything we recover associated with that," I said.

"Cut me in?" The duke's voice lifted. "And you say this map is inside the canister?"

"That's right," I said.

The duke smirked, then licked his lips. I sensed the wheels turning in his shiny little head.

"Well," the duke said. "This has been lovely, but as I said, I have an engagement I must depart for—"

I jumped to my feet and squared off in front of him. "We need answers, now—"

"Buck!" Harry said.

"My ex-, ah, current girlfriend is being held by the Sect and if we don't produce the canister by the end of tomorrow, they'll kill her—in fact, they've threatened all of us—"

"Buck, please," Harry said. His fragile smile was betrayed by his wild eyes.

I hovered over the Duke. "Did you *look* inside the canister?"

He raised his hands as if to block a blow. "Freddy showed me the documents before we left from Scotland—I demanded to know what it was he wanted hidden. I'm not a fool, Mr. Reilly—"

"Where the hell's it at?" Lenny shouted over my shoulder.

I turned and Lenny was on his feet with his fists balled.

The duke held his hands together, fingers extended, and he tapped his fingertips together. "If I tell you that, how can I be assured you'll cut me in, as you put it?"

Harry held his hand up in front of me. "I give you my word, your Grace," he said.

The old bastard was more cagey and bold than I expected. I'd lean on him harder, but Harry was already flustered, so I pressed my lips tight.

Duke Conway said, "Freddy's package, er, your package, I suppose, Sir Harry, is in a remote location in Norway."

"Norway?" I said. "Why there?"

"Jesus," Ray said.

"How far away's that?" Lenny asked.

"My great-great-grandfather was a renowned mountaineer and there's a monument established in his honor there. I was asked by the queen to attend an international event there in 2014, so Freddy joined me, and we saw to the placement of his—your—package at the same time."

"Son of a bitch," I said. "We're running out of time—Norway? Goddamn." I remembered the details behind Freddy's death. "In Oslo?"

The duke licked his lips repeatedly. He loosened the solid blue tie he was wearing and unbuttoned the top button of his shirt. "Not mainland Norway, the Archipelago of Svalbard, which has the northernmost city on the planet. The Seven Islands to the north, to be exact, very close to the North Pole."

"Hooooly shit," Lenny said. "The North freaking Pole? How the hell we gonna get there and back tomorrow?"

Ray was already on his phone researching information. "The only city with an airport near there is Longyearbyen, Svalbard," he said. "Which is the northernmost city you mentioned."

"Precisely." Duke Conway paused, then said, "You can't fly to the Seven Islands, there are ice floes, icebergs, and glaciers all over the place. You must travel by a boat with ice breaking capacity. We chartered the M/S Sjoveien, which wasn't luxurious, but it was substantial enough to cover the distance in relative comfort."

"Those islands are 183 miles from Longyearbyen as the crow flies," Ray said.

"The monument for Sir Martin Conway, my relative, is on the island now known as Parryøya."

"Sounds Russian," I said.

"It's named after English explorer William Edward Parry who visited Svalbard during his 1827 expedition to reach the North Pole—of course, Sir Martin was there in 1897, but none of the islands were named after him."

The duke's statement revealed a sense of bitterness over the naming of islands. Talk about first-world issues.

"Sir Martin's expedition there followed the first crossing of Spitsbergen, which is the formal name for Svalbard. He was the first explorer to cross the island mass. He was very well known as a result, and I see it as my duty today to ensure not only the continuity of the family name, but also the baron's accomplishments."

"Hence why the queen asked you to attend the event you noted there."

"Correct. I used the opportunity to place a Conway-family time capsule at the marker on Parryøya."

"And the canister?"

His nose quivered like a rabbit. "Seek and ye shall find," he said.

"Smart ass." Lenny said that under his breath, but I heard it, and the duke extended his lower jaw as if he had too.

"Wonderful," Harry said. "Thank you so much for your assistance—"

"I will hold you to the offer of participating in the recovery of whatever is associated with Robert I's map you noted." Duke Conway paused. "Or, since I hid it safely, perhaps I will go recover the canister and share the findings with you."

"That won't be necessary," I said.

Harry stood up and nodded toward the door.

"One last question," I said.

Harry rolled his eyes.

"Freddy died in Oslo as the result of falling off a building. He must have been on his way home from your trip to Svalbard."

"What's the question?"

"Was he murdered?"

"Buck!"

The duke didn't appear surprised. "Freddy did get greedy in his older age, which also loosened his lips, so while I would say it is entirely possible, the local authorities there concluded his death was suicide."

"Could the Sect have pushed him off the building?" I asked.

The duke hunched his shoulders.

I again stood, and Lenny and Ray followed suit.

We thanked the duke and hurried out of the massive home. The sun was approaching the horizon on what had been a very long day. Ray was already on his phone, I assumed to file a flight plan to Longyearbyen.

"You'll never reach Parryøya in time, Buck," Harry said. "Can you negotiate with the Sect?"

"I have an idea about that," I said. "Anything you can do?"

Harry had a look of determination on his face, and he walked with more purpose, speed, and agility than I had seen in him do in years. He stopped suddenly and spun to face me.

"As I said when you came to Hampshire Manor, I regret not being more forthcoming with you when you first asked about your, ah, Catherine, but I was trying to protect you."

I exhaled a deep breath. "I understand."

"But like you, I now see the importance of taking a more aggressive approach."

"What are you saying, Harry?"

A shrewd smile bent his lips. "I'm long overdue for a visit with my dear in-laws. I'll fly to Edinburgh tonight and be off to Inveraray in the morning."

It was the first smile I'd had all day.

"Give them my warmest regards."

"It will be my pleasure."

SECTION 4:

IF YOU WANT BLOOD

20

HARRY DROPPED US AT OXFORD AIRPORT AND WE
PROMISED EACH OTHER WE'D report back from our respective
next steps. As Ray, Lenny and I made our way to Big Mama, I tried to
imagine Harry visiting with the Duke and Duchess of Argyll—his in-
laws—at Inveraray. I'd love to be a fly on that wall, but our next step was
far more challenging.

Ray walked purposefully around the outside of Big Mama,
conducting a thorough preflight inspection. He found peace in routine,
which was a blessing for him. I, on the other hand, flourished in
adversity, which unfortunately I'd had more than my fair share of. Lenny
sat in Big Mama's open hatch where he chewed on his fingernails. Lenny
was a gifted orator, even if his choice of vocabulary was coarse and often
insulting, but I always thought that his direct manner of speech was the
secret to his popularity.

I noticed a man peeking out from behind another plane on the
apron, which took a second to register, but when it did, I realized it was
the guy who'd knifed me at the Glasshouse Hotel. He kept his distance
but didn't appear to be trying very hard to hide.

Did that mean Roger was here, with Heather in tow?

Or was Knife just following us with instructions to keep Roger
informed?

I'd been thinking about how best to engage Roger and the Sect in
our next steps, which as Ray had noted, was highly unlikely of succeeding
in the remaining time we'd been allotted. One of my chief operating
mantras was to stay ahead of the curve but given the current
circumstances, it was not possible. However, seeing Knife gave me an
idea on how to do that.

It was time to contact Roger on the burner phone he'd given me
through his kidnapping associates. After three rings, someone answered
but said nothing. I spoke up.

"This is Buck Reilly. I need to speak with Roger."

What sounded like a hand going over the phone was insufficient to cover up the voices in the background, even though I couldn't understand what they said. Then, someone took the phone and listened for a moment, before speaking.

"You've been a busy lad, haven't you?" Roger said. "Cotswolds, Amsterdam, Oxford … I hope you're not out sightseeing."

I wanted to get his attention right away. "We've discovered the location of the canister, but it's going to take a couple days to recover it."

"No extensions, Reilly—"

"I'm calling to invite you to join me on the final leg to actually recover the canister."

"Hmm, how kind of you," Roger said.

"But only if you bring Heather along, too."

"I make the rules here—"

"Or, I'll collect the canister late, and if you do anything to hurt her, I'll make sure the London Times has a scoop on the documents, which from all I've learned, will cause several issues to both history and the monarchy in Scotland and England, for that matter."

"We don't respond well to threats, Reilly. Plus, how do I know you're not lying?"

"Call your pal who stabbed me in the back. He's watching us from a hundred yards away here on the tarmac at Oxford Airport."

The line fell silent, but after a few run-ins with Roger, I knew he was fuming.

"Where do you think the canister is?"

"I want to speak with Heather first," I said.

Roger must have held the phone away, but I heard him speaking to someone. Next thing I heard was a familiar but distant voice.

"Buck, I'm okay. I hope you're making progress!" Heather said.

Roger placed the phone back against his ear. "Now, where are you going?"

I hesitated. Could her voice have been recorded? I didn't think so.

"The canister is in northern Norway. An archipelago called Svalbard, or Spitsbergen as its also known. Meet us at the main town there, Longyearbyen, early in the morning."

"Longyearbyen?" Roger asked. "I know the place. Former mining town."

"We have to go farther north from there."

"There's a Radisson Hotel in Longyearbyen. Stay there and we'll meet you in the morning," he said.

"Good. We're leaving to go there shortly," I said.

Roger hesitated. "I don't suppose you'd give my man a lift?"

I laughed out loud. "The son-of-a-bitch who stabbed me in the back? No way."

"Fine. See you in Longyearbyen tomorrow."

"Be there early."

I clicked end.

Ray had climbed aboard the plane and fired up the left engine first; thirty seconds later, he started the right one. I climbed the ladder, retracted it, closed and locked the hatch, walked through the fuselage past Lenny and climbed into the right seat.

"The flight plan has us on the ground for forty-five minutes in Oslo, then moving on to Longyearbyen," Ray said.

"Perfect, thank you."

I texted the Norwegian detective I'd left a voicemail inquiring about Freddy's death for previously and let her know I'd be in the airport in an hour, briefly, and could she come meet me. She responded immediately and said she'd be there. By the time Big Mama shuddered her way into the sky, I was confident that we had a plan, but still needed to book passage to the Seven islands tomorrow.

While Ray flew Big Mama, I searched the internet for different options to take us farther north. National Geographic and Lindblad Expeditions had a boat departing tomorrow morning from Longyearbyen to travel north, but it carried 138 guests. It would be pretty hard to impose our need to control the itinerary with that many people.

The Duke of Oxford mentioned the name of a ship named *M/S Sjoveien* that they chartered from Longyearbyen. My search for that led to the ship's owner, Polar Quest, and their website showed that it had been chartered by Terra Incognita Ecotours and was also departing tomorrow. I checked the operator's website, which noted there was still availability, so I called their number.

"Terra Incognita Ecotours." The man had a British accent.

"Hi, my friends and I are in Svalbard and looking to join a tour destined for the northern parts of Spitsbergen," I said. "Your website says you have a tour aboard the *Sjoveien* departing tomorrow. Do you have any availability?"

"Wonderful timing," he said. "My name's Ged, I'm the tour operator. We're starting an eight-day cruise aboard the *Sjoveien* tomorrow."

"What's your itinerary?"

"We'll travel up the western coast of Spitsbergen, following the ice and darting into different fjords in search of wildlife," Ged said. "How many people are in your group?"

I hesitated and thought that through.

"We'd need two cabins for four people."

"Just so happens that we have two cabins available." Ged's sing-song voice had me wishing this was a vacation for me and Heather.

"One other thing," I said. "We're in a hurry to get to the Seven Sisters up north. It's the anniversary of Sir Martin Conway being the first explorer to cross Spitsbergen, which he followed by going to Parryøya. There's a marker there, and the Duke of Oxford, James Conway, asked us to hold a ceremony in his honor." Now the life-or-death question. "The timing is important to coincide with other celebrations, so would you be willing to cruise straight up there first thing?"

Ged hesitated on the other end of the line. "We typically work our way north, stopping to search for polar bears, reindeer, arctic fox, rare birds, and walrus, but I could talk to the captain and expedition leader."

"It's imperative for us, so a deal breaker if the captain won't agree. I'll give you my information and you can text me to confirm, but let's assume the answer is yes. I can give you a deposit now."

I pulled out my money clip and removed my American Express card.

"By the way, what are the details of the boat?" I asked.

"The *Sjoveien* is 144 feet long and has cabins to handle up to twelve guests."

If they still had two cabins available, our renting them would make the trip much more profitable for the operator, so hopefully that would give us some leverage to alter the itinerary. I gave him my credit card number and he said to meet at the Radisson at 10:00 a.m., where coincidentally, they were also staying. I'd read that Svalbard only had a full-time population of 2,000 people, so there must not be many hotels.

I ended the call satisfied that the plan was coming together. By the time I checked our location, we were well over the North Sea on a northeasterly heading toward Norway. The mic clicked on, and Lenny's voice boomed in my ears.

"You know it's the White Nights up where we're headed? It doesn't get dark for months." He paused. "How the hell we gonna sleep?"

"Hopefully we won't be there very long," I said.

"And those seven islands are way farther north than where we're flying into—"

"You and Ray will stay in Longyearbyen. I just booked the same boat that the duke and Freddy used previously to take me, Heather, Roger and his henchman up there."

"That sounds like a stupid idea, man," Lenny said.

"I agree with Lenny," Ray said. "Safety in numbers, right?"

"Yeah, man," Lenny said. "We'll come too."

"I have some other assignments for you guys that may be mission critical," I said. "So stay in Longyearbyen and don't stay up partying all night just because its light outside."

Ray gave me a loopy smile and nodded his head.

It took another hour for us to reach Oslo Airport, which was a significant facility with one main terminal, two parallel runways, and a lot of commercial traffic. Like other European airports, it had a long history of military and cargo usage but had been rebuilt into a modern architectural masterpiece in the late 1990s.

Ray followed the instructions from Oslo Air Traffic Control and set Big Mama down on runway 01L and then taxied to the location designated by the operator, Avinor.

"We need to tie up out here on the apron," Ray said. "Avinor will send a car for us."

I checked my watch. The flight took longer than expected so the detective was probably already here. I texted her that we'd arrived, and she responded that she was inside waiting.

"The detective who handled Freddy's investigation is waiting inside the VIP terminal. Since we'll be flying to Longyearbyen right after I meet with her, you might as well just wait out here," I said.

A black BMW sedan pulled up next to Big Mama and I saw the name of the operator, Avinor, on the rear passenger door. A blond man in a dark suit stepped out of the car, clutched his hands in front of himself, and stared at Big Mama, ready to assist.

"I'll be back soon," I said.

I popped open the rear hatch, lowered the ladder, and climbed down.

"Mr. Reilly?" the driver asked.

"That's me, let's go."

"Are there any others?"

"They're staying here. I'm just going inside for a quick meeting."

"Yes, Detective Pedersen is waiting in one of the conference rooms for you."

The drive to the private terminal was quick, and the driver escorted me inside and to the conference room where the detective was waiting. I walked in and she stood from her chair. Tall with black hair and bright green eyes, I was initially taken aback by her stunning looks. She looked like she should be on TV, not in a police precinct.

I held my hand out to her. "I'm Buck Reilly."

"Sonja Pedersen."

"Thanks for coming out from downtown, I didn't realize the airport was twenty miles away."

"Not a problem. I live out here and it's after working hours, so it wasn't out of my way." She paused. "Can you explain to me why you're interested in Frederick Lassiter?"

Aside from being attractive, her English was flawless. Seems that everyone in Europe speaks perfect English nowadays.

"Sure. He did some work for my birth father in the '80s and I recently met his widow while searching for some documents my birth father had given him for safekeeping. I'm trying to get the documents back now, which is when I learned he'd, ah, perished here in Oslo."

"Who is your father?"

"Birth father. His name's Sir Harry Greenbaum."

"I remember the name from my research, but he wasn't a 'Sir' back then."

"If you were doing research, does that mean you didn't believe it was suicide, or did you conclude that he did jump off the hotel here?"

"I always felt he was pushed but couldn't gather sufficient evidence to prove it."

"What made you think that?" I asked.

"The circumstances. He had just returned from Svalbard, he was just connecting in Oslo and there were reports of two men asking the front desk for him, but there was no video or information on their identities." She hesitated. "And who commits suicide by jumping off a five-story building?"

"Yeah, that is questionable, I would agree."

I noticed a folder on the table that she must have brought with her.

"You said you might have some information for me?" she said.

"Maybe, but before I share that, did Freddy have anything of interest in his possession?"

She glanced at her envelope but didn't reach for it.

"You tell me what info you have," she said, "and if I believe you, or it helps, I have something I can share with you."

She was playing a game of quid pro quo and wanted the "quid" up front. I didn't have much choice and knew I had to tantalize her for any hope of her telling me why she thought he was murdered.

"Did you speak at all to the Duke of Oxford while you were investigating Freddy's death?"

Her face turned blank and then she leaned back from me. "I don't know anything about any duke. What's his name?"

"James Conway, Duke of Oxford. Freddy had accompanied him on the trip to Svalbard for some type of ceremony. The duke didn't step forward for you to speak with him?"

"Never heard of any duke associated with Freddy."

"Pretty sure they were here in Oslo together, but they were definitely in Svalbard together before coming here."

"And why do you think this duke is a person of interest?"

"I just met him earlier today and he's one of those slippery guys who is always ready to lend a hand if he has his other hand in your pocket. Freddy had given the duke something of great value, at least to some, and my guess was that the duke wanted to erase all the evidence associated with its provenance."

"Why did you meet the duke today?" she asked.

"Same reason I'm here now. As I said, I'm searching for what Freddy had purportedly given the duke."

"I see."

She glanced down at the folder on the round conference table, then picked it up. "I can't give you this, but you can take a picture of it."

Detective Pedersen opened the brass clasp on the back of the envelope, reached inside, and removed a couple items. One was a credit card receipt for $10,000, US, from Polar Quest, which I assumed was his ticket for the *Sjoveien* and referenced cabin 202; another was a map of Svalbard that someone had used a blue ballpoint pen to keep a record of where the boat traveled, and the last was an odd sketch of what almost looked like three scuba tanks side by side with a small "x" on the left cylinder. Could that have been a map from the site where Conway buried the canister and his time capsule?

She handed me the sketch. It was contained in a plastic covering so it wouldn't take on additional fingerprints or dirt. I studied the drawing, which was more precise than I would have expected from Freddy but had no idea what it could be.

"You said I could take a picture of this?" I asked.

"Go ahead."

I laid all three of the items on the table and used my phone to take pictures. If he had just come from Svalbard, it must have something to do with his being there with the duke.

"Do you recognize anything about the drawing?" she asked.

"Unfortunately not, but I'm heading to Svalbard next, so will see if I can find a connection." I picked up the credit card receipt, also contained in clear plastic. "Did you speak to the boat company and learn anything about the itinerary when Freddy was onboard?"

"I did. They sent me a map of their expedition. The ship stopped at several fjords where they spent a night in multiple locations. They traveled to the Seven Islands north of Svalbard where they hiked, but they didn't share anything else useful to me."

Maybe it hadn't helped her, but confirming they had indeed gone to the Seven Islands was good news for me since I didn't trust anything Duke Conway had told us. A tinge of guilt curled my fingers, but I couldn't mention anything about Seven Islands until I went there myself to search for the canister. If successful, I'd alert her after the fact.

"Anything else about Freddy's death that made you question it?"

She hesitated, and her eyes narrowed as she looked into mine, which surprisingly disarmed me. Maybe it was because she was such a natural beauty, and her scrutiny made me nervous, or maybe it was because I feared she knew I was holding out on her.

"Like you said, jumping off such a short building seemed questionable to me as well. He must've landed on his head because his neck was broken."

She watched for my reaction.

"Broken from hitting the ground, or before?" I asked.

"That is the key question, Mr. Reilly." She stared at me for a long moment. "If you learn anything more in Svalbard, I'd be very grateful for your help." She pumped her eyebrows once. "In fact, come back to Oslo and we could discuss the case over dinner."

I felt my face get hot and hoped I wasn't blushing like a school kid. "I'll let you know."

MAP OF SVALBARD

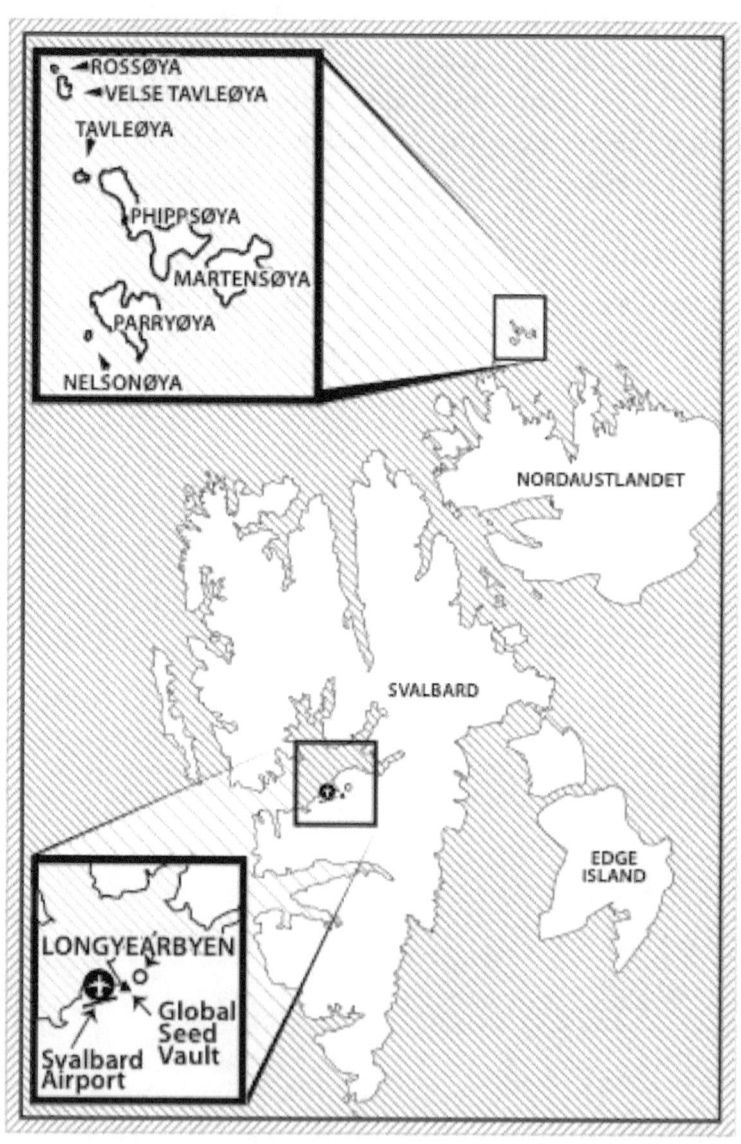

21

THE FLIGHT TO LONGYEARBYEN TOOK ANOTHER COUPLE OF HOURS. This time of year at this latitude there was constant daylight caused by the midnight sun, which is both bewildering and exhausting.

It was nearly 11:00 p.m. local time as we approached the airport, but with the sun shining, it felt much earlier. The heat was on inside Big Mama, but my frayed nerves were causing me to perspire more the closer we got to Svalbard, or Spitsbergen, whichever name you wanted to call it. Between that and the perpetual daylight, I was fired up and anxious to get to the Seven Islands where we would hopefully put this business with the Sect behind us once and for all.

I'd never had much interaction with a so-called secret society, and frankly considered most of them as overblown myths, but the deeper we had delved into the situation of the missing canister, and met people in the know, there was no doubt in my mind that regardless of how well cloaked the organization was, the Sect was very real, and they took their mission very seriously.

As we approached the rugged archipelago, I was taken aback by the raw beauty of the snow-capped mountains, the barren landscape and ultimately, of the very basic airport below. The single runway was 8,146 feet long, and as Ray had briefed me during the flight, the airport didn't meet international standards since there were no runway lights and could only be used during daylight, which this time of year, of course, meant twenty-four hours a day. However, given the location, there was only an average of one commercial flight per day coming to Svalbard. As a result, we had the entire air space to ourselves.

The airport was perched near the northern edge of the broad fjord that Svalbard's only city, Longyearbyen, was situated on. It had a small terminal, but no taxi-way along the runway, and a relatively large apron where there was room for many larger jets than would typically be here. Just past the airport, farther east along the coast, was a port with multiple ships, and then the valley where Longyearbyen was situated. The town made Key West look large, but this one had a small ski area on the mountain to the east that looked over the city.

"Man, can we get any more isolated than this?" Lenny's voice came over my headset.

"Nope," Ray said. "Like that duke said, this is the northernmost city in the world."

"Damn," Lenny said. "That's kind of cool, when you think of it that way."

"Speaking of cool," I said, "pile on whatever clothes you have. It's thirty degrees outside."

"Say what?" Lenny said.

"We're almost to the North Pole," I said.

"Ho, ho, ho." Lenny said this under his breath, but his mic still caught the comment.

"We'll get some warm clothing from one of the stores in town," I said.

While Ray attended to the landing checklist, I saw that there were two voicemails that just popped onto my phone. Svalbard was 400 miles from the northernmost point of continental Norway, and there was no cell service as we flew north across the Norwegian and Barents seas.

I clicked speaker and then played them on my phone.

"Mr. Reilly, this is Ged from Terra Incognita. I'm pleased to tell you that Gary, our expedition leader, has modified the itinerary to accommodate your request to head straight up to the Seven Islands. We will then work our way back south. It will be a long run the first day, but we will keep everyone engaged with wildlife presentations in the salon."

Good news.

Ged's message continued. "That being the case, I went ahead and booked the two cabins to your credit card. We'll see you tomorrow morning at the Radisson Blu hotel."

"Sounds cozy," Lenny said.

"You still want to go all the way up to the polar ice cap with us?" I asked.

"Hell no. I'm going to find me a nice little bar with a fireplace going and catch up on the last two weeks of emails and prayer requests." He shook his head. "I've totally abandoned my flock over this crazy-ass shit."

Lenny's candor made me smile. "Couldn't have described it better myself."

The second message was far briefer.

"Buck, it's Harry. I met with the Duke and Duchess of Argyll. Call me whenever you get this, no matter the time."

Shit. The run of good luck started with the tour operator's call may have just hit the wall.

I hit redial and called Harry.

The phone was picked up, but a clatter followed, and I grimaced at the sound over my phone's speaker.

"Hello, Buck? Is that you?"

"Yes, Harry, returning your call."

"Bloody late, isn't it?"

"It's only 10:00 your time, 11:00 here, and your message said to call any time."

He cleared his throat and sighed, probably at the effort it took him to sit up in his bed.

"So I did, so I did," he said. "So you're on Spitsbergen?"

"I'm calling it Svalbard, and we're on final approach now."

"You left Oxford nearly six hours ago. How slow is that bloody antique plane you insist on flying?"

"We had to make a stop along the way, Harry. We're exhausted but nearly to the airport. Did you meet with your in-laws?"

He groaned. "I did and they were bloody well shocked to find me at their doorstep, I assure you that. Their expressions were priceless."

"How did it go?"

Another grunt came across the line. "As you would expect. They continue to harbor hatred toward me, and even though they said they found it interesting to meet you, I'd describe their sentiment toward you as a rung below indifferent."

Lenny, who was sitting with me, curled his face into a confused twist. I could feel my own features contort similarly.

"'A rung below indifferent,' you say?"

"They still want the bloody canister back, and while it was not stated, I believe they'll kill to get it, or possibly even after they get it to cover up the bloody existence of the wretched thing."

"Lovely. Did you confront them about the Sect?"

"Of course. The old bastard didn't say a word, but his mischievous smile when I asked if he was on the Council spoke the truth, at least to me."

"So my son-of-a-bitch grandfather actually tried to kill me," I said.

"I wouldn't put that in the past tense just yet, my boy. It was one of the more chilling meetings of my life and given that I have bought and sold well over one hundred companies, which in some cases were hostile takeovers, that's saying something."

"How did the meeting end?"

"While they admitted nothing, when I shared you were following a strong lead to the northern ends of the earth, he didn't exactly appear surprised. My guess is he's in communication with and possibly controlling the man who has been dogging you."

"Roger. He's the asshole who is holding Heather hostage."

"Quite."

"Is that it?"

"Bit of a cat-who-ate-the-canary smile at the news of your progress searching for the canister, and when I reiterated you needed some more time, he raised his eyebrows and lifted his hands as if he had no idea what I was speaking of, but I could tell he certainly did know."

"I've arranged for space on a boat to take us to the Seven Islands tomorrow, but it's a long trip that will push us outside of the window they gave me."

"What does that mean for Heather?"

"She and Roger are meeting us here in the morning. I booked him a cabin on the same boat and offered for him to join us to buy time."

"Brilliant." Harry paused. "Let's do hope that the information his Grace provided was accurate. I can't imagine how this Roger will respond if the Conway time capsule does not contain what they're after."

My stomach suddenly turned over. I hadn't thought of that given the duke's certainty over its placement. "Do you think the duke was bullshitting us?"

"As I told you, he's a shrewd and greedy one. Nothing would surprise me."

If I thought I was going to get any sleep during this sunny polar night, Harry's observation just wiped that idea clean. It did remind me of something the duke had said in Oxford.

148

"I'm a little concerned about the duke's lack of recollection related to Robert the Bruce's supposed treasure map that was purportedly in the canister—which you'd confirmed," I said.

Harry cleared his throat again, which further raised my antennae.

"Yes, well, that was many years ago. It should be there."

"I certainly hope so, but even if we do find it, none of it may save our collective skins."

"Hopefully you will have succeeded by this time tomorrow night. I have every faith in you, my dear boy."

I got suddenly choked up. Harry had called me that for as long as I'd known him. But now, knowing that he'd been my birth father all along, the phrase caused a chill down my spine.

"I'll touch base tomorrow." I paused. "Watch yourself, Harry. They included you in their tally of who would die if we're not successful."

A sardonic laugh preceded his next statement. "I have added an armed security detail here at Hampshire Manor and won't be going anywhere until this is over. Godspeed, dear boy."

I ended the call.

Lenny shook his head slowly from side to side. "Remind me to find a new best friend who doesn't put me in life-threatening situations when—if—I get back to Key West."

"Gotta have faith, Lenny."

"Oh I got plenty faith in God, it's people I got no faith in. Especially greedy old rich bastards like this bunch."

Our altitude dropped steadily as Ray had Big Mama on final approach. He set her down smooth and we cruised the length of the runway to reach the terminal at the far end. As we got closer, I realized there was an additional plane here—a private Jet—a Cessna Citation XLS, tied down where we were headed. While it could have belonged to anyone, a Norwegian entrepreneur, politician, or a visiting gazillionaire, my gut told me the plane belonged to the Sect and they'd beaten us here. As long as Heather was with them, I hoped it was them, especially since I needed them here before the *Sjoveien* set sail in the morning.

Ray parked next to the Citation, which I now saw had no tail numbers. Given the proliferation of apps that provided detailed ownership information on planes, owners had begun not to include numbers on the tails of their planes. That omission didn't mean the owners or charter company were up to no good, it just meant they wanted to be left alone.

We completed the postflight checklist quickly, and when we climbed out of Big Mama, I couldn't keep my eyes off the Citation. I walked around it but even though it was one of the smallest private jets, the windows were too tall to see inside the plane. I put my hand on the left, tail-mounted Pratt & Whitney turbofans.

"Still warm," I said.

"Freaking freezing out here, man," Lenny said. "I'm going inside— I hope we're not locked out."

Ray shivered next to me. "I love our Grummans, but wouldn't it be nice to have a jet?"

He winked at me and then hurried after Lenny.

A gust of wind cut right through my thin clothing. I hustled after the guys and entered the vacant terminal. There was no Passport Control here, so it only took a few minutes to pass through the small terminal and arrive at the glass doors that led to the front of the airport.

"I called a taxi," Lenny said. "I'm staying inside until it arrives."

The airport felt abandoned and given its remote location outside of town, there was no car traffic, so when the pair of headlights came up the long straight driveway, it was safe to assume it was our ride. What turned out to be a van traveled past the terminal, on the other side of the empty parking area and pulled up to a stop by the door marked for Arrivals.

After a moment, the driver stepped outside.

We walked out and found the driver standing by the open tailgate. She frowned when she saw us. "No baggage?"

"Just passing through," I said.

The woman's lips silently repeated my explanation. Without further explanation, Lenny slid open the side door and climbed inside. Ray followed him and I jumped into the front passenger seat, followed by the driver, who turned the fan up on the heater for us.

"First time in Svalbard?" she asked.

"Can't you tell?" I asked. "We're headed to the Radisson Blu, please."

She grunted and drove down the long road away from the airport. It wasn't even a driveway, it was just the road itself that had dead-ended at the airport, and now led to the coast. After a short drive we came to a large area enclosed by tall chain-link fencing and the driver slowed and pointed to it.

"Almost everyone lives in rented homes here and we're not allowed to keep dogs inside, so they stay in these kennels."

There were numerous double-decker dog houses, each with a small deck where the animals could sit outside. Several dogs were currently out on their little porches, oblivious to the cold. There had to be a hundred of them here, largely huskies and border collies.

"How cruel," Ray said.

"Most are sled dogs and perfectly accustomed to the cold. They're well taken care of, I assure you."

She continued toward town, slowing once more at a triangular road sign of a polar bear against a blue background, with a broad red border along each edge. Under the sign was another one that read: "*Gjeder hele Svalbard.*"

"What's that sign say?" I asked.

"It means there are polar bears all around Svalbard." She glanced toward me. "It's against the law to leave town without a gun."

"Without a gun?" Lenny asked. "The NRA must love this place."

"Polar bears outnumber people here," the driver said. "They're the apex predator and will hunt people down from a very far distance to kill and eat them."

"Screw that," Lenny said. "I'm not leaving the hotel."

The road continued through the port area where shipping containers were stacked up three high and three rows deep. A long dock ran parallel to shore with ships of various sizes moored on both sides. I assumed that's where the *Sjoveien* was located. As we continued toward town, there was absolutely no sense of architecture, just small buildings where necessities were sold, and it seemed like every other one carried snowmobiles.

"Popular form of transportation?" I pointed to a snowmobile dealership.

"There are also more snowmobiles than people here. It's the best way to travel in winter, and nimble enough to evade predators."

"How cold's it get here in the winter?" Lenny asked.

"Typical winter is minus thirteen degrees to minus twenty degrees Celsius. But from November through January, it never gets light. The opposite of the midnight sun that is coming to an end in the next month or so."

"How close are we to the North Pole?" Lenny asked.

"From Longyearbyen, it's about 800 miles," the driver said.

We turned right just before the North Pole Expedition Museum on the left and the Svalbard Museum, which was situated in a radical bit of modern architecture, on the right. We passed a strip center of dark shops, one of which was the Husky Café, and then took the first left and found the Radisson Blu on our left. The hotel was a two-story, gray composite structure with very basic windows and looked like low-quality subsidized housing, but then again, almost everything here looked like that. The northernmost city in the world was utilitarian, under siege by polar bears, either 100% light or 100% dark and colder than a witch's tit.

I smiled. Exactly how it should be.

We climbed out of the vehicle after I paid the woman with kroner I'd gotten at an ATM in the FBO in Oslo. A cold wind urged us into the hotel—we were greeted immediately by a stuffed polar bear in the lobby that stood at least ten feet tall with its arms outstretched as if it might reach down and pluck one of us up to tear in half.

I saw Lenny shudder, whether from the bear, the cold, or both.

My concerns were more focused on Roger, Knife, and whether Heather was safe. I glanced around and saw no sign of them. We checked in and the rooms were cheap, so we got three deluxe rooms, which inside were more like college dorms. Deluxe, it seemed, was code for no-frills.

Now midnight, the sun was still well above the horizon and would continue to move laterally until it climbed again. Light bled around the curtain on my room's window, but I was too exhausted to care. Tomorrow was going to be a critical life-or-death expedition to the edge of the polar ice cap, and somehow, I needed to sleep to be as sharp as possible.

But sleep would not come easy, there was just too many details running through my mind.

22

THE MIDNIGHT SUN LIFTED HIGHER AND SIGNALLED THAT DAY HAD BEGUN. I'd checked the time on my phone no less than a half-dozen times during the brief period I'd attempted to sleep, and awoke with a start, anxious to find Heather. If for some reason she didn't accompany Roger, I wasn't sure what I'd do, but I was certain it would be violent.

Still early, I lay in bed and unfolded the detailed map of Svalbard I bought in the hotel's gift store after checking in last night. The topographic detail made it very clear that the archipelago was one mountain peak after the next, and due to the multiple fjords on the western coast, there was as much water as there was land that comprised the island. In fact, at this scale, I now saw Svalbard was comprised of multiple islands, the vast majority of which was covered in snow, ice, and permafrost.

Way at the very top, I finally found the small island chain of the Seven Islands, which was referred to here as Sjuøyane. Parryøya was the southernmost island in the chain and appeared tiny compared to the balance of Svalbard. I couldn't find any detail on where the monument to Sir Martin Conway was situated in the chain, so needed to make sure that the captain of the *Sjoveien* knew where it was, before we departed, or I'd need to call the Duke of Oxford.

That line of thought led me to consider what would happen when we found the Conway time capsule and the canister. Harry speculated the Sect may wish to kill us to contain the knowledge of its existence even if we did turn it over. There would be at least a dozen guests on the boat, and with crew, probably closer to twenty people, so Roger couldn't kill everyone, could he? Given the importance they have attributed to the contents of the canister, though, I couldn't take anything for granted.

That epiphany made me consider our exist strategy. If things got ugly, how would Heather and I escape from the one of the northernmost islands on earth? They'd certainly be covered with snow and ice, as well as surrounded by ice floes, icebergs, and other hazards that would make it impossible for Ray to rescue us in Big Mama. I jumped out of the bed and cranked up the shower in the little bathroom. Afterwards, my mind was still focused on contingencies as I got dressed. Tourist information in the room noted there were several sports stores in Longyearbyen and given that it was the starting point for expeditions of many types, whether on boat, foot, snowmobile, the stores opened early.

I checked my phone and Ray had texted to see if I was awake yet. I wrote him back and told him to meet me in the lobby in ten minutes so we could get some cold-weather gear. He may be staying behind, but Heather and I needed to make sure we didn't freeze to death searching for the damned Conway monument.

Once dressed, I left my room at the end of a long hallway and hurried to the lobby. I only had an hour before I was scheduled to meet Heather and Roger, so had no time to waste.

Ray was there waiting, staring up at the big polar bear.

"Think you could outrun him if he was chasing you?" I asked.

"No, but maybe I could outrun Lenny." He paused. "Or at least trip him."

"You're terrible, Ray."

"Survival of the sneakiest."

We stepped outside onto the gravel parking lot and the wind slashed at us like a frozen machete. We didn't even have sweaters, much less jackets.

"Holy shit," he said.

"Let's run."

I took off at a jog across the street and up to the pedestrian path that had shops, a couple of restaurants, a post office, grocery store, and a few sports stores dotted along each side. I could hear Ray huffing and puffing behind me. He wasn't big on physical fitness, and I can't imagine the last time he may have run anywhere, but extreme cold has a way of making you dig deep.

Fortunately, we came to a small shopping mall with several stores, a salon, coffee shop, and sports store inside. I ripped the door open and waited for Ray to catch up. When he did, his face was bright red, his breathing shallow, and his mouth spewed fog from his breath changing from gas to water vapor to water droplets. He practically fell into the vestibule, placed his hands on his knees and stayed bent over for a minute as he caught his breath.

I waited as my mind ticked through a shopping list.

Ray stood up straight, exhaled hard, and nodded to me. We entered the interior of the shopping area, and the sports store was straight ahead. With no interest in fashion, I grabbed parkas and snow pants for both me and Heather, along with gloves, wool hats, thick socks, sweaters, and long underwear. Ray did the same for him and Lenny.

In the back of the store was a gun case with several rifles and large revolvers.

"That taxi driver said we're supposed to have guns if we leave the populated areas," Ray said.

I hesitated and studied the armory. It seemed the .308 was the popular rifle caliber and .44 magnum the most common handgun. If I bought one, Roger wouldn't be the wiser and I doubted they'd check what little luggage I had to bring on the boat.

"Can I help you, sir?" A young female store clerk inquired.

"I'd like to buy one of these revolvers," I said.

"Are you a permanent resident of Svalbard?"

"No."

"Have you applied to the governor's office for a license to possess a firearm?"

"No, how long does that take?"

"It's quick, only a few days." She smiled.

"Ahh, well, that won't work. My boat leaves later this morning."

"Don't worry, sir. If you're on a commercial excursion, your guides will have weapons."

I hesitated. If a gun wasn't possible, I needed some type of weapon. There was a display of knives of all sizes. I picked a large one with a black handle.

"That's a good skinning knife," the clerk said. "You going hunting?"

"I like to be prepared."

I paid for everything, we donned our heavy parkas, wool hats, and gloves and set back out to the hotel. My mind was still lost in contingency planning as we walked. I saw a group of snowmobiles parked together and imagined what it would be like to drive one through the vast snowfields here. That thought gave me an idea.

"Ray, I need you to check on something after we leave this morning."

"What's that?"

When I told him, he first thought I was crazy but given the circumstances, he understood. He was quiet for the rest of the walk, but as we approached the hotel, I stopped, and he did too.

"I have no idea what to expect from this situation, but odds are that Roger cannot be trusted," I said. "You heard what Harry said about his meeting with the Campbells, and since we know Colin is on the Sect's Council, we should assume the worst case."

"You're right. I'll see what I can figure out." He paused. "Do you think Lenny and I are safe here?"

My exhale condensed into fog, which momentarily blocked Ray's face.

"I think we need to presume that we're all in mortal danger and plan accordingly. You and Lenny should make yourselves scarce until I get back—there's no cell coverage where we're headed, so it will be impossible to communicate."

"Then how will your idea work?"

"We set a schedule and hope for the best."

He just stared at me.

"Have some faith, Ray."

He pursed his lips and then said, "Hopefully Lenny has enough for both of us."

"All of us," I said.

We walked inside the hotel lobby—

"Buck!"

My mouth fell open as Heather ran from the seating area and jumped into my open arms. I squeezed her tight, and felt my throat constrict as I buried my face into her neck. When I opened my eyes, I saw Roger behind her, the same newsboy cap on his head, a cast on his left arm, and his expression tight and impatient.

"I'm so glad to see you," she said.

"Have they hurt you in any way?" I asked.

"No, they haven't touched me. I've been locked in a castle somewhere in Scotland this whole time. They drove me there after capturing me at the airport. Took forever."

I lowered Heather to the ground and stood tall in front of Roger. Knife, as I called him, was there too. Was that all, or did others meet them here? I'd ask Heather when we had a minute.

"I see you've been shopping," Roger said.

I handed Heather the bag. "I bought you a jacket and supplies to keep warm."

I noted that Roger and Knife were already dressed in warm clothing, and I assumed they brought whatever they needed for the climate. If they froze to death, however, it wouldn't bother me in the least.

I checked my watch. "The tour group we're accompanying up to the Seven Islands is meeting here in the lobby in thirty minutes."

"Tour operator? Screw that, let's take your plane," Roger said.

"Too much floating ice for water landings. It would sink us."

"How long's the boat ride?" he asked.

"I persuaded the operator to take us there straight away, but even so, it's gonna take all day to get there." I paused. "It never gets dark though, so when we do arrive, we can get out to where the, ah, canister is buried and collect it."

"And then all day back again?"

I didn't want to tell him it was an eight-day cruise as he would pitch a fit and throw a wrench into the spokes. He'd find out once we got on board, and then he and Knife could enjoy a romantic voyage in their cabin. The vision gave me a brief smile.

"That's right," I said. "But it's a beautiful place, so we can enjoy the return trip and see some wildlife."

"Bloody cold and stark here," Roger said. "Makes Scotland look lush."

"Everyone needs to collect whatever gear you brought and be back out here in twenty minutes or you'll miss the boat." I said. Then to Heather. "That's a different outfit than what you were wearing yesterday morning."

"There were some clothes at the castle."

"When did you all arrive?" I asked.

"Last night aboard a small PJ," Heather said.

"I saw it at the airport. Citation." I turned to Roger. "You a pilot?"

He held the arm up that was in a cast. "Even if I was, I got a broken flipper thanks to you."

"They have a pilot," Heather said.

"Come with me to my room to get my—"

"Sorry, Reilly, she stays with us," Roger said.

I looked at Knife. "You have a name?"

His eyes were black marbles. For someone who appeared to be in his late twenties, he had a hardened visage that made him seem ageless.

"Call me Liam."

"Right, well, why don't you gather your belongings, and we'll meet back here. The boat we're taking is run by a tour operator and there are only twelve guests."

Roger and Liam exchanged a glance which worried me, so I added, "And a crew of ten. You gents will be sharing a cabin, as will Heather and I."

"No funny business on the boat, Reilly," Roger said. "We're a couple soldiers from a much larger army. Anything happens to us, then more will follow, and they won't be nearly as accommodating."

An idea struck. "Don't worry. The Duke of Argyll—you know, my grandfather—already told me that if we cooperated, then his men wouldn't hurt us."

"Did he now?" Roger asked. "Isn't that cozy."

"Helps to have relatives on the Council," I said. "My friends and I have zero interest in getting involved in anything that would be contrary to the Sect's mission, so we're totally motivated to help you find the documents and then go home."

"I know I'm never coming here again," Ray said.

Roger glanced at Ray for a moment, and then held his hand out to Heather. "Let's go collect our bags and get back out here. We wouldn't want to miss the boat, now, would we?"

We all walked down the hall. They took the stairs down to the lower level and Ray and I continued down the long corridor toward our rooms.

"Do what I told you, Ray, even if you have to go back to mainland Europe to find what you need." I hesitated. "Their pilot may be here, or he may be at the airport watching his plane and ours, so be careful."

"Understood. We'll be fine," he said. "You watch your ass. These creeps have no conscience. Figure out a way to maintain the upper hand."

"That's where you come in, my friend."

I held out my hand and Ray hesitated, and then leaned forward and gave me a tentative hug. I don't think we'd ever hugged before.

"Be careful, Buck."

"You too, partner."

23

OUR GROUP BOARDED THE BUS LAST WITHOUT MEETING OTHER GUESTS, and it took us to the port where we joined the ship. Since we were last on the bus, we were first off and navigated the shaky gangplank onto the ship's bow where we were guided inside. I found Ged, the operator, first thing, and requested cabin 202, the same one that Freddy had, according to the receipt that Detective Sonja Pedersen had allowed me to photograph in Oslo. The cabins had already been assigned, but he was very amiable and since most were similar, he agreed to shuffle the deck and give me and Heather the one I requested. I didn't bother asking about Roger's cabin, but hoped he'd be as far away as possible.

The *Sjoveien* was not new or luxurious but based on the size was exactly what we needed. If this were a vacation for Heather and me, I could understand the allure of the smaller boat, compared with the bigger Nat Geo/Lindblad ships, which were much larger, carried ten times the number of passengers, albeit did have greater amenities. The Polar Quest website said our ship had two Zodiacs with 50-horsepower engines, which was sufficient for all the guests to be able to go out to make landings or reconnaissance trips for wildlife at the same time. My research on the bigger ships revealed that they had a lower ratio of boats to guests, so people had to take turns rather than go all at once.

However, this was anything but a vacation, so the smaller size also meant we had more flexibility in controlling the situation, and worst case, put fewer people at risk. Ged returned a few minutes later.

"Buck, you and Heather are in cabin 202 on the main level." He smiled at Heather. "Very nice to meet you and welcome aboard."

"Roger and Liam, you are in cabin 203, directly across the hall from Buck and Heather."

"Perfect," Roger said.

"Your bags will be brought to your cabins, which we encourage you to wait in until we get underway, at which point we ask that all guests meet in the salon for introductions and a briefing."

Ged then greeted the people behind us, and I grabbed Heather's hand.

"Let's find our cabin, honey."

"We're right behind you, Reilly," Roger said.

"No, you're right across from us, like the man said." I smiled. "Hope it's cozy for you two lovebirds."

He stared daggers back at me and followed us past an open hatch that led to the port side of the deck. We turned right and there was a stairwell that led to the cabins below, and then we turned left and found cabins 202 and 203. I opened our door, then let Heather pass by me to enter and I pivoted to face Roger.

"We'll see you in the salon with the others when we cast off. Let's keep this chill and act like we're here for fun. If you act like a gangster, the ship captain won't go anywhere, least of all up to the Seven Islands," I said.

"We'll play the game, but you and the woman keep your mouths shut. If you double-cross us, your friends at the hotel will be dead before lunch."

I closed the door behind me and locked it.

Heather fell into my arms, and I felt her body convulse. Was it from crying or relief? She exhaled hard and pulled back to gaze up at me. There were no tears on her cheeks.

"What the hell are we doing here?"

I rubbed my face with both hands. "A lot's happened since we were so rudely separated. Bottom line is we met with Freddy's widow in Amsterdam, she gave us the name of James Conway, the Duke of Oxford, who Harry happened to know, and we met with him back in the UK."

"Is this damned canister really up here on top of the world?"

I exhaled hard. "Conway said he buried it in a family time capsule next to a monument for a distant relative of his who was an explorer here in the late 1800s."

"Good that Harry knew him," she said.

"Harry then paid a surprise visit to the Duke and Duchess of Argyll."

"Your grandparents."

"His in-laws. Colin was cagey, of course, but Harry tested him and walked away certain that he was a part of the Council that runs the Sect. The Duke of Oxford said the same."

Heather processed that for a moment, then looked up with sad eyes. "He must've given the order to have you killed back at the hotel then."

I nodded slowly.

"I'm sorry, Buck." She hugged me again.

"Yeah, well, I wasn't really looking for a new family anyway. These old families date back a thousand-plus years and are very incestuous. They're all about maintaining the status quo—"

"Of course they are," she said. "It's the Golden Rule. They have the gold, so they make the rules."

"Freddy, it turns out, accompanied the Duke of Oxford here and then supposedly committed suicide at an airport hotel in Oslo, presumably on his way home. We stopped there on the way, and I met with the detective who handled the case."

"What did he say?"

"She thought he was murdered, but there wasn't any evidence. She shared a few things with me though, including a receipt for him being on this ship, in this same cabin, when he and the duke went to the Seven Islands."

"So you requested this cabin on purpose?"

She glanced around at the small space that had two small, single bunks set perpendicular to each other. She frowned.

"If Freddy was murdered, maybe he knew he was at risk. If so, I was hoping he may have left a clue on board here."

A whistle sounded and the ship lurched as it left port.

"Best thing we can do now is keep Roger and his stooge calm by acting like tourists on an adventure. Let's go out to the briefing, meet the other guests, be charming and inquisitive, and make sure Roger doesn't do anything crazy like commandeer the ship," I said.

"Both he and Liam have guns, Buck." She paused and studied my face. "Will they kill us after you deliver the canister?"

I recalled what Harry said after seeing Colin Campbell.

"We have to assume they might try to, Heather, which is why we need to stay ahead of the curve, appear cooperative, but be ready to pivot."

"How the hell are we going to pivot up here in the middle of nowhere?"

"I have Ray working on contingency plans, and he can also contact the authorities, but the best outcome is we find the damned canister and get the Sect off our backs. Otherwise, the next batch of Rogers and Liams will show up and we won't know when or where."

Heather ran her fingers through her hair. "Then let's go make some new friends."

I leaned forward and kissed her. Heather had once again become an integral part of my life, thanks to the fact that we'd both matured, become less self-focused, and people from our past who had manipulated us were no longer in our lives.

"I'm sorry to have gotten you into the middle of all this," I said.

"Not your fault. Once Harry dropped the bomb about being your birth father, I was pushing to learn more, so am equally culpable for the situation." She shook her head once. "Who knew your birth mother's relatives were aristocratic lunatics."

"Exactly. Like C.S. Lewis said, 'you can't go back and change the beginning, but you can start where you are and change the ending.'"

She kissed me again.

"Let's go meet our shipmates," I said.

As I reached for the door there was a knock. With no peep hole, I unlocked it and opened it blindly. Roger stood there, newsboy cap, cast and all.

"Let's talk, Reilly."

I pulled the door wide, he entered, and I closed it again. There was a single chair by the small desk under the oversized porthole. I pointed to it.

"Grab a seat."

Once I sat on my bunk, Heather sat on hers and Roger reluctantly sat on the chair.

"What's on your mind?" I asked.

Roger removed his cap and set it on the desk. His hair was dark and matted, and he looked like a totally different person without the hat. "I know you went to Amsterdam and met with the widow Lassiter—"

"Per your suggestion, thank you," I said.

"From there you went to meet the Duke of Oxford, who I know had a relationship with that wanker, Lassiter. Sir Harry met you there, too."

"You're well informed."

"What I don't know is what his Grace said to you that resulted in this voyage to the hinterlands."

"When Harry gave the canister to Freddy after my, ah, Catherine died, Freddy apparently realized he was in no position to keep the material safe. Maybe you guys roughed him up, I don't know, but he asked the Duke to hold it for him."

I paused to study his eyes. Still cold and unyielding.

"Some years later, again, I don't know why, but the Duke and Freddy came here to Svalbard and buried the canister in with a Conway family time capsule up on a northern location here at Svalbard."

"Why here? They're British, not Norwegian."

We held each other's gaze as I considered how to answer his question. Finally, I sat forward. "I'm not going to give you the details until we get there, Roger."

His eyes narrowed. He glanced over at Heather.

"You need to be patient," I said. "We'll be at the location tonight, we have twenty-four hours of daylight, so we should be able to dig it up and then Bob's your uncle."

"And Fanny's your aunt," Heather said.

Roger scowled. "You think that's your insurance here? Keeping me in the dark?"

"Afraid so, but hey, we're all on the same ship, headed to the same place."

"You bring a shovel?" Roger asked.

Shit.

"Ah, no, I didn't, but I'll ask Ged, the tour operator, what they have on board. Speaking of which, they're waiting for us in the salon."

"So you believe what his Grace said about all this?" he asked.

"Let's just say I extracted the information from him. He's more interested in making money and notoriety than getting hurt or killed, so I don't think he'd have lied about it."

Heather stood up. "We should join the others to avoid attracting attention. Buck and I already discussed blending in by being friendly." She paused. "You should do the same."

"We're not the friendly types," Roger said. "We'll be watching you, though."

I stood and Roger followed suit. We exited the cabin, and he walked across the hall and into his. Heather and I navigated the corridors back to where we boarded. The dining area and salon were just past there, toward the stern of the ship. Several people were already seated on the couches and chairs there, so we walked toward them through the dining area, which contained one long table where meals would be served community-style.

Ged saw us and waved. Others looked over toward us—

"Buck Reilly?" A voice from the couch sounded.

"No way!" A woman's voice followed.

As I got closer, I couldn't believe my eyes. A couple I knew from Key West was seated there amongst six other people.

"Bill and Linda Klipp? I'd say I'm surprised to see you, but this is your typical kind of trip."

Heather nudged me from behind. "Who are your friends?"

"Heather Drake, meet Bill and Linda Klipp, two world-renowned wildlife photographers and adventure travelers who live in Key West."

"It's a small world amongst explorers," Ged said.

"Nice to meet you," Heather said.

"And I recognize you from being on so many of my favorite magazine covers," Linda said.

Heather bowed slightly, and it set off a small chain reaction of whispers amongst the other guests. Introductions were made all around. There were two women in their late sixties traveling together. A woman in her forties and another one in her seventies, both traveling by themselves. An Australian brother and sister in their early thirties and another couple who were Americans.

We squeezed onto the couch next to Bill and Linda. Bill nodded toward the last couple across the salon seated in chairs. "That's our friend, Ralph. He's a Nat Geo photographer and often leads trips like these. Ann, his girlfriend, is also an accomplished photographer."

Roger and Liam walked in gritting their teeth and not making eye contact with anyone. Ged announced them and another round of introductions ensued. They stood behind us.

I turned back to see them.

"Coincidentally, some friends from Key West are here on the ship," I said.

Roger's eyes narrowed and he was no doubt assessing whether this was all some kind of set-up. Bill and Linda were in their sixties, and as I recalled, had been retired from big jobs in finance for twenty years, or more. They didn't look threatening, but I wanted to set Roger's paranoia at ease.

"Several of the folks here are highly accomplished photographers, which is a great sign that we're going to see some extraordinary wildlife," I said.

Roger raised a brow, gave everyone a nod, but pinched his lips.

Ged and his wife, Teresa, handed out pre-poured champagne glasses and offered a toast to everyone for what he said would be a remarkable journey. I gulped mine hoping his words would come true, albeit with a totally different outcome than what he was referring to. He then introduced Gary, the expedition leader, and Anders, the naturalist. Teresa ran us through the typical meal schedule on board the boat.

Nobody had any questions, so Ged asked Gary to provide a summary of the trip's itinerary. Gary was an American that had lived in Australia for twenty years and traveled the world leading wildlife expeditions.

"We're starting the trip by heading up to the northern area of Svalbard, and over the next eight days will work our way back to Longyearbyen," Gary said.

I heard a grunt behind me, followed by a poke to the shoulder. I glanced at Roger, and he mouthed the words, "Eight days?" His eyes were wild.

I hunched my shoulders, turned around and caught Bill's glance. He nodded toward Roger with a "what's his problem" expression on his face.

I rolled my eyes.

Gary continued to describe that the ship would travel in and out of fjords and noted that all the guests were expected to use their binoculars or telephoto lenses from the observation deck atop the ship to help search for wildlife on the shores and ice floes as we traveled. There was a question for a show of hands of anyone who didn't want to be awoken during nighttime hours if a polar bear was spotted.

Nobody raised their hand—until Liam did.

"Need my sleep, mate," he said.

Roger grunted again—Liam jumped.

"Ow! That was my foot," Liam said.

I bit my lip to contain a laugh. The situation in total was just too weird to comprehend. Had I not decided to stop in Edinburgh to research my birth mother after Harry blew my mind with the news that he was my birth father, my friends and I would be back in Key West by now. There was nothing funny about the Sect, their mission, and intentions to kill us if we were not successful though, so the moment of humor didn't last.

The briefing broke up and everyone went out the hatch in the back of the salon that led to the rear deck. Heather and I lingered, as did Roger and Liam, until we were the only four left inside.

"Eight fucking days, Reilly. What the hell were you thinking?" Roger asked.

"No other way to get to where the Duke of Oxford buried your damned canister," I said. "You think we want to be on here with you? Let's focus on finding the damned thing and then maybe we can figure out a way to return sooner."

He patted the bulge under his jacket. "Oh, don't worry, I'll get us back to town tomorrow afternoon, believe me."

"Just relax, will you, Roger?"

"That word's not in my vocabulary, Reilly. My original offer had you turning into a pumpkin tomorrow night. If your information is bogus, then this'll be a one-way trip for you and your lady friend here, and maybe this whole damned boat."

I licked my lips. I hoped Ray would have success looking into my idea as there was no way this could end well with Roger, given the circumstances.

I stood and extended my hand to Heather, helping her up too.

"Let's go out on deck and watch the mountains go by. Maybe we'll see some orcas, whales, or polar bear."

Roger's teeth were gritted. "That water's bloody cold, lad. Doubt you or Heather could survive longer than a minute if you fell in." He let that sink in. "Better watch yourself."

I steered Heather toward the hatch.

"Same goes for you and Liam. I'd hate for you to get hurt."

24

THE EXPEDITION LEADER AND NATURALIST PROVIDED MULTIPLE SESSIONS ON the wildlife of the region, safety, photography, and other topics during the day at sea, but Heather and I skipped most of them. Roger and Liam ignored them all.

When we weren't confined to our bunks due to heavy seas, Heather and I thoroughly searched our cabin for anything that Freddy may have stashed there. We took the bunks apart, the desk, chairs, the closet, and anything that was bolted down but found nothing. We also removed the covers from the electrical sockets, air conditioning vents, and light fixtures and discovered nothing but dust.

"Did the detective in Oslo, or the Duke of Oxford imply that Freddy may have hidden something specific?" Heather asked.

"No, I was just hoping that maybe he had."

"Great, well, we've trashed our room based on your hopes."

"I understand that but given that we're rapidly approaching the zero hour with the Sect, anything we can do to improve the situation is worth pursuing."

It took us a couple of hours to put it all back together again and we then went out to the salon just in time to catch the tail end of Gary's history on *Sjuøyane*, which translates into English as Seven Islands.

"The islands are named after various explorers who had used the area for different expeditions," he said. "For example, Phippsøya was named after the Englishman, John Phipps, who was there in 1773 during an attempt to reach the North Pole. Parryøya was named after William Parry, who also attempted to reach the North Pole in 1827. During that trip, he made it up to 82°, 45' north latitude, which was the record for the highest latitude ever attained and wasn't broken for forty-nine years."

I leaned into Heather. "That's the island we're headed to."

Gary continued. "The satellite reconnaissance photos that the Norwegian government provides daily tracks the movement of fast ice, ice floes, pack ice, etc. as it generally moves northward. The satellite photos over the last few weeks shows drastic change and movement northward, which is fortunate, or we'd never make it to the Seven Islands."

"Is that attributed to climate change?" Heather asked.

"Some would say that, but one of the interesting aspects about the Seven Islands is that the northernmost branch of the Gulf Stream concludes there, which brings warmer water in that melts the ice faster," Ralph, the Nat Geo photographer said.

"Hard to believe the Gulf Stream starts south of Key West and meanders its way all the way up to here," I said.

"We live there and have meandered here as well," Bill said.

That caused some giggles from the group.

"The landscape in the Seven Islands is barren and rocky with some coastal plains, but otherwise mountainous with steep slopes that drop straight to the water."

"Are there polar bears up here?" Michael, the Australian asked.

"Absolutely," Gary said. "And since we're almost there, let me mention our gun safety protocol." He glanced around the room. "Both Anders and I will carry rifles when on shore in case any polar bears confront us. We have permits for the guns and nobody else is allowed to touch them, so please, don't even ask to."

"Are there glaciers on the Seven Islands?" Heather asked.

"Surprisingly not," Gary said. "We've passed many glaciers today, south of here, but again, due to the Gulf Stream, there are none on those islands. Aside from snow, you'll see driftwood on the shore, flowers, lichens and unfortunately, trash that has traveled up the Gulf Stream."

Ged got up and walked past us and out of the salon.

"Wait here," I said to Heather.

I hurried after Ged and caught up to him out in the hall near the hatch that went out to the port deck. "Hey, Ged, quick question for you."

He smiled and his gray beard arched upward. "What can I do for you, Buck?"

"The monument we're looking for on Parryøya—"

"Good news about that. The captain knows where it's located on the northern shore of the island where there's a deep-water bay, so we can get close with the ship and then go ashore on the Zodiacs," he said.

"Perfect, that should save us time." I paused. "What I wanted to ask was whether there are shovels or digging tools on the ship? We didn't have time to get any beforehand."

"That shouldn't be a problem. All these exploration vessels carry a wide array of tools for many reasons. I'll speak with the captain." Ged smiled. "After you first called me, I did some research on you, *King* Buck."

Oh gawd.

"Are you looking for buried treasure up here?" His smile was broad. I guessed—hoped—he was kidding.

"Nope, not on this trip. Just searching for a time capsule that memorializes Conway's achievements."

"That's exciting. He's one of the explorers?"

"Sir Martin Conway, who the monument is for, was an explorer, but no, the time capsule was placed there in the last fifteen years by a distant relative of his. We're seeking to find it to confirm its contents."

"Long way to travel to see a new time capsule," he said. "Are Roger and his friend members of the Conway family?"

"No, they represent the organization interested in the information though. They, ah, tapped me to help them, but with the deadline being tonight, it's been a challenge." I frowned. "They're both a bit grumpy as a result."

Ged nodded. "I thought I detected something along those lines. We'll be there soon now, so not to worry. I'll have whatever excavation tools they have on board placed onto one of the Zodiacs before we head to shore."

As he said this, the sound of the ship's engines changed in pitch, and we began to slow.

Ged smiled again. "Sounds like we're close. I'm going to see the captain, but you may want to gather your friends and don your gear. You'll go in the first Zodiac with both Anders and Gary, and after Gary drops you, your friends and Anders to search for the monument, the others will go see a walrus community nearby." His smile faded. "Since you'll have both armed guides on your boat, we'll have to delay the others going to shore until you return, so please be as quick as you can."

He winked and I attempted to smile back at him.

Truth was my nerves were increasingly frayed the closer we got to our destination.

What if we couldn't find the monument?

Or we find the monument but not the time capsule?

What would Roger do?

I was worried for Heather's safety, and that of Ray and Lenny if Roger is true to his word. Failure wasn't an option, so I brushed the thought aside, and focused on next steps.

Everyone from the salon came out toward me as the lecture had ended.

Heather walked straight for me, followed by the Klipps and Gary brought up the rear.

"Time to gear up," Gary said. "We'll meet on the bow in twenty minutes where we'll hand out your one-piece flotation suits and life preservers."

Bill stepped forward. "Let's all get in the same Zodiac," he said.

"Sounds good," I said.

Having some other friends on board might dissuade Roger from pitching a fit if we failed to find the time capsule.

Back in our cabin, I tried my cell phone, but it was on SOS with no service. The ship's Wi-Fi wasn't working either. Not many places left on earth where there's no cell coverage or Wi-Fi, which most people, including me, would normally relish, but not now. I was hoping to check with Ray to see if he'd had any luck with the plan we'd established. I'd have to rely on faith at this point.

If it didn't work out, we'd improvise.

The shades were open on the porthole, and we could see Parryøya ahead. It was a steeply mountainous island covered in snow. "We're going to freeze out there," Heather said.

"It all comes down to having the right gear," I said. "The parka and pants I got you are top of the line, which combined with the long underwear, sweater, and gloves, should keep you warm. Especially if we have to walk a distance and then try and dig up the frozen earth."

Heather had stripped down and was layering up. Aside from worrying about the cold, she hadn't complained about a thing, including being held hostage. My estimation of her ability to withstand challenging circumstances had continued to escalate these past few days, and I was both proud of her and encouraged for our future together. Life with me wasn't easy for a lot of reasons, and if she could hang through all of this, it proved our compatibility, at least to me.

She, on the other hand, may run away to New York City as fast as she could once we got out of here.

If we got out of here, that is …

I hadn't shown Heather the knife I purchased in town and stashed it now in my jacket pocket. The knife was so long I couldn't zip the pocket shut, so I placed it in an interior pocket where I could reach for it, if need be.

Fully geared up, we stepped out into the hall. I knocked on Roger's door, and he pulled it open. He was still wearing the clothes he'd come in.

"We're at Parryøya and about to go to shore," I said. "Are you coming?"

"Nobody told us. We'll be ready in five minutes."

"We're meeting up on the bow. See you there."

"Moment of truth, Reilly. If you dragged us up here for nothing, it'll be a one-way trip."

I bit down so hard it could break a molar. There was no sense in trying to reason with him as his orders came from the aristocratic leaders of the Sect who called the shots from the ivory towers in their ancient castles. If anything, I was glad he reminded me of the urgency of the situation as I'd need to pivot quickly if what the Duke of Oxford told me wasn't true.

"See you on the bow," I said. "And hurry up. I convinced the operator to change their entire itinerary to accommodate your demands, so let's get this over with."

"Ay, laddie, one way or the other."

His cabin door slammed shut and I saw Heather shudder.

I rubbed my hand on the outside of my jacket and felt the knife underneath.

One way or the other, indeed.

We walked out onto the deck where the cold wind whipped our faces. I pulled the wool hat onto my head and zipped my jacket up to cover most of my face. As Ged had said, the ship was now anchored in a wide bay that was surrounded on both sides with tall, snow-capped hills that led to taller mountains. The shoreline looked to be flat in the center of the bay, which is where he had indicated the Conway monument to be.

A burst of acid reflux suddenly burned my throat.

I said a quiet prayer asking for guidance and help to find what we'd come for, the ability to keep Heather safe and to navigate whatever happened next and emerge unscathed. It was a lot to ask for, and Lord knows I was unworthy of such grace, but you don't ask, you don't get.

We found several of the others on the bow where red, one-piece suits were piled up according to size. There was a hot tub, and I had a momentary fantasy of sitting in steaming water with Heather and enjoying a cocktail. That wasn't likely on this trip, no matter what we found on the island.

Heather and I collected our one-piece suits and inflatable flotation devices that we wore around our necks, and then walked over to where Bill and Linda Klipp stood with Ralph and Ann, all of whom had cameras with long lenses draped around their necks, with backpacks full of additional gear over their shoulders.

"No cameras?" Linda asked.

"Just iPhones, unfortunately," I said. "We happened to be in Svalbard and set this excursion up spontaneously."

"I like the way you roll," Ralph said.

He was a tall man who had appeared quite serious during Gary's presentations. Out here now, dressed and ready to go, he seemed to be totally in his element, with joy evident in his speech and sense of humor.

"You must have done a lot of trips like this," I said.

"Five or six a year for the last twenty years, so yeah, you could say that."

"You too, Ann?" Heather asked.

"I was doing a couple a year when I met Ralph, what, six or seven years ago?" she said.

Ralph nodded.

"Since then, I've accompanied him on most of the trips."

"You don't work?" Heather asked.

"I sold my business," Ann said. "So now just consult, but I'm even paring that down at this point." She had a warm smile and bright blue eyes. "Once you start doing trips like these, it's all you'll want to do."

Roger and Liam appeared and were dressed in black jackets and pants. Liam collected a one-piece suit, but Roger didn't. They walked up to us, and I immediately sensed something wasn't right.

"So what's with the stop in Parryøya?" Ralph asked. "Ged said you and your group were looking for something specific here?"

"We're here to find a monument to an explorer named Sir Martin Conway from the late 1800s," I said.

"Bill said you're a treasure hunter," Ralph said. "Do we get a cut if we help you find it?"

A dry laugh shot from my mouth. "It's just a monument—"

"Mind your own business there, laddie," Roger said. "Plenty of birds and reindeer for you to take cute pictures of."

The smiles in our group immediately faded.

Way to go, Roger. Rather than keeping everything light to not draw attention to our mission, the asshole just pissed on everyone's shoes.

"Sorry about Roger here, he's under a tight schedule to confirm the presence of some historic documents in the time capsule, which is why he asked us to come help."

That may have taken a slight edge off Roger's sharp comment, but I could tell by Ralph's scowl that from here on out, Roger was dead to him. If only I had the same luxury.

I looked Roger up and down. "You need a one-piece and life preserver."

He held his cast up. "I can't get my arm in one of those suits, so Heather and I are going to stay behind while you and Liam search for the monument," he said.

"I want to go," Heather said.

Roger's eyes narrowed and I realized he wanted to maintain control by keeping us apart. While our eyes were connected, he patted the breast of his jacket to let me know he was armed. I bit the side of my mouth.

"That's a good idea," I said. "Liam and I will take the first shift out searching and digging and you guys can stay warm and go next if we're not lucky."

Heather shook her head and looked from me to Roger and back to me.

"Fine. I'm going inside where it's warm then." She walked away.

Gary walked up along the starboard rail and waved to us. "The first Zodiac's in the water, so Anders will take the group going to shore, and I'll stay onboard with Bill, Linda, Ralph, and Ann and cruise along the shore to search for wildlife."

We followed him down the rail toward to an open gate and gangplank with stairs that had been lowered to the water. One crewman stood at the top, and another at the bottom to help guests climb aboard the rubber-hulled boat. We went down the rickety metal walkway, one by one, starting with Gary, followed by Ann, then Ralph, followed by Bill and Linda, then me, Liam, and Anders, our guide, who had a stainless-steel rifle over his shoulder. The guests all sat on the round edges of the boat's hull, half on the starboard side, and half on the port, with Gary in the rear to operate the engine.

There were two shovels and a pickaxe bungeed sideways across the stern next to Gary. I again took in a deep breath and sought to control my breathing to remain calm and focused. I didn't like Roger's game of divide and conquer even though it kept Heather on board rather than being with them on the island. He wanted to stay a step ahead and keep me off balance, and there was little I could do about it.

A crewman released the carabiner that held our boat to the ship, and Gary backed us slowly away. The moment allowed me to absorb the incredible beauty that surrounded us. Snow-covered mountains, blue water, calm seas, the omnipresent sun hovering over us and a complete lack of humans aside from the small group of stalwart explorers who had come to the northernmost part of the planet to witness rare wildlife, brave the challenging environment, and be at one with the unique remoteness that was increasingly rare on the earth today.

For a moment I felt completely free of the anxiety that had gnawed at me these past few days as I soaked in the raw beauty, reveled in the cold air that buffeted my face, and savored the anticipation of the unknown that tickled my heart in a way I hadn't experienced since the glory days of e-Antiquity.

I glanced at Liam, and he had no interest in the sights and was focused exclusively on me. The buffoon had the subtlety of a silverback gorilla and zero appreciation for the surroundings.

A laugh sounded and I realized Bill was watching me.

"There are probably less than fifty people on the entire planet at this high of a latitude right now," he said. "Enjoy it."

"I am," I said.

I wished Heather was here.

Back to Liam, who was staring me in the eye, his face deadly serious. He reached down and parted his jacket to reveal his gun holstered to his chest so only I could see it.

What an idiot, I thought.

25

THE *SJOVEIEN* HAD ANCHORED A HUNDRED YARDS FROM THE SHORE, so the ride didn't take long. We saw none of the floating ice in this bay that we'd encountered throughout the journey from Longyearbyen, and I was again amazed that the Gulf Stream reached all the way up to here. The bottom dropped off precipitously from the island, which allowed us to drive the boat right up onto the rocky shoreline.

Anders, with his rifle over his shoulder, held the bowline and jumped over the edge onto the rocks. He pulled the Zodiac in farther up the shore and then turned to me.

"Be careful getting out."

He held up his hand, but I didn't need it. I tossed out the shovels and pickaxe, then swung my legs over the side and landed firmly on the rocks, which were metamorphic, sedimentary, and volcanic. There was schist, gneiss, and granite of all sizes, rounded from eons of getting tumbled by the waves and snow. The snow field was maybe another fifty feet inland and continued in a sheet as far as the eye could see. If I didn't have on sunglasses, there would be no way to avoid snow blindness.

"Give me your hand," Anders said to Liam.

Liam accepted his offer and stepped more cautiously over the bow. He wasn't wearing eye protection, and I hoped he'd go blind out here, which would make him easier to manage if things went awry.

"Radio me if you need anything, or when you're ready to return to the ship." Gary shouted over the revving Yamaha 50-horsepower engine on the stern of the Zodiac. "We'll come back in two hours, either way."

"Good luck," Linda shouted.

They backed away and turned bow first into the light surf. I suddenly felt more alone than I ever had before. Anders was from Denmark but spoke good English, and Liam was a useless knob here solely to monitor my activities, so I didn't expect any help from him.

"Do you have any idea where the monument is?" I asked Anders.

"There's a mark on my map of the island." He pulled out a paper map that had been folded up inside his breast pocket. "I picked this up once Ged told me we were coming here to search," Anders said. "Take a look."

He held the map up to me and there was a small symbol of a cross, or maybe it was an X, near the bay where we'd landed, straight up the shore, and in toward where the topography angled upward.

"It's the only symbol on the map for all of Parryøya," Anders said.

"Let's hope that's it," I said. "What do you think, Liam?"

"Better be."

I picked up the pickaxe and a shovel and took the lead. The knee-high rubber boots provided onboard the ship crunched easily through the snow. Buried underneath were more of the rocks like those on the beach, which made the footing difficult.

Liam stumbled repeatedly.

"Take your time," Anders said from behind us. "Don't break your leg."

Liam used the other shovel like a walking stick to help keep his balance. We continued down the shore for twenty minutes. Anders consulted his map frequently and then called for us to stop. He held the map up for us to view.

"The symbol's just below the peak up there." He pointed up the hill to the highest point, and then down the tight topographic contours on the map. "We should turn inland now. Whatever is noted here should be right at the base of that hill up ahead."

I turned toward the mountain and plodded on through the snow. We crossed animal trails, found reindeer droppings, saw an arctic fox observing us from a rock formation. There were even small, purple flowers that popped up from exposed patches of dirt. The raw beauty was incredible and was like nothing I'd ever seen before.

Nearly halfway to the hill, I saw some large impressions in the snow and realized they were footprints. I paused to wait for Anders to catch up.

"What are those from?" I asked.

He grimaced. "Those are polar bear prints." He knelt and touched the snow. It was soft around the prints. "Fresh, too."

"You any good with that rifle?" Liam asked. "If not, give it to me. I'm a crack shot."

Anders smiled. "We're not allowed to let the guests handle the guns. Don't worry, I'm a good shot."

"Have you ever had to kill a polar bear before?" I asked.

Anders paused, sniffled his nose, then ran the sleeve of his arm across his face. "I've scared bears away with warning shots before but have never killed one."

"Bloody great," Liam said.

I continued onward. There were additional animal tracks, including more from polar bears, but now that I knew what they were, I kept my comments to myself. Time was of the essence. I didn't like leaving Heather on the boat with Roger, and the longer this took, I feared the other guests would get agitated, which could trigger Roger doing something crazy. This was our sole shot to get the Sect off our backs, and I was determined to make it happen, come Hell or high water.

After another fifteen minutes of trudging through knee-deep snow, we were close to where the ground shifted sharply upward. Anders went back and forth from his map to his compass and then used his binoculars.

"What's that, up ahead?" he said.

He handed me his binoculars. I focused them in to where he was pointing. I spotted three black poles pointing straight into the sky. "They look like trees, but without branches or leaves," I said.

"Look around," Anders said. "There's no trees anywhere on this entire archipelago."

"Let's check it out," I said.

I picked up the pace and after another ten minutes, we arrived at what was clearly a monument.

"Are they steel?" I asked.

"Poured-in-place concrete," Anders said. "They must have fabricated them here and added stain to the mix to make them black."

"That makes sense. I was wondering how they could have hauled steel beams on the boat and out here."

Liam was breathing heavy. "Get on with it then."

We closed the distance and once there, I concluded that Anders was right. They were concrete and in the center one, was an inscription. It read: "Sir Martin Conway, Arctic Explorer, 1897."

I dropped the pick and stretched my arms. "Let's use the shovels to clear the snow away and see what's beneath," I said.

Liam grumbled, checked his watch, and must have seen we were short on time so helped me remove the snow. Thankfully, the snow was dry and light. It didn't take long to get down to the ground where there was a plaque. It read: "Conway family time capsule, 1890 – 2014."

Anders had a big smile. "Congratulations."

"We need to dig it up," I said.

Anders's smile faded. He checked his watch. "We have about thirty minutes before we need to go back."

"Get to it, Reilly."

My shovel wouldn't penetrate the frozen earth.

Shit.

I dropped that and took up the pick, which I swung with all my might, repeatedly, until the earth started coming loose in frozen chunks. I pounded and pounded to break up the ground, and Liam used his shovel to remove the loose clumps. Before long I was soaked with sweat inside my snow pants, down jacket, and waterproof jumpsuit, but I continued with the pick until I was down three feet where the ground softened. Not wanting to impale the time capsule, I switched to the shovel.

I stopped to catch my breath and wished I'd brought a jug of water. I saw that Anders had taken up a position on top of a rock behind us, maybe fifty feet away, and was scanning the periphery in all direction with his binoculars.

"We ain't got all day, Reilly," Liam hissed.

"Screw you, asshole," I said. "My damned back still hurts from where you stabbed me."

"Imagine how a bullet would feel."

I exhaled hard and continued digging. The soil was softer, and since it had been dug out previously, was relatively free of rocks. When the hole was down to nearly four feet, I suddenly heard Anders shouting. I looked up to Liam who still hovered over me, but he was focused on clearing the dirt that I'd tossed out of the three-foot square hole.

Liam glanced over toward Anders, who I could still hear yelling, in what, Danish?

Liam stood up, glanced back and then spun around to look in the opposite direction of Anders.

"There's a bear coming!" he said.

"What? Where?"

"He's running toward us—huge bastard!"

"Where's Anders with the rifle?"

"Back on a rock pointing it straight toward us." He glanced down at me, and I saw terror in his eyes. "We're right in between them."

Liam dug what looked like a .38 caliber revolver out of the inside of his jacket.

Hell of a lot of good that pea shooter will do—

BOOM!

Down in the hole, I couldn't see what happened, but Anders must have fired the rifle.

"Did he hit the bear?"

"Shot over its bloody head for a warning." Liam's eyes were wild. "Bastard's still coming. Damned monster must've heard all that bloody digging noise you're making."

Crap.

Liam extended his arm with gun in hand toward where the bear must be coming from.

"Don't shoot him with that thing, you'll just piss—"

BOOM! BOOM!

"… him off! How far away is he?"

BOOM!

Anders fired again.

"We're in the way and the bloody guide can't get a clean shot! He's still shooting over his head." Liam raised his arm again.

"Get down so—"

BOOM! BOOM!

"Think I hit him!" Liam said.

From my perspective inside the hole, Liam's eyes grew even wider with terror. I could hear Anders scream in the background, but my ears rung so bad from Liam's gunfire, I couldn't make out what he was saying.

Suddenly, Liam took off running.

Shit!

I was a sitting duck in this hole.

The ground shook as if a stampede of buffaloes were coming at me.

BOOM!

"No!"

The terror in Liam's voice now matched what I saw on his face.

BOOM!

Click … click … click.

"Get down!" Anders voice was finally clear. "Get down, so I can …"

"Aaaaggghhhh! Help! Aaggghhhhh."

An ungodly scream erupted. I hunkered down in the hole as far as I could.

There was no playing hero against a polar bear.

BOOM!

The sound of Anders's rifle was closer and far deeper than Liam's little snub nose.

Silence followed.

I crouched frozen in the hole and listened for any sound.

Had the bear got both of them?

I held the pick over my shoulder ready to defend myself—

Static sounded. The radio. Then muted voices.

I pushed the pick down to help me climb out—clunk—it hit something. I bent down and kicked more dirt away and found a handle on a box. I bent over and brushed more dirt away. The box was solid and looked to be in good condition.

Where was the bear?

I stood and peeked up out of the hole. Anders was hunched down next to the bear—a massive giant—but there was no sight of Liam.

What the …?

I was about to climb out, but quickly used the shovel to pry around the box in the hole, and then jammed it to the side of the box and angled it to the side. The box lifted.

Now loose, I reached down and pulled it with all my strength.

It came free.

The box was heavy, maybe a foot wide and a foot deep. Items clunked around inside it. I hoisted it up and out of the hole where it landed with a clank outside. I pulled myself out, threw the shovel down and ran over to where I found Anders in tears.

The bear had been shot several times and red blood matted its yellowish-white fur. It was as big as a Volkswagen Beetle.

I glanced around, not seeing Liam.
Did he get away?
Then I saw his foot.
He was under the bear.
Lying in a pool of their mutual blood.
I had to look away.

SECTION 5:

HELLS BELLS

26

ANDERS AND I CARRIED LIAM'S LIFELESS BODY BACK TO THE SHORE.

Anders was inconsolable.

"It's not your fault," I said. "You did everything you could."

"Why did he shoot the bear with that pistol?" Anders said. "I could have scared him away."

I'd picked up Liam's gun when we got him out from under the beast and placed it inside my jacket. I had the time capsule in one hand and my arm around Liam's waist with the other as we carried him out. A bullet fell out of Liam's pocket as we bounced along. When we stopped for a break, I reached in his coat and found a handful more and shoved them in my jacket. I'd reload the gun and have protection against Roger.

We saw Gary's Zodiac coming in from the west, and the other one from the boat speeding toward us with only two people aboard. I felt bad for all the passengers as this would ruin their expedition. Liam, on the other hand, got what he deserved.

Polar bear attacks were infrequent here because people were well informed and carried the necessary weapons. The tour operator had done a good job in briefing us and was armed appropriately, but the unique circumstances that drove us deep into the island, away from the boat, and with Liam foolishly wounding the bear, created a situation far outside of their control. The operator would no doubt be distraught, but this was not their issue.

We all arrived simultaneously on the shore. Ged and a crewman from the *Sjoveien* jumped out of the Zodiac that came from the ship, and Gary, Bill, Linda, Ralph, and Ann climbed out of the other one. Few words were spoken as the situation was clear. Once we had Liam loaded into Ged's Zodiac, we stood in silence, their eyes on my blood-covered clothes.

"It wasn't Anders's fault," I said. "The bear came in from the only angle he couldn't defend, and Liam had a low-caliber pistol and shot the bear, which only pissed him off."

"Passengers are prohibited from carrying guns for that very reason," Ged said. "He broke the rules and it cost him his life."

Gary stepped forward. "We're going to take pictures to document the bear and the direction it came from." He paused. "Anders, are you up to showing us where this happened?"

Anders took a deep breath and nodded. He took shells out of his pocket and reloaded his carbine. Gary carried a similar rifle and the six of them set off along the path we'd made through the snow.

"Be careful!" Ged called after them.

We climbed inside the Zodiac, Ged took the helm, the crewman pushed us off from shore and we set off for the *Sjoveien*. It was impossible not to look at Liam lying in the middle of the boat. The bear had slashed his neck with its island-sized paw, and Liam had bled out quickly. His jacket was covered in blood, as were my clothes from carrying him.

I looked away, letting my eyes glaze over the natural beauty of the landscape and dark colored sea. There'd be no forgetting the site of Liam, his screams, and the freight train of a bear.

I'd been resting against the time capsule, which I refocused on now. The box itself was made from hard plastic, which made sense given the frozen environment it had been placed in. It would never have deteriorated, but it won't be getting re-buried.

We arrived back at the *Sjoveien* and tied up at the lowered gangplank that rose up and down in the waves. The other guests were lined up on the rail and I spotted Heather with Roger pressed up against her. Their faces were serious, and Roger was chewing his lip, no doubt with fury. He probably suspected I had something to do with Liam's demise.

Other crewmembers hurried down the gangplank and brought blankets and a stretcher with them. They handed me a blanket, and I realized they wanted me to cover myself so I wouldn't horrify the other guests. I wrapped one blanket around me, and another around Liam's body, picked up the time capsule and scrambled onto the shaky, aluminum stair as the crew descended to attend to Liam's body.

Heather's cries hit me halfway up, and once I reached the top, she jumped into my arms. Her sobs filled my ear where her head was pressed into my shoulder.

"It's okay, honey," I said. "I'm all right."

Having been in the midst of the situation, my emotions had been in check, but with her clutching me now, I felt my knees weaken. The bear could have just as easily killed me. Roger's glare behind her, though, refocused me on the moment.

"Buck, I'm so glad … you're all … right." Heather's voice broke.

I could hear the ruckus of the men carrying Liam's body onto the gangplank behind me and wanted to clear the way for them to pass.

"I need to get out of these clothes," I said.

Heather squeezed me again before relinquishing her grip. She took me by the hand and Roger's eyes were locked onto mine as I brushed past him, the time capsule firmly in my grip.

"I'll be at your room shortly to see the contents of that box," he said.

I felt I should say something about Liam, but given Roger's vicious stare, I didn't. The feel of Liam's gun in my coat leveled the playing field.

Heather led me toward the stern of the ship and the other guests cleared a path, their eyes wide, some crying at the situation, and others just aghast. I cinched the blanket tight as we walked through the salon, dining room, and the corridor to our cabin. Heather entered first and then hugged me again once inside. I didn't want to traumatize her with my bloodstained clothing so kept the blanket wrapped around my coat.

"I'm going to shower and change," I said. "Can you get me a trash bag for these clothes and put some new ones in the bathroom please?"

She nodded quickly.

Once inside the small bathroom, I unwrapped myself from the blanket, appalled at my blood-soaked reflection in the mirror. I reloaded and hid Liam's pistol in the stack of towels on the shelf, stripped down, took a hot shower, and once finished, found fresh clothes sitting on the sink. I placed the jacket and pants that'd I'd turned inside out when I'd taken them off, into the black trash bag.

When I opened the bathroom door, I found Roger standing there, with Heather seated on her bunk. The time capsule was on my bunk, still closed.

"The crew briefed me on what happened," Roger said.

"I hope you faked more emotion than you're showing here."

"Liam was a soldier. He's not the first to die for the cause and won't be the last."

I swore a silent oath that Roger would be next if he reneged on the deal about my finding the canister to eliminate the Council's intent to kill me. But with Heather here, I just wanted to get him out of our lives as soon as possible. That reminded me of my plan with Ray. I checked my watch. It was 12:15 a.m.

"Am I keeping you from something?" Roger's sarcasm was ever present.

"The rest of my life," I said. "Let's open this damned box so we can all move on."

I sat on my bunk with the time capsule in my lap. I rotated it looking for a clasp, but it was sealed shut. Roger pulled a large knife from his pocket.

"We'll cut it open along the seal," he said. "Hold it tight."

He lowered the knife toward me, which caused me to tense up. I was ready to spring toward him if the knife came too close to me, but he shoved it into the narrow gap along the edge near the top. The sound of air rushing out was a good sign that the contents were safe. It had only been underground for ten years, but if not sealed properly, all the contents would have been ruined.

Using his good arm, Roger angled the knife up and down, and I rotated the box around as he cut the seal. With three sides sliced, the lid popped up enough to get my fingers under it. I placed it on the floor for better leverage and pulled hard on the top. The screech of plastic and the rubber gasket gave way, and I was able to wrench the lid off.

We all peered inside.

I removed the contents, item by item. There were different pieces related to the Conway family history, including a family tree, a plaque with their crest, ancient copies of books that Sir Martin had written, and a scrapbook.

Roger stood up straight. "The canister's not here," he said.

The expression on his face changed from surprise to anger to determination in a millisecond. Liam's gun was in the bathroom, and the knife I bought in Longyearbyen was under my pillow on the opposite end of the bed. I'd have no chance to dive for it with Roger holding his own knife.

I swallowed hard.

"Let's look at all this more closely," I said. "Maybe they emptied the canister because it wouldn't fit in the capsule."

I opened the scrapbook and quickly determined it was in chronological order from old to new. There were sketches from Sir Martin's mountaineering to gratuitous photos of various Conways with other aristocrats in diverse settings filled with pageantry. As I turned pages, I slowly coiled myself to lunge at Roger if he so much as hinted at violence. The last couple of pages were about James Conway, the present Duke of Oxford, which was no surprise since he was behind the time capsule.

"Nothing there, Reilly." Roger's expression was all business. "Wouldn't have mattered anyway."

My heart thudded in my chest. I glanced at Heather, seated on the edge of her bunk, her eyes wide.

"So you were going to kill us anyway?" I asked.

"Orders is orders."

I positioned the still-opened scrapbook to block his knife if he sprang toward me.

The last picture was the most recent. It was of the duke, and another man …

"Wait a minute," I said. "I saw a picture of Frederick Lassiter at his widow's home in Amsterdam. Same beady eyes. That's the guy Harry gave the canister to, who then gave it to the duke, who he's standing next to in this photo." I read the caption. "It says: 'The Duke of Oxford, James Conway, at the dedication of select species from the United Kingdom at the Global Seed Vault, Svalbard, Norway, 2014.'"

Freddy held something in the picture.

"Let me see that."

Roger ripped the scrapbook from my hands.

Liam's gun was too far away in the bathroom, so I edged toward the other end of my bunk, closer to where my knife was under the pillow as I watched Roger's face. He held his knife as he gripped the scrapbook and pulled it closer to peer at the photo.

"*Jings*," Roger said. "*Help ma boab*."

I slowly placed my hand under my pillow and gripped the handle of my knife. "What the hell's that mean?"

"It bloody well means that's the canister that Freddy's holding."

My heart skipped a beat.

"Maybe they placed it in that Global Seed Vault," I said.

"His Grace didn't tell you that?"

I thought back to what he'd said. "No, come to think of it, he said something like, 'seek and ye shall find.' I assumed he meant it was in the time capsule."

Roger grunted. "Did he know what was inside the canister?"

"Harry told him." I paused. "The old bastard's eyes lit up as if he'd discovered a winning lottery ticket."

"Cripes," Roger said. "That old bastard is well known by the Council for being untrustworthy and self-serving. Could he have been using misdirection to throw you off?"

"I have no idea."

"Where's this Seed Vault? This article says Svalbard."

"I saw it when we drove to town from the airport."

A smile slowly creased Roger's cheeks.

"Why do you look so happy?" I asked.

"I have a helicopter on the way to pick Liam's remains and me up." He clucked his tongue. "I'll have my pilot take me to the Seed Vault first."

"Wait, there's no cell service up here, how'd you call in a helicopter?"

Roger patted his breast pocket. "Satphone, mate. Never leave home without it."

The sound of an engine penetrated the cabin. An airplane engine.

I hoped that was a sign that the escape plan I'd set in motion with Ray was upon us, and that events were going to move quickly now. Adrenalin shot through me. I had to get of the jump on Roger.

But how?

There was only one way ...

I lunged for Roger and punched him hard in the stomach as he studied the photograph. Caught by surprise, it knocked the wind out of him. The Conway album fell from his grasp, and he tried to recover by blocking me with his cast and slashing the knife toward me, but I'd already grabbed him around the middle and slammed him hard into the desk.

Heather yelped in surprise.

I grabbed his hand with the knife and cracked it against the edge of the desk—the weapon fell to the ground and from the corner of my eye, I saw Heather dive for it.

Standing above me, Roger pounded my back with his cast, but I lifted my head up fast and caught him on the bottom of the chin with the crown of my skull—a loud thunk sounded—Roger dropped like a sack of laundry, unconscious.

"Oh my gosh, oh my gosh, oh my gosh," Heather said.

I quickly rifled Roger's pockets, but his gun wasn't there. I took his knife, threw it under Heather's bunk, and grabbed mine from under the pillow.

"Get your jacket, we need to go!" I said.

"Where are we going?"

"We need to get off this boat."

"To where, we'll freeze out there!"

I snatched the photo out of the scrapbook, ducked into the bathroom and grabbed my parka, and the gun, then ran back to the cabin door.

"Now, Heather, move!"

27

I PULLED HEATHER AT AN URGENT PACE through the back of the ship. Several guests were seated in the salon, and a few jumped up as we approached.

"Oh my gosh, I'm so sorry about what happened," Michael said.

I'd learned the Australian was an international radio and television journalist, and I feared what he'd say about all this once he got back to civilization.

We rushed past him. "Thank you, yeah, it was awful," I said.

Ged stepped forward. "A helicopter will be here within the hour to retrieve the body—"

I nodded to him but pushed past. God knows what expression Heather had on her face, because Ged's brow furrowed as he watched us rush toward the door to the aft deck.

Other guests just watched us with their mouths open. Once outside, I glanced up and saw that our Zodiac had already been placed on the storage rack on the upper deck.

Dammit!

When I looked down over the rail, I saw that Gary's Zodiac, with the others that had stayed behind to photograph the bear, had returned. The last of them was just coming up the gangplank. I pulled Heather toward them and came face-to-face with Bill Klipp.

He stopped in his tracks as we approached, a puzzled look on his face. "You okay?" he said.

I paused. Since we knew each other from Key West, I knew I could count on him. "Actually no. Too long of a story, but that guy, Roger had kidnapped Heather and is trying to kill us. We're getting out of here, so anything you or the others could do to slow him down, would be very much appreciated." I paused. "Just be careful, he's armed and dangerous."

Bill's expression was matter-of-fact as if he dealt with these types of things all the time, but ever since I'd known him, I'd never seen him get ruffled or angry, so his response was in character. He did raise an eyebrow though.

"What do you mean you're getting out of here? We're hundreds of miles from Longyearbyen."

As if on cue, the airplane I heard from our cabin circled again at low altitude. Bill looked up and gave me a knowing smile.

"Apologize to Ged for me, will you?" I said.

"Good luck."

I yanked Heather and we ran to the open gate in the rail that led to the gangplank. A Filipino crewman stood at the top and was reaching for the line being lowered from the crane to attach to and pull the Zodiac out of the water where it would be stowed next to the other one. I dashed through the gate.

"What are you doing?" the crewman said.

"Ah, we left something on board."

"You can't …"

Heather followed me onto the Zodiac, but as I tried to drop her hand to reach for the engine, she yanked it back toward her.

"What on earth are we doing? We can't make it to Longyearbyen on this—"

I pointed to the sky as the plane flew toward the island at low altitude.

"Untie us from the ship and push us off," I said. "Fast, before the crew realizes what we're doing."

Already warmed up, the engine started easily.

"Hey!" the crewman shouted. "You can't take the boat!"

"You can pick it up back on the island."

I shoved the gear lever into reverse and twisted the handle to give it gas—too much gas—freezing water splashed up over the transom and soaked me. I popped it in drive and spun the handle to give it gas again and the boat jumped forward—Heather toppled onto the floor.

More shouts followed from the rail, but I didn't look back.

The single-engine airplane was descending toward the island. The plane had snow skids instead of wheels or floats. It looked like a Pilatus PC-6 Porter, which was the ideal plane for these conditions. Ray must've been able to rent one, per my plan. While it turned out there was no ice here in the bay, Big Mama required two pilots to fly safely, so he wouldn't have been able to use our plane anyway.

"Heather!"

My shout caused her to jump. She looked back and I pointed to the plane approaching the snow field behind the rocky beach.

She shook her head. Was that a smile, a frown, or shock?

The Pilatus pulled up suddenly and began to circle around.

"Come on, Ray, land that bitch!"

Halfway to the island, a sharp sound rose above the clatter of the four-stroke engine. I intuitively ducked and glanced back over my shoulder toward the *Sjoveien*. Roger stood in the open gate by the gangplank with a rifle to his cheek. A burst of flame exploded from the barrel of the gun aimed at us, which was followed again by a sharp report.

THUD!

A chunk of the rubber Zodiac blew off next to my knee.

"Get down!"

Heather hunkered low and I twisted the accelerator handle as far as it would go, and the boat picked up speed. I zigged and zagged in an evasive manner, which slowed us down.

I put my bare hand on the hole and felt air rushing out of the left pontoon.

We're going to sink out here!

I glanced back when I heard another shot—Roger suddenly tumbled overboard—his arms flailed, the rifle flew from his grasp, and they both splashed into the water.

Bill stood behind him and I couldn't see his face, but he waved to us.

I couldn't help but laugh. I owed him a beer if we made it back to Key West alive.

With the boat now pointed straight toward the island, I saw Ray again descend closer to shore. The plane's skis settled onto the snow just as our boat began to waffle and lose speed.

"What's wrong?" Heather shouted over the sound of the engine. "Why are we slowing down?"

"The hull's punctured. We're not going to make it!"

"*What?*"

"Take your coat off so you can swim!"

I'd never seen greater surprise on Heather's face in the decade I'd known her. We continued to slow, now fifty yards from shore. She pulled her coat off, cursing aloud as she did.

I was already wet, and my adrenalin was pumping so fast I hardly noticed the cold, but that was about to change. The boat started to buckle, and I killed the power. Zodiacs were supposed to be unsinkable, even if the hull's punctured, but we may have taken more than one hit and if we collapsed suddenly, I didn't want either of us to get tangled underneath, or for the propeller to rip one of us in half.

We came to a stop thirty yards from shore and the left pontoon totally sagged flat. I could try and paddle us, but that would take longer, and Roger had probably already climbed back on the gangplank by now and we were totally exposed. He probably has an army from the Sect aboard his incoming helicopter, so we had to expect he'd come after us.

The sound of the plane engine grew louder, and the Pilatus was pointed toward the water now and taxiing our way.

If he came too far, the skis would get stuck in the rocks.

"We have to swim for it," I said.

"Are you insane?!"

I gave her my most charming smile. "You can't come to the High Arctic without taking a polar plunge."

"What about my cell phone?"

"The pants we're wearing have waterproof pockets. Stick it in there and zip it up tight."

I stowed my phone, stood and nearly lost balance. The boat had become unstable. I sucked in a deep breath, counted to three, and rolled over the side.

The thirty-three-degree water sucked all the air from my lungs.

I surfaced quickly and treaded water as I waited for Heather to jump.

I heard more cussing followed by a loud splash.

"Aagghh! It's freezing!"

"Hurry ... and get ... to shore." My teeth chattered from the frigid water. "The plane'll ... have ... heat."

We swam with all our strength through the freezing waves. Orcas were abundant in these waters, which was in the back of my mind, but fortunately none were likely here close to the island.

What maybe took a couple of minutes felt like an eternity and by the time I crawled onto the rocks, my extremities were numb, and my breathing labored. I turned around and helped Heather crawl onto the shore. The sound of the plane beckoned from behind us.

I wrapped my arm around her, and she shook like a wet dog, but from cold, not trying to shed the water. We stumbled through the rocks and boulders toward Ray, who thankfully was only another fifty feet away. He spun the plane as we approached so he'd be ready to take off. He popped the right-side hatch open as we arrived, and then extended his hand to help Heather aboard.

Her lips were blue, and she shook like a palm frond in a hurricane but pulled herself inside with Ray's help and squeezed between the front two seats and fell into the back. I shook as well, dove inside the door, pulled it shut and leaned around to check that she was okay.

"You guys are nuts!" Ray said.

"I'm never traveling north of New York City again," Heather said. "Especially with him." She wagged her thumb toward me.

There were blankets and plastic tarps in the back of the plane, which Heather wrapped herself in, and then handed me one up in the right, front seat. The plane had eight seats including the pilot.

"Perfect timing, Ray." My teeth clattered. "Now get the heat on and get us out of here."

Ray gradually ran up the engine and then released the brake and we began to slide across the snow. The surface wasn't as smooth as it looked, which resulted in a bumpy ride.

"There are big rocks under the snow, so keep an eye out," I said.

A moment later, Ray pulled back on the stick and the plane lifted into the air.

"This Pilatus is a great short runway plane," Ray said. "We may need to add one to Last Resort's fleet."

The name of our company, Last Resort Charter and Salvage, never felt more appropriate. I never expected to be one of the salvage jobs though.

"Check the radar, will you?" I said. "Any company coming our way?"

Ray toggled the digital instrument panel in front of him. "Looks like a helicopter in-bound, maybe fifty miles away."

"Shit," I said. "We need to beat it back to Longyearbyen."

"At 119 knots cruising speed, we'll be at the airport in seventy-nine minutes.

"Pedal to the metal," I said.

"How'd you ditch Roger and his henchman?"

I exhaled a deep breath and explained what happened while I was digging up the time capsule, and that I brought it back to the boat and opened the box under Roger's supervision.

"I knocked Roger out and we fled."

I didn't want to freak Ray out by saying Roger would likely be coming to the Seed Vault. We should have enough time to retrieve the canister and get out before he arrived, but that would require some extraordinary measures.

"What about the canister?"

"I believe it's in the Global Seed Vault near the airport. That's where you need to land."

He turned toward me fast. "You mean at the airport?"

"No, at the Seed Vault."

His mouth dropped open. "I saw that place, it's built into a mountainside. We can't land there."

"Sure you can, Ray. You're a hell of a pilot and this is a hell of a plane—"

"That doesn't change any—"

"We have no choice, okay? Roger will be on his way there in that helicopter and if we don't get control of that damned canister before he does, we're dead meat." I let that sink in. "If there's no plateau to land on, we can set down on the access road that leads to the Seed Vault."

Ray gave me "another fine mess you got me into" stare, and I couldn't blame him for being pissed but there wasn't anything we could do about it other than stay ahead of the curve.

"This damned trip's going to kill us yet," he said. "We need to get back to the peace and quiet of Key West."

"I promise you, that's the plan after we find the damned canister."

He glared at me, and if I could read his mind, I suspected it would say 'I've heard that before …'

"Where's Lenny?" I asked.

"At the hotel waiting for news. I bought him a satphone so we can communicate."

"Do it."

Ray produced another satphone and dialed Lenny up. He put the phone on speaker.

"You got 'em?" Lenny asked.

"Hey," I said. "Yeah, we're on the way, ETA in forty-five minutes."

"You coming to town from the airport, or should I meet you there?"

"No, meet us at the Global Seed Vault, but you need to get some bolt cutters or other tools so we can break into it. Heather and I need jackets too, if you can find any."

"Break in a seed vault? The hell you talking about, man? And it's the middle of the night, ain't no stores open."

"That's where the canister is. Liam got himself killed and Roger's going to be coming for us so there's no time to waste. Haul your ass to the store, break in if you must, and get whatever you can find to bust into that damned seed vault."

"You trying to get me arrested now? Shit, man, if it's a vault, like a bank or something, wire cutters ain't gonna do squat."

"Figure it out, Lenny. We're coming in hot, and our lives depend on it—*all* our lives."

The only sound that followed was him blowing into the phone.

I hit end and shook my head. "Heather, keep checking your phone for cell service and when you get it, look for a website on the Seed Vault. Maybe there are pictures, or better yet, a floorplan so we can try to have some direction when we get there."

"On it," she said.

"I'll search for any info on why James Conway was involved with the ceremony there back in 2014."

"And I'll yard-dart us into the mountain by the damned vault," Ray said.

I smiled. "Come on, Ray. You like a good challenge. Just pretend this is one of your video games. I'm sure you've accomplished more difficult feats on those."

He grumbled something inaudible.

When we were twenty minutes out, I was able to connect to the internet.

"I'm in, Heather. You should be able to as well."

A moment later, she said, "Got it. Their website says the Seed Vault's purpose is to 'offer free, safe and long-term storage of seed duplications from all gene banks and nations participating in the global community's joint effort to ensure the world's future food supply.'"

"Great, but we don't really care about their purpose, we need to navigate the damned place. Is there a floorplan or anything?" I asked.

"Hang on." She pecked away in rapid fire on her phone. "Oh boy, yeah, there's some detailed photos—jeez, this place looks like a serious end-of-the-world concrete bunker set into the side of a snow-packed mountain."

"I told you so," Ray said.

"What about inside?"

"Yeah, hang on." She scrolled. "There are three chambers that look like concrete bomb shelters with rows and rows of racks that are three levels high. Each one's stacked with crates that must contain the different types of seeds. Looks like Fort Knox in there, and cold."

"What do you mean cold?" Ray asked.

"The pictures of people inside are dressed like it's a deep freeze. There's a long tunnel that must go deep into the ground." She paused. "Damned place looks impenetrable."

"Don't worry," Ray said. "Lenny's picking up some tin snips and scissors, no problem."

"Cut the sarcasm, okay, Ray?" I said. "Is there any detail on what's in the three chambers? Like where specific country's deposits are located?"

"Hold on," she said. "There's a virtual docent, but I can't hear what she's saying." She paused. "I can click on each chamber, and if you click on a box, it lists what country has deposits in there, not that that will help us."

"Why do you say that?" I asked.

"I'm telling you, there's hundreds if not thousands of crates per chamber!"

"You're not being helpful, Heather," I said. "Give me your phone—"

"No, you're supposed to find out why the duke was there—holy crap."

"Now what?"

"I found a map. This thing is right out of a James Bond movie. It shows the entrance, which is a triangular concrete structure at the above-ground portal, and then a long tunnel going deep into the rock. There are pictures of each section, and the passageway looks like it's from

Battlestar Galactica—a round tunnel with a metal grating with long tubes along its ceiling. It's gotta be a hundred yards long and there are literally vault doors at the end before you get into some kind of pre-chamber, then more metal doors leading into each of the three vaults."

"Piece of cake," Ray said.

"Ray, stop it!" I said.

"Call Lenny back and tell him to bring dynamite," Heather said.

I inhaled a deep breath, held it for a moment and then exhaled. "What kind of locks are on the chamber doors or inside the tunnel?" I asked.

"Let me zoom in." She paused. "Wait, there are no locks, they're just big heavy, metal doors."

"See?" I said. "You guys are so negative. They're probably just airtight so the seeds aren't compromised."

"Okay, Mr. Optimism, what did you find on Duke Douchebag?" Heather asked.

"I found an article, but I've been listening to you, so let me read it."

"We're ten minutes out from the airport and the mountainside bunker," Ray said.

"The article's about the event where the duke and Freddy were captured in the photo. There's no mention of Freddy or the canister, but what it said about the duke is explanatory enough. Says here that 'the United Kingdom was represented by the Duke of Oxford, James Conway, a relative of the first man to cross the Spitsbergen archipelago, Sir Martin Conway, to deposit 101 seed samples from eighteen different crop species, among these onions, lettuce, carrots, and different kinds of brassicas.' That's pretty much it."

"So is your hypothesis that he stashed the canister in with the carrots?" Ray asked.

"Harry said that the instructions to Freddy were to hide the canister in a place that wouldn't be discovered until a date in the distant future, or at a time it wouldn't matter anymore," I said.

"What better place than a doomsday seed vault?" Ray said. "Post-Armageddon, nobody will care about silly power-sharing agreements between bigshot families or treasure maps. They'll be trying to grow onions and cabbages to survive."

I glared at him, irritated by his attitude, but he was right.

"That's right, Ray. Makes sense."

We were flying low to stay under the radar, and Longyearbyen had been growing closer on the horizon. The runway of the airport was now visible ahead. I couldn't quite make out the Seed Vault yet, but based on what I recalled, it was just above the eastern end of the runway. Ray was right, the mountain it was situated on looked steep.

Crap.

"You see what I see?" Ray asked.

"Yeah, make a pass and see if there's any place to land."

"No planes on the radar," Ray said.

"We've got that going for us," Heather said.

I bit my tongue.

We closed the distance quickly and the Seed Vault had turquoise prisms of glass that illuminated its roof. The structure itself was quite narrow, but per Heather's description, that was only the entryway that led to a long tunnel that had been cut deep into the earth. Ray circled around it, and it was indeed positioned on a steep mountainside, but the road that led up to it was long and flat. There was a car in the parking area a couple of hundred yards away.

"Could Lenny be here already?" I asked.

"Either that or maybe security," Heather said.

Security, good grief. I felt the bulge in my pants pocket and was glad I'd grabbed Liam's gun before we fled the boat.

"That service road looks doable, what do you think?" I said.

Ray craned his head to peer out his window.

"Maybe."

"The Pilatus is a short takeoff and landing plane, right? We should be fine."

"And there's a perfectly good airport just over there." Ray pointed to the big runway a quarter mile away.

"No time for that. C'mon, Ray, you got this."

"Shit," he said. "Buckle in tight and hang on."

He vectored the Pilatus on its left wing and carved a tight circle while descending toward the Seed Vault's concrete entry. There was another brown building adjacent to it that looked like it held offices and maybe an air filtration system, but it was nearly two in the morning, so there wouldn't be any staff present, aside from security, maybe, but I didn't want to worry my friends.

The lone car, however, was a concern.

The plane straightened out, and just like Ray had professed earlier, we were aimed toward the snow-covered access road like a yard-dart falling toward its target. If we missed, we'd either roll down the hill, or clip a wing on the uphill side, cartwheel and be ripped into tiny pieces.

Heather reached forward and grabbed my arm.

"Are you sure about this?"

I took her hand and squeezed it.

"Hang on, baby!"

28

THE PLANE'S SKIDS TOUCHED DOWN AND BOUNCED OFF THE SNOWPACKED SERVICE ROAD.

I gritted my teeth and hung on as Ray reduced speed further. The plane settled down again on the snow, and then Ray pulled back on the stick, but not enough for the plane to lift off. The wheels had brakes, but if applied too hard on the snow, we could spin out. Ray was patient and let the friction from the snow on the skids slow our momentum.

We continued down the short access road from the parking area toward the Seed Vault.

"Good job, Ray," I said. "I knew you could do it."

"What choice did I have? Our lives depended on it."

Heather patted him on the back.

"Our lives also depend on getting that damned canister," I said.

Ray taxied past the brown building on the left, which I concluded must contain air filtration. He continued to the end of the service road and turned the plane around.

Good idea in case we needed to make a hasty getaway.

Another search of the perimeter didn't reveal anyone from either the brown building or the car in the lot. I realized there was no snow on top of the car, but there was evidence of fresh snow leading up to the vault entry. There were footprints in it.

Could they be Lenny's?

Would he have already broken in to get out of the cold?

That would save us time—

"A van's coming up the hill," Heather said. "It's got a taxi light on top."

"Must be Lenny," Ray said.

Shit.

I glanced back to the entry of the vault and realized there were multiple footprints in the snow. Could Roger have beat us here? Or did he have reinforcements in Svalbard?

The taxi drove all the way over to the plane.

"Heather, you stay inside the plane and be our lookout. Call me if anyone else shows up, or if you see the in-bound helicopter—"

"I'm not staying out here—"

"Please! I'll need Ray and Lenny's help to break-in. You hide here—Roger will be in too much of a hurry to check the plane if he arrives before we leave."

"Fine, I'll stay. Jesus," she said. "Don't treat me like a girl."

"That's not the point." I tried to control my breathing. "After already being kidnapped once, I'm just trying to keep you safe. I'm counting on the tour operator back on the ship to have delayed Roger after he shot at us, so we should have time, but we need to get moving."

Lenny climbed out of the taxi carrying a bag that had handles from the bolt cutters protruding from the top. The taxi driver also got out. Was she going to be a problem?

"Miss the runway?" she asked.

"No." I conjured what I hoped was a warm smile, even though I was still damp and freezing. "We're from Crop Trust. Here to make a surprise inspection."

"Really? This guy said it was some kind of emergency." She nodded toward Lenny.

I cleared my throat. "We treat all surprise inspections like emergencies, part of our protocol." I paused. "Thanks, but you can go now."

"He's not going to need a ride back to town? I don't mind waiting, there's not much work for me at this hour."

"No, he'll be flying out with us."

The taxi driver finally loaded up, backed into a snowbank, turned around, and drove slowly out. Ray climbed out of the plane, and Lenny joined us.

"They say there's no crime in this town," Lenny said. "Until now."

He removed the bolt cutters from the bag along with two black parkas. I pulled one on and handed the other to Heather, who had moved up to the front right seat of the plane.

"Let's get this over with," I said.

I followed the other fresh footprints in the snow that led to the main entrance. It looked like one pair of shoes and one pair of boots. There were cameras on the exterior of the building, and I wondered what security protocols they had in place.

Would motion-sensitive alarms sound, either here or at a remote location?

It was a fifteen-minute drive to town, so even if a car was dispatched immediately, we might just have enough time to get inside and figure this out, and then return to the plane and take off.

Super tight timeline with no margin for error.

The height of the concrete entry was taller than I expected. There were more of the triangular-shaped turquoise glass panels mounted to the top front of the building for art, and they sparkled in the light. The entry feature was quite narrow, maybe ten feet across, just wide enough for two eight-foot-tall, stainless-steel doors.

"Those doors have key locks, man," Lenny said. "These bolt cutters are useless."

"Damn," I said. "Now what?"

Ray reached over and grabbed the long vertical pull bar on the door. "Let's see how strong they feel."

He pulled hard, and the door swung right open, which nearly caused him to fall over.

"Son-of-a-bitch," Lenny said. "Broke into that store for nothing."

"Somebody must be here, guys," I said. "That car, the fresh footprints, and now the doors are unlocked." I scrutinized the two key locks and there was no sign of tampering.

I exhaled hard.

"Let's go see what's going on."

"What if it's the police?" Lenny said.

"Then we're just stupid tourists who can't sleep due to the polar night."

"What if it's Roger or his ilk?" Ray asked.

I didn't want to spook the guys, but we couldn't delay any longer and I needed them to be confident. I opened my coat to reveal the gun in my waistband.

"You gotta a gun?" Lenny asked. "Oh man, we're going to jail for sure now."

"Relax. Emergency, lifesaving purposes only."

"I've never even seen you hold a gun before," Ray said. "You know how to use it?"

"Of course. Look, I don't want to shoot anybody, but these assholes intend to kill us, so I'll use it in self-defense, if need be." I paused. "Now let's go."

I stepped inside. The interior was illuminated with fluorescent tubes in the center of the ceiling, and there was a three-level cable tray suspended to the left side of the lights. Every surface of the entry was a flat, gray concrete. There was a complex fire protection system control box on the wall to the left, and a TV screen showing multiple security monitors in all directions on the outside of the building on the right.

Wait until they checked the recording and saw a plane land out front.

At the end of the corridor, which was maybe thirty yards long, there was another set of stainless-steel metal doors, and a metal stair next to it that led up to a mezzanine that had a ladder to a roof hatch.

"Heather exaggerated what she saw on their website," I said. "She said it was a hundred-yard-long corridor that looked like something out of *Battlestar Galactica*."

We hurried forward to the next set of doors and found a coat rack next to them. There were boots, overalls, and multiple blue work jackets with the Global Seed Vault name and logo on the breast pockets.

"Let's put these on to make ourselves look more official," I said.

"Or more guilty," Lenny said.

Once dressed, I faced the doors. There were two heavy-duty, manual, sliding locks that were also not locked. I pulled them both up and then pulled the door open—it squeaked loudly, which caused me to wince.

My eyes bugged out at what I saw next.

"Crap."

"Here's your hundred-yard tunnel," Ray said. "Looks like a space station or nuclear submarine or something."

"Let's go."

I jogged forward, wary of the time this was taking. Our feet clanked on the metal grating that comprised the floor, and I wondered whether anyone could hear us beyond whatever was behind the next set of doors.

We got through the long tunnel, opened that door and entered a room that had been carved out of the rock. There was an additional fire control panel, fire extinguisher, and the continuous cable trays that were half-full of green wires. There was a square open entryway that did not have any doors, and I realized the doors I'd seen ahead were inside yet another chamber. We stepped through the open doorway, into another chamber that had one set of gray metal doors here.

"This feels like a trap," Ray said.

"A rat trap," Lenny said.

I opened that one and stepped into yet another hollow that was much wider. There were three more doors there, one at the far right, one in the middle, and one on the far left.

"It's the journey to the center of the freaking earth, man," Lenny said.

The door to the far left was propped open and the lights were on inside. I held my finger up to my lips, and then whispered, "Heather had said there were three different vaults that held racks and racks of seeds."

I dug into my pants pocket and pulled out my phone and found the photo of the hand-drawn map I got from the detective in Oslo. I previously thought the diagram looked like three scuba tanks and the one on the left side had an "X" on it but it was a drawing of the three chambers here.

The "X" on the drawing was the same chamber to the far left with the open door.

Now that I held my phone, I realized I should check on Heather.

There was zero cell in here though, of course.

What did I expect inside a bunker?

I waved for the guys to follow me and walked quietly toward the open door. I peeked around the corner and there was yet again another chamber carved out of the rock, and another open door ten feet inside it. Racks were visible inside there.

We walked slowly toward the next open door.

"My heart's beating like a steel drum." Lenny's whisper was a hiss in my ear.

I again held my finger up to my lips.

Voices were audible in the next chamber.

I peered through the door and saw five rows of large warehouse-style racks, each with three shelves and each shelf holding three stacked bins.

In the second aisle on the left, about halfway down, I could make out two men in discussion but couldn't see their faces.

At the close end of the rack, I peered around the corner and my jaw fell open.

Son-of-a-bitch.

I waved to the guys to follow, turned the corner, and was halfway to the two men before they noticed me. One was wearing an official jacket like the ones we had on, and the other was wearing a Saville Row, custom-tailored suit. He spotted me first and his jaw dropped open and he stopped speaking. The other man must have heard us because he also stopped talking and turned to face us.

"I'm sorry," the official said. "The vault is closed, what are you doing here at this hour?"

I ignored him and looked to the one in the suit. "I was just about to ask you the same question, your Grace. Back to collect the canister you and Freddy hid here in the vault? Was that just before you pushed him off the hotel roof in Oslo?"

The official's eyes bulged wide.

The Duke of Oxford's mouth curved into a sneer.

"That is a libelous statement, young man."

In front of them was a blue crate with the lid opened. There was a sticker of the British flag on the lid.

"Thanks for saving us the time to sort through all these boxes," I said. "Of course, if you'd just been honest with me in the first place, we wouldn't have had to take a boat almost to the North Pole, dig up your self-serving time capsule and a man would not have been killed by a polar bear in the process."

"Dear Lord," the official said.

"Shut up, Ingemar," the Duke said. "Had you been able to get me in here yesterday when I arrived, we would have been long gone by now."

"I told you I had important—"

"Shut up, I said!"

The official, who was named Ingemar, crossed his arms.

A lifetime of privilege and using his title to manipulate people and matters to his own self-interest hadn't likely produced many situations where the duke had been spoken to with such candor.

"Who was killed?" he asked. An irritating smile bent his lips. "Sir Harry, perhaps?"

"Strike one, Chompsky. One of the Sect's hoodlums there to guard us. Shame really, but when Grandpa Duke of Argyll finds out it happened needlessly due to your attempt at misdirection, their little Council might not be too happy with you."

The duke rolled his eyes.

I stepped forward. "What's in the box, boys?"

"Just seeds, I'm afraid," the duke said.

"Strike two."

I turned to Ingemar. He was an older gentlemen with round glasses, gray hair and a close-cropped beard.

"Uh, well, um." Ingemar stammered.

"If you don't want to be considered an accomplice to murder, I suggest you step aside," I said.

The man glanced quickly from the duke to me. He took a large stride backward. I took his place and peered into the carton. There were several individually wrapped packages, but sitting on top of all of them was another item that had been wrapped in the same type of packaging, but now lay exposed. It was an old, pewter-colored oblong tube that I saw had another pewter box attached to it on the top, and on that was a keyhole.

"What do have we here?" I asked.

No response.

I picked it up and given what I expected the contents to be, it was heavier than I expected. As I held it closer, I heard a liquid sound splash inside it.

That's not good.

"Does it have water in it?" I asked.

The duke's obnoxious grin returned. "Acid, actually. You see that contraption mounted to the top? It's an old-fashioned security device that if tampered with releases the acid into the canister, thereby destroying the contents." Now he batted his eyelashes coquettishly. "No key, no access."

"We'll see about that," I said.

His smile changed abruptly to a sneer. "That's British property and you will do no such thing."

I glanced at the device's keyhole and saw that it was for an old-fashioned skeleton key. A warm sensation washed over me, and I reached inside my jacket—

The duke raised his hands and stepped back. "There's no need for violence—"

I retrieved the skull key that Lenny and I had found in a secret compartment in my mother's gravestone at Dunfermline Abbey.

"I have the key, because the canister and its contents belong to my family—"

"You have no family, you're a bloody orphan, cast aside like day-old bread."

"And you're an asshole," Lenny said.

I bit my lip. Conway was right on many levels, but hell if I'd allow him to believe he scored a point. I held the key up for him to see and even showed it to the official for good measure. If the contents were destroyed, I'd send it all to my charming grandfather, and blame his blue-blooded compatriot, the Duke of Oxford.

"In my country, possession is nine-tenths of the law," I said. "I have the canister and the key, so the contents are mine."

"Go ahead," the duke said. "Ruin the bloody lot. My understanding is it's your only chance to keep your pathetic little group—including Sir Harry—alive anyway."

I held the key up to the hole and hesitated.

"You sure about this, man?" Lenny asked.

"Don't get acid on yourself," Ray said.

I had the canister in one hand and the key in the other. I slowly placed the key into the hole, and it fit. I glanced around at the other men, and let my gaze fall on his Grace.

I turned the key and there was a loud "click."

Inside, the small box must be spring activated, because it popped open. An ampule of yellow liquid was inside of it, but it remained intact. The small device slid off the top and there was a latch under where it had been, which I twisted and the canister lid opened in half, like an oblong jewelry box.

"Well, well, well, how about that," I said.

Inside there were a few sheets of yellowed paper, or some material serving as paper. I carefully pulled a page out. On top was an ornate, handwritten wording that read: "Alliance between Clan Campbell and Clan Stewart."

"That should make for fun reading," I said.

The next document appeared even older and was made from some type of skin which felt quite fragile. On top of this one was more old-fashioned cursive, but the words were readily legible: "Codicil to the Last Will and Testament of King Robert I."

"I do believe we've found some potentially history-changing documents here. The Council will be thrilled—well, that is if they ever see them," I said.

There was one last page that I expected to be the treasure map. I turned it over.

What?

It was the signature page for the Codicil.

I turned all three pages over again, and there was nothing else.

No treasure map or anything resembling one.

A flash of perspiration preceded an epiphany. Freddy had hidden the key, could he have taken the map for himself?

The duke raised a finger to signal that he had something he wanted to say.

"I daresay that you have no equitable negotiating position with the Council. Your own grandfather, by birth, has given the order for you to be killed, so I doubt very much that he would entertain any overtures directly from you."

I handed the canister to Ray and pumped my index finger to indicate for him to take photos of the documents with his phone.

His Grace continued. "Therefore, I'm willing to act as your intermediary to present the documents and your case to his Grace for exoneration."

"There's nothing for me to be exonerated from, asshole. All I did was be born."

"In exchange," he continued. "I would make the case to join the Council, where I will further defend your right to, er, well, exist." He waved his hand as if it were a trivial quid pro quo.

"I just have to give you the canister and its contents so you can do all that for us?" I asked.

"Absolutely, young man."

I laughed. "The old guard like you thinks you can get away with anything, don't you? Including double-cross and murder—"

There was a flourish by the door and Ray and Lenny jumped aside.

Roger was there and had Heather in front of him.

He had a gun to her head.

"Did I hear you say double-cross and murder?" Roger said. "That's my department."

Oh, shit.

29

"THERE'S NO SEAT AVAILABLE FOR YOU ON THE COUNCIL, YOUR GRACE," Roger said.

Roger had his arm with the cast around Heather's neck and the gun in his other hand pointed at us. Nobody moved and we all just stared at each other for a moment.

"This is getting old, Buck," Heather said.

Lenny laughed out loud. "You can say that again."

Roger loosened his grip on Heather. "I'll release her, but she'll be the first to die if anyone tries anything stupid."

I heard a grunt from the duke. He probably thought that was an acceptable buffer.

Roger pushed Heather toward us and stayed behind her as they came forward.

"I'll take the canister, Reilly," he said.

I took the canister from Ray and handed it to Heather, who was still between us. It was impatience and fatigue on her face now and she looked like anything but a famous cover model. She held it up over her shoulder and Roger plucked it from her grasp and pushed her toward me. I stepped up, took Heather by the arm, and moved her behind me. I wasn't going to do anything further to risk her, or any of my friends' lives.

Roger held the gun in one hand and the canister in the other.

"The Duke of Argyll said that there was an acid-box on top, and that his daughter had stolen the key to unlock both that and the canister," Roger said. "Where'd you find the key?"

"Dunfermline Abbey. Hidden in my mother's gravestone."

"Splendid."

"Bloody Freddy lied to me," his Grace said. "He'd be alive today had he just told the truth."

"So you did kill him?" I asked.

"Disposed of a rodent is a more appropriate summary."

Lenny whistled behind me. "Cold, man."

215

"Is everything still inside?" Roger asked.

"The agreement between the Campbells and Stewarts is there, plus the Codicil to Robert the Bruce's will, but no treasure map," I said.

Roger laughed at that. "You don't know what happened to the treasure map, do you?"

"I'm sorry," I said. "How would I know?"

"We're certain that Harry Greenbaum, your father, kept it after Catherine died. If he'd given them all back at the time, I wouldn't be here to kill you."

He paused and his smile grew wider as my brow buckled in confusion.

"You really are a fool, aren't you, Reilly?" he said.

My stomach churned. "I'm sorry, Roger, what am I missing?"

"Sir Harry found the treasure. How do you think he first became wealthy?"

My jaw dropped open.

What?

Harry?

He'd kept that from me all these years? He may have just dropped the bomb on me about being my birth father, but why had he left out this critical detail when we were on the run for our lives? When Heather was being held captive?

"Guess he didn't mention that, huh?" Roger laughed again. "Nothing more dangerous than a man chasing a title. England's full of them, eh, your Grace?"

The Duke of Oxford cleared his throat. "I have a question, if you don't mind."

"Be my guest," Roger said.

Roger's joviality either meant we were all going to walk away and laugh about this—not likely—or that he was going to kill us and leave us to freeze here in the vault.

"Why the cooperation agreement between the Campbells and Stewarts?"

Roger nodded his head. "A very good question, your Grace, and one of the main reasons the Council exists."

"Do tell us then," the duke said.

216

"It was established to prevent the Campbells from contesting King David II from taking the throne after Robert I passed away. The Campbells were given a guaranty for privilege, money, lands—in fact those where Inveraray Castle are—and an eternity of titles for their clan to continue."

"What's the hitch?" I said. "Why would the Campbells be granted all that? What was the quid pro quo?"

"Always to the point, aren't you, Reilly? But, yes, another logical question. That's best answered by understanding the Codicil itself."

He held up the canister.

"That was my next question," the duke said.

"Royal putz," Lenny said.

"Robert the Bruce failed to have a son with his first wife, Isabella, having only a daughter, named Marjorie. He did have several dalliances, though, as he galivanted around the countryside, but one woman captured his heart, and she gave him his first son."

I swallowed.

"Her name?" the duke asked.

"Catherine Campbell," Roger said. He turned to me. "Not your biological mother, of course, but a distant relative in the same genetic line of Campbells that still continue all the way to the Duke of Argyll."

I felt Heather's hand on my back. "And what did the Codicil to his will state?" she asked.

"Years later, Robert's second wife, Elizabeth de Burgh, produced a son, David, who would ultimately go on to become the next king, David II. Only problem was that David was four years old when his father died. Up until then, Robert had remained steadfastly in love with Catherine, and their son, Alexander was twenty years old by then."

My mouth had gone dry.

"Isn't this juicy," the duke said.

"The Codicil changed Robert I's Last Will and Testament to make Alexander his legal heir to the throne."

All eyes turned toward me.

"And that would have made Buck ..." Ray said.

"A lot has happened in the last 700 years," Roger said. "But had the House of Bruce remained in power, it would have put you in line for the throne."

"Damn," Lenny said. "We're talking serious King Buck shit now."

"The continuity of kings and queens were admittedly serpentine in those earlier centuries, until the House of Stewart assumed power," Roger said. "Which upon David II's death, there was still no male heir, so it went back to Robert I's first daughter, Marjorie, who had married Walter Stewart. Their son, Robert, became King Robert II and began a very long line of Stewarts who reigned for centuries."

Quiet befell the chamber as that history-dump sank in.

"Bottom line is," Lenny said. "Buck's birth mother's family got screwed over."

"You could put it that way," Roger said.

"And all the land and titles and cash behind this cooperation agreement was just hush money to bury Robert the Bruce's desire to have Catherine's son, Alexander, become his heir," Ray said.

A bit dizzy from all that, my gut was getting increasingly knotted up. I didn't like where this was headed. "So what happened to Catherine and Alexander?" I asked.

"Right to the heart of it again, Reilly. I like that about you." He paused. "This takes us to why the Sect was established. The Codicil was never made public because his second wife had hidden it so her son David would become king. Once the agreement between the senior Campbells and Stewarts was established, Catherine and Alexander were murdered. They were the first of many to die over the centuries. The Sect's job ever since has been to ensure the continuity of the monarchy and to prevent any of these sordid little details to become public information."

I tried to swallow, but my mouth was now dust dry.

"What's he mean by that?" Lenny asked.

The duke had slowly moved behind me, out of Roger's line of site.

"He means we'll be the next to die as they can't let this information become public or it could topple kingdoms and create feuds amongst royals around the world," I said.

"You are quick on your feet, lad," Roger said.

"I did what I said I'd do, and you've got the damned canister and documents," I said. "We—I especially—have no interest in any of this crap, so just let us go, and we'll forget all about it."

Roger took a few steps back toward the end of the aisle and raised his gun.

"I'm afraid that's not possible."

30

A METALLIC SOUND CLICKED NEXT TO MY EAR AND HEATHER GASPED.

It was a gun next to my shoulder.

"Not so fast, Roger," the duke said.

I glanced to my right and saw what looked like a .44 magnum revolver pointed at Roger from behind me. The hammer was cocked and ready to go.

The breath froze in my chest—I was a human shield for the duke and that meant Roger would have to shoot through me to get to him. Or, if the duke shot first, my right eardrum would be shattered permanently.

"Drop your bloody gun. And you—" the duke pointed the gun toward Ray who was closest to Roger. "Take the canister back from him."

Roger hesitated but must have recognized that he couldn't shoot us all fast enough not to be shot by the cannon aimed at him. He tossed his gun over toward the door where it clattered on the concrete floor. Ray then stepped forward and took the canister and hurried back to stand behind me, the duke, and Heather. Lenny was frozen in place.

The Seed Vault official's eyes had been so wide at all the goings-on, I wondered if he was in shock. He hadn't said a word in minutes. The duke was alternately pointing the gun at all of us, and I could sense rusty wheels grinding in his narrow, shellacked head.

"I've been thinking here," the duke said. "Planning how to conclude this nasty business we find ourselves in, and I've arrived at a solution."

"This should be good," Heather said.

The duke, who had now stepped toward Roger, had the giant .44 magnum pointed toward him.

"If I kill Roger with this gun," he raised the magnum slightly, "and then use his gun to kill the rest of you, then nobody will ever know about all of this, except me."

"Yo, dude, you got Tourette's or something?" Lenny said. "You're saying all this shit out loud."

"Then," the duke continued, "When I deliver the canister and the news you've all been disposed of, I believe the Council would see things my way, wouldn't they?"

"Why are you doing all this?" I asked.

His eyes became sharp, and a sneer peeled his lips back. "I'm bloody tired of living in a borrowed apartment on an estate where I'm considered a nuisance!"

The duke's voice was shrill, and I could see in his eyes that he'd come unglued.

"This is my destiny, to reclaim my family's prosperity, to have our own bloody estate and further the repute begun by, Sir Martin Conway, here on this barren rock amidst the bloody frozen Arctic."

He whipped his attention toward me. "Yes, I killed that rat, Freddy, after we left here last time because I was furious that he'd hidden the key to that wretched canister—which you obviously found."

"We have a confession," Lenny said.

"Shut up, damn you!" The duke pointed the magnum toward Lenny.

"James, you mustn't hurt anyone," the Seed Vault official said.

"Quiet!"

Roger edged backward toward the end of the rack. I slowly unzipped my blue Seed Vault jacket, and then the parka Lenny had brought me from town. I reached inside and got a grip on Liam's revolver.

The duke noticed that Roger had moved and then pointed his gun toward him.

"You stay right there, boy!"

I smoothly pulled my gun out from the layers of jackets and lifted it to the duke's head as I cocked the hammer.

"Freeze, *lad*," I said.

The duke jumped, the magnum, now pointed over Roger's head, went off—

BOOM!

The sound was so ear shattering, I flinched—Roger took off out the door.

"Stop!" I yelled.

He ignored my shout but since the duke was still holding his gun, I couldn't chase after him. I shoved the barrel of my gun into the duke's bony back and he cringed.

Ray took the magnum from the duke.

"Goodness gracious," the official said. "Has everyone gone mad?"

The duke's gunshot in the rock and concrete chamber was so loud, I could hardly hear what anyone was saying, but everyone's lips were moving at the same time, and they were waving their hands toward me.

Finally, I was able to read Ray's lips. "What about Roger?"

I pulled the canister out of the duke's grasp, shoved it under my arm, and grabbed Heather by the hand.

"Let's get the hell out of here!"

We hurried toward the door, and I realized that Roger must have grabbed his gun as it was no longer on the floor. I slowed my pace—Lenny and Ray crashed into my back.

"What are you doing?" Ray said.

"Roger must've picked his gun back up," I said.

I peered around the corner of the chamber's door that led to the area where all three storage vaults were accessed, and I noticed that the far vault door was askew.

"I think he's in the last chamber. He's either hiding or watching for us to exit so he can come out shooting." I paused. "Lenny, take the duke's .44 magnum and run out to the exit corridor in the middle and stop—"

"Why me?"

"Because you can then provide cover fire from that angle so we can follow. Ray, you and Heather will go next and keep running until you get to the plane and get it started."

"With pleasure."

Lenny inched up next to me and glanced around the corner. "That exit corridor's out in the middle of that damned cavern. I'll have to run straight toward that asshole to get there. What if he shoots me?"

"I'll cover you, plus If he comes out shooting, you shoot back."

His jaw rippled as he clenched his teeth. If this damned experience didn't end all our friendships and my partnership with Ray, then nothing would, but right now, I just wanted to get everyone safely extracted from this damned tomb.

I checked again. The door at the far end was cracked open a couple inches. Roger would have to push it open and take aim at Lenny while he was running, and since he'd be coming toward him, it was an easy shot.

"Ray and Heather, once Lenny's in place, you follow after him," I said. "If Roger sticks his nose out, Lenny and I'll both shoot at him to provide you cover."

Lenny lifted the magnum up and down. "Damned thing's heavy, man."

Heather got herself in a crouched position as if she was about to start a race, and Ray stood behind her.

"On three, Lenny," I said. "One, two, three!"

Lenny leapt into the open space and moved like a wide receiver running a fly route, pointing the gun in front of him as he ran. It took several seconds for him to get to the corridor, but he did so without issue. He stopped and leaned against the rock wall there and glanced from the far door to us, and back.

He gave us a thumbs-up.

"You guys ready?" I said. "Run all the way to the plane. Don't hesitate and don't look back, no matter what happens behind you. If we don't come out in ten minutes, take the plane, and get the hell out of here, okay?"

"No, it's not okay," Heather said. "I'm staying with you—"

"Heather, this is a straight-forward escape plan, please don't complicate it. We've taken too long already."

Whether it was fear or anger that contorted her expression, I wasn't sure, but she leaned down and gave me a hard kiss, then backed up to look me in the eye.

"And you follow right behind us."

"I will, now get ready."

Heather nodded and Ray groaned.

"One, two, three, go!"

Heather sprang forward, followed by Ray, who even though he'd lost a lot of weight in the past several months and had even been working out, was anything but fast. I crouched out in the open space with Liam's gun pointed toward the far door, but again, nothing happened.

Heather and Ray disappeared around the corner and presumably kept going.

Lenny gave me another thumbs-up. I was suddenly worried that if Roger wasn't in the far chamber, could we all be running into a booby trap?

A sound clanked behind me—it was the duke holding a metal pipe over his head ready to crash it down on my skull. I jumped out into the open space, hesitated, glanced toward the duke—but out of the corner of my eye saw movement on the far end—

Roger had pushed the door open—

BOOM! BOOM!

Rock splintered next to my head and I pivoted on my toe and dashed forward toward the exit corridor—

BOOM! BOOM! Lenny returned fire.

His cannon of a pistol sounded like a bazooka.

Roger retreated behind the now perforated door.

Already short of breath, I crashed into the wall next to Lenny.

"Get out of here," I said. "I'll bring up the rear."

Lenny darted around me, gun in hand, and ran up through the open door into the long space-station-looking corridor. I raced after him, but he was younger and faster, so he pulled away.

BOOM! BOOM!

Shots followed me.

The corridor was so long, I felt like a fish in a barrel.

Lenny darted through the door on the far end.

I got to the door—

BOOM!

A searing pain tore through my right shoulder, and it spun me around and down to the metal grating floor where I hit hard.

"Ah, shit!"

A quick glance down the corridor—Roger was running toward me.

Pain ripped through my upper torso, and I wiped a hand across my shoulder. It was bloody but seemed to be high enough not to have hit any organs.

I tried to raise the gun in my right hand, but my arm wouldn't work—my scapula screamed. The bullet must've broken a bone.

I reached over with my left hand and grabbed the gun, but it wobbled as I tried to raise it toward Roger closing in on me—

BOOM!

The cannon blast came from behind me.

Lenny.

Roger dove or fell to the ground.

Lenny crouched next to me and tried to pull me up. Stars shot through my eyes from the pain—I dropped the gun to grab his outstretched hand to balance me.

BOOM!

Roger fired again as Lenny dragged me through the door at the end—he slammed it closed, and we were in the final corridor with the stairwell to the mezzanine, and the door to the outside was up ahead.

"You okay?" Lenny asked.

"It hurts, let's get out of here."

I could hear the plane engine running outside. Then I heard the door behind us squeak open just as we pushed through the final door to the outside, which we dove through, and Lenny again slammed it behind us.

Dizziness overwhelmed me and I fell to the ground—the soft snow broke my fall. My mind reeled and my blood pumped out as I lay face up under the charcoal sky.

A muffled gunshot sounded from inside the vault, and a hole tore through the metal door just over where I lay.

"Buck, get up, man!"

Lenny hurried back over, pulled me upright, and with his arm around me, carried me to the plane.

Heather jumped out upon seeing me struggle to walk and pressed her hand against my shoulder—pain caused lightning bolts to flash behind my eyes—she yelled something, but her words were lost in the engine's run-up.

Lenny let me go and spun back around.

Heather grabbed a hold of me and pulled me to the plane.

I glanced over toward Lenny, who faced the Seed Vault's door.

The door began to swing open—

Lenny raised the cannon.

BOOM! Click.

Lenny put a round right in the door's center and it closed again. Unfortunately, the click that followed meant he was out of ammo.

A helicopter suddenly lifted from behind the Seed Vault and darted around behind us—Roger's chopper. There must not have been an army on board, after all. Just a pilot who didn't want to get into a firefight.

Lenny ran up and gave me a final boost into the plane.

The door wasn't even closed yet when Ray released the brake and pressed the throttle forward. The plane slid smoothly on its skids over the snow, gaining speed, as Lenny, Heather, and I fell into a ball in the second row of seats.

"Ugghh," I grunted.

"You're bleeding everywhere!" Heather's voice was panicked.

I clenched my teeth and peered out the window.

"Can you … do … something … about that?"

The plane bounced on the uneven surface as we gained speed. The parking area with the lone car came up fast on our left and Ray had to use the rudder to steer us away from where the mountain turned sharply upward, which pointed us down toward the airport.

He pulled back on the stick, and we were airborne, but going down the hill not up.

I winced at the pain and saw blood on the seat as Heather clasped my seat belt.

"Hang on everyone!" Ray yelled over the noise of the engine as he banked the plane toward the water, and then over toward the airport, as we continued to descend.

He had us aimed toward the center of the runway.

Big Mama sat ready at the far end of the asphalt strip.

I hoped the old girl would start smooth and fast to get us the hell out of here.

"You're losing a lot of blood," Heather said.

She pulled my jackets open and slid them over my shoulder—

"Oww!"

"Don't be a baby!"

Yaw pushed the plane sideways as we dropped toward the runway, and Ray fought to keep it going aloft and straight.

Heather felt around the wound—I jerked at the pain.

"The bullet entered an inch below the top of your shoulder," she said. "Went clean through, but your collarbone's broken in half and sticking out."

She heaved for a moment and placed her hand over her mouth.

"Don't … puke … on … me."

Dizziness pushed my head back into the seat.

The tail of the plane suddenly shifted in a wind gust just as Ray was about to set it down—he pulled up—got her straight, lifted the skids and pressed the wheels hard against the asphalt.

"None of this'll matter if we don't survive this landing," I said.

The tips of the wheels protruded through the bottom of the skids just enough to catch rubber, which allowed takeoffs and landings on hard surfaces but didn't get in the way on snow.

Lenny still clutched the empty .44 magnum as he scanned the hilltop back toward the Seed Vault. I couldn't help but smile through the pain, and the tears that had welled in my eyes.

"Good job back there, Lenny."

He nodded. "Yeah, man. I love this gun. Bitch'd stop an elephant."

"Or a polar bear."

Ray taxied straight up to Big Mama. The Cessna Citation XLS that had been here when we first arrived was still there.

"We flew here on that," Heather said. "Looked like the same pilot that was in the helicopter."

"My baby always rides in style," I said.

She grimaced and glanced toward Big Mama.

"*Almost* always," she said.

"Big Mama's topped off and ready to roll," Ray said. "Can he travel or do we need to get him to—"

"I'm fine—"

"The pressure's helping to stop the bleeding," Heather said.

Ray killed the engine, hopped out, and jogged over to get our Albatross running. Lenny popped open the rear door on the Pilatus, climbed out and he and Heather helped me down. I held my right arm close to my chest and tried not to move it but was suddenly concerned about the canister.

I felt my left side pocket—nothing.

My breath caught.

I reached around with my left hand and felt a bulge in my right pocket.

Whew.

After all this, I would've hated to have lost our ticket to freedom.

Big Mama's right engine fired up and a blast of black smoke shot out the exhaust.

"Can we go back to Key West now?" Lenny said.

"You'll be in a first-class seat home soon, Lenny, I promise," I said.

He smiled but then the corners of his lips dropped.

"*Soon*, you say?"

"I've got a couple loose ends to wrap up." I grimaced at him.

He shrugged. "Yeah, I guess you do."

31

HEATHER AND I STOOD IN FRONT OF THE MASSIVE DOORS of what could only be described as a castle. My shoulder still ached after the collarbone had been set and the entry and exit wounds from the bullet had been sutured closed. Aside from the broken bone and loss of blood, it had been a relatively clean hit, but that didn't diminish how much it had hurt. A sling now held my arm at a favorable angle, and while it only happened a few days ago, we'd been too busy getting our ducks in a row to allow any downtime to commence the healing process.

I used my left hand to grasp the huge brass knocker and pounded it three times to announce our arrival.

"You ready for this?" Heather asked.

"Ready as I'll ever be," I said.

The door swept open and a man in a gray tuxedo greeted us with raised eyebrows.

"I'm sorry, but visiting hours are over." His pedantic stare lingered. "Can I help you?"

"I'm Buck Reilly and this is Heather Drake. Tell the master of the house we're here."

"That's Heather Drake, ah, Reilly Drake, actually," Heather said. "We were married."

The man bowed, opened the door wider and we stepped inside. He ambled off to deliver the message that guests were here.

"Was that necessary?" I said.

"I just want them to know you're not alone in this. And that we, ah, have history."

"History." I chuckled. "That's an understatement."

The sound of footsteps echoed through the art- and antique-filled two-story entry, and I took a couple of deep breaths to calm my heart. I never imagined this happening, and wished with all my heart that it didn't have to, but when confronted with inescapable facts, the choices were to run and hide or face them head-on. I've always been more of a head-on kind of guy, and in this case, it was the only true option.

The footsteps got louder, and a man appeared from the main corridor. He stopped and studied us for a moment, glanced over his shoulder, held up a hand as if to tell someone to stay back, and then continued toward us. Once he arrived, his gaze lingered for a moment on my shoulder and then let his eyes meet mine. His were steady and unwavering.

Mine simmered in their sockets.

"Mr. Reilly. To what do I owe this honor?" the Duke of Argyll asked.

"Honor, is it?"

"As I recall, you were in some kind of race against time to find the documents your birth father had given away." He paused. "I'm surprised to see you here."

I bit my tongue. Heather held a straight face. We'd discussed it in advance, and I'd emphasized it was important to handle the meeting delicately as his reaction could confirm our suspicions or keep us wondering.

I reached into the top of my sling—the duke stepped back as if I was grabbing a weapon.

That in itself was a tell.

I pulled out rolled-up photocopies and handed them over.

"What you now have in your hands are copies of the conspiracy between the Campbell and Stewart clans, dated in the late 1300s, along with the Codicil to Robert the Bruce's Last Will and Testament, from the 1320s, that had named Alexander Campbell, your forefather, the king's rightful heir to the Scottish throne."

Colin Campbell, the duke, or my grandfather, take your pick, briefly opened the folded papers, shuffled through them, and then folded them back in half. He expertly maintained a blank expression, even though his eyes wavered slightly.

"My lawyer has the originals in a safe place, with digital copies prepared for distribution to every major British and international news agency, should you not agree to my terms," I said.

His eyes blinked rapidly a few times, and his jaw clenched, but he otherwise held a blank stare into my eyes.

"You can report the situation to the others on the Council, and of my demand that the Sect must immediately cease to follow, threaten, or harass me and my friends, or the documents will be shotgunned to the press, with your name as the contact person for questions."

His nose began to twitch.

Men accustomed to great power do not readily accept adverse terms. They're far more accustomed to dictating them.

I held my tongue, waited, and watched.

The duke finally licked his lips.

"What about the treasure map?"

Bingo.

My heart fluttered and Heather shuffled her feet.

"Your goon, Roger, had a theory on what had happened to that, and frankly, I don't give a damn."

"Roger's in the hospital in Svalbard until he stabilizes and can be transferred to Oslo for surgery. He suffered from a rather nasty gunshot wound—in addition to his broken arm, I'm afraid, and hasn't been able to communicate."

"So sorry to hear that."

My smile conveyed my true feelings.

The duke's eyes hardened.

"I don't want anything from you, aside from you calling off your ancient bloodhounds and leaving us to live our lives in peace." I let that sink in. "Otherwise, aside from releasing the documents, I believe we've established ourselves as formidable opponents that you'd be better off to leave alone. Otherwise, next time we'll go on the offensive."

His eyebrows lifted higher.

We stared at each other.

Heather gave me a slight nudge on my slinged arm which made me flinch in pain.

"Oh, and I want the picture of my mother that's on the piano in that ghastly study of yours."

The duke inhaled a deep breath, held it, and then let it out slowly. He considered me, up and down, and it wasn't lost on me, or I assumed him, that we were the same height, had similar bone structures in our faces and very similar builds, albeit being forty years apart in age. He glanced over his shoulder and nodded to someone that was out of my line of sight.

"What if you're lying about the map that had accompanied the Codicil?" he asked.

"I'm not, and if Roger's correct, then you already know that. But in any case, you know where to find me. You can come yourself or send your henchmen to Key West. I'll be ready."

We stood appraising each other in silence a moment longer. Then the duchess strode into the room holding the photograph I'd demanded. Like her husband, she was quite sharp for her age, and I had no doubt she was eyeballs-deep in the Council with him.

She handed the framed photograph to the duke, and then turned her steely gaze to me, then Heather, and back to me again. There was no emotion, empathy, or curiosity in either of their eyes. They'd clearly written me off before I was even born, which was fine with me, but admittedly, it did sting.

How people could be so cold was beyond me.

"Had things gone differently, and Catherine not died, you would have been the next Duke of Argyll," Colin said.

I cringed. "You know what they say, things happen for a reason. And regardless of all this—" I swung my good arm wide. "I wouldn't change a thing."

Colin cleared his throat. "Alright then," the duke said. "We have an agreement."

I felt like saying just like the Campbells and the Stewarts had done 700 years ago but held my tongue.

He extended his right hand, and then glanced at my sling, so he switched to his left hand. I gave him as firm a grasp as I could, then he handed me the photograph, which I couldn't bring myself to look at.

The duchess nodded to me, and while I sensed she leaned forward, her feet remained planted solidly on the ancient rug that was as large as my entire suite at the La Concha in Key West. Heather and I returned their nods and turned to leave.

The butler appeared and opened the door for us.

No goodbyes, good lucks or safe travels …

Once outside, I let out a long breath.

Heather snuggled up to my side and grabbed my hand as we walked up the long gravel path that had wide swaths of green grass on each side, and then turned to find our car in the large lot to the side of the castle.

"You okay?" she asked.

"That was surreal, but, yeah, I'm fine."

Heather drove the rented Range Rover into town and past the Inveraray Inn.

"Still wish we could stay there sometime," she said.

"We won't be back."

We continued past and drove to the pier on the point. Big Mama was tied up at the end, where she rested in the flat water of Loch Fyne. There was a crowd of people on the pier checking her out. Heather parked and we got out.

Ray started the left engine, and moments later, the right one spun to life. A murmur passed through the crowd as Heather and I approached.

"Be kind to your subjects, King Buck," she said.

"Very funny."

"Almost time to go home."

"One last stop," I said.

Ray opened the rear hatch from inside the plane and lowered the ladder. I felt relief at the meeting with the Campbells being over and was already overcome by the dread of the next one, but it had to be done.

Heather climbed aboard first, and once I struggled up using one hand, I turned around to find the strangest thing. The crowd waved to me, to us.

It was that image I chose to remember about Inveraray.

The turrets of the duke's castle were visible high above the tree line.

I shook my head and closed the hatch.

"Goodbye, Scotland."

32

HEATHER DROVE ME TO HAMPSHIRE MANOR FROM COTSWOLD AIRPORT. The charming village, stone walls and rich umbers and greens of the countryside flashed past in a blur. My thoughts, however, were focused inward. My history with Harry had run the length of my entire life, and as I'd learned recently, had begun with my conception. He'd been an old family friend, investor, advisor, and after my parents were killed, a paternal mentor. His confidence in me, encouragement and even risking, making, and losing millions by supporting us at e-Antiquity, had always meant the world to me. After my parents—my adopted parents, that is—of all the people I'd ever known in my life, Harry had been held in my absolute highest regard.

Until the epiphanies of this past week.

Now it was all different, muddled, confused and very potentially, changed beyond all repair. Could we reset our relationship now that most if not all the cards had finally been placed on the table?

It would depend on what happened next.

We arrived at the half-mile-long gravel driveway that ran through a forest of spring foliage and sentinel-straight conifers that reached to the heavens with their shoulders stooped from decades at attention. We emerged from the woodlands and followed the drive along the large lake where Harry's massive estate, Hampshire Manor, reflected at the far end like a mirage. White swans swam away from the estate, distorting the reflection, which like a delusion, was either real or a figment of fantasy.

She parked the Rover near the front door, next to the burgundy Rolls Royce that Harry had owned as long as I could remember. Past the symbol of wealth, aristocracy, and British history was the entry portico. My heart skipped when I saw Harry standing there, dressed in a gray flannel suit, his hands clasped on top of his ample belly, waiting for me.

His son.

"Here we go again," Heather said.

"This is different," I said.

She squeezed my right quad. "Whatever happens, just know I'm here for you."

I turned to look into her eyes. Our relationship had certainly been complicated over the years, but in the end, she'd become a stalwart supporter, friend, lover, nurse, and partner. A rush of emotion caused me to reach for the door handle with my good arm. My feet dropped onto the gravel, and I practiced deep breathing as I rounded the vehicle and met her there. She looped her right arm through my left one and our feet crunched through the brown pea gravel as we walked toward Harry, who stood erect with his expression as inscrutable as a sphinx.

"Buck, Heather, so very glad to see you."

Harry studied my slinged arm briefly, then held his arm out to the side. "Come, let's go inside."

We entered his vast foyer, and staff were lined up on both sides, nodding to us as we passed. My eyes focused straight ahead, assuming we were headed to Harry's immense study.

Percy was at the end of the line. "Master Buck, Ms. Heather, can I get you anything?"

"No thanks, Percy," I said.

I entered the study to find the fire blazing in the hearth, a third leather chair now placed in a semi-circle with a round table in the middle, which was set for a meal. I heard Harry issue subtle orders behind us as I chose to sit in his worn chair, which was farthest from the fire. The discussion would have me sweating enough without assistance, and I wanted to throw him off his game from the outset. Heather sat to my right, which left Harry to sit closest to the flames.

Perfect.

More deep breathing as Harry poured brown liquid into three snifters, carried them on a tray, and placed them on the table before sitting down in the stiff chair.

"Thank you for letting me know you were successful—I had no doubts," he said. "I want to hear all about it." He reached down and took a sip from a snifter. "Please start with what happened to your arm."

"I was shot. A couple inches to the left and it could have broken my neck."

"Dear God. How awful."

Heather reached over and placed her hand on mine. "I'd never been more scared in my life."

"I can't imagine." He paused. "So you were there too?"

Heather nodded.

"Heather, Ray, me, and Lenny, who saved us all with cover fire."

A shiver ran through Harry's stout frame, and he balled his fists to stave it off. His eyes fluttered, and I could tell he was as concerned about this meeting as we were, which is why the truth was all that mattered.

"Where did all this happen?" he asked.

"At the Global Seed Vault in Svalbard."

He sat back in his chair—which let out a squeak in protest.

"His Grace had said the canister was in those islands north of Svalbard—"

"He lied."

"Bastard." Harry humphed.

Another first. In all my years of knowing Harry, that was the first time I'd ever heard him curse.

"I won't replay the entire long, sordid journey, except to say that by the time we figured out he'd placed the canister at the Seed Vault and were able to get there, the duke had beat us to it and nearly got away."

"He was arrested for the murder of Frederick Lassiter when his plane landed in Oslo," Harry said. "Was he the one who shot you?"

"That's good to hear," I said. "No, Roger from the Sect arrived shortly after we did. Let's just say it got more complicated from there." I hesitated. "But Roger also provided clarity to the duke and me which changed the trajectory of the discussion."

"How so?"

"The key I'd found in Dunfermline disarmed the canister's acid-latch…"

His eyes opened a fraction wider at the mention of that. Another detail he hadn't told me about previously.

"Were the documents in good order?"

"They were. We've since made many copies and depending on how the Council responds, we may blast them onto the internet."

Harry's belly jiggled from a deep laugh. "That would be an appropriate response."

Silence fell between us, as if we both knew what must come next.

"Of course the map that had originally accompanied the Codicil was gone," I said.

"Yes, I'm aware," Harry said.

I watched the flames of the fire dance high in the hearth and imagined Harry's temperature must be on the rise. He'd lied to me before saying he thought the map was still in the canister.

"Roger told me that you'd profited from whatever map had been in the canister, and that had become the launchpad for your financial success. He stated that unequivocally in the Seed Vault, just before he shot me."

Harry squirmed momentarily in his chair, coughed into his fist and then cleared his throat. "That is, ah, somewhat true. I had already had some success, on a far smaller scale, before I met your mother, but after she died suddenly and you had been adopted by the Reillys, I needed something to help me dig out of the pit of despair I'd collapsed into."

I waited. Harry licked his lips.

"As I already told you, I gave the canister and the skeleton key to Frederick for safekeeping as leverage to protect myself from the Sect. Meanwhile, I'd kept the map, which was quite inexplicit, but gave me something to pursue to take my mind off the disintegration of my family."

"So you went treasure hunting."

"Indeed." Harry smiled briefly. "Where do you think you inherited your archeological skills from?"

I frowned, and Harry's smile faded.

"There was just enough information for me to deduce that Robert the Bruce had hidden something of great value near the former location of Dunskellie Castle in East Dumfries and Galloway," Harry said. "Back then, Dunskellie belonged to Sir William Irving, who happened to be Robert's standard-bearer at the Battle of Bannockburn, but it was years before that when Robert had met your mother's distant—"

"I know all about the cooperation agreement between the Campbells and Stewarts, and even the codicil," I said. "What'd you find?"

"Allow me to at least provide the context behind all that. Robert had suffered a battlefield loss in 1306 and was forced into hiding. He spent three months in a cave near Dunskellie, which is where he met Catherine Campbell and fell madly in love with her. They were inseparable, and seven months later, she gave Robert his first son, albeit an illegitimate one."

"I know he sought to make Alexander, her son, his rightful heir to the throne and that the powers that be after his death didn't want to lose power, so they had Catherine and her son killed," I said.

"Quite."

"So, what did you find there?"

"Not there but based on cryptic notes and references on the map, I found an amazing cache that Robert had hidden for Catherine and Alexander near the Kirtle Water, or river, as you would call it, several years later."

"What was—"

"There were 10,000 special coins that Robert had minted with Alexander's face on them to become currency after his illegitimate son's coronation." He paused. "Needless to say they were never placed into circulation so appeared brand new when I found them."

I inhaled a deep breath. As an archeologist, I imagined that would have been very valuable.

"I've never heard of the existence of these coins, or seen a copy," I said. "What did you do with them?"

"They have never seen the light of day due to fears of the Sect," Harry said. "I sold them to a private investor in 1990 for the sum of 10,000,000 British pounds."

I absorbed the information but rather than admiration, I felt a surge of anger.

"The Campbells and even the Stewarts must've searched for the cache previously," I said.

"Of course, but without success. Suffice it to say they would have killed to keep the coins and information a secret."

"I know," I said. "They've been trying to kill me—all of us—for days now."

"I'm dreadfully sorry about that, Buck. You must believe me."

"Why didn't you tell them, so the situation would've vaporized years ago?"

Harry exhaled hard. "I had no choice. I was under confidentiality from the buyer—"

"Is that agreement more valuable than my life—"

"—who is also a titled individual who would have been murdered by the Sect—"

"So his life is more valuable than mine? Or Heather's? Or our friends?"

Harry sat forward. "By letting them believe there was a chance that the treasure was still out there, it kept them more focused on finding it than on revenge," he said.

"Until you outed me as your biological son and they decided to kill me—or use us to find the bloody canister—"

"As you said, they always suspected that I had somehow monetized the map, but never had proof—"

"Why didn't you tell *me*!"

"I knew you had the capabilities to find out what Frederick had done with the canister but had no idea that he and that buffoon James Conway had placed it in the Seed Vault—quite brilliant actually—and with the cooperation agreement and codicil in hand, you could do as I had done and leverage them to leave you—all of us—alone."

I sat back in Harry's chair. My eyes were fixed on his, and my teeth clenched tighter and tighter.

"So you put us all at risk and used us to unwittingly negotiate a settlement? After you'd already found the coins decades ago and sold them for 10,000,000—"

"I'll write you a check for all of that right now—"

"I don't want your money, Harry!" My mouth hung open. "You've lied to me in more ways than I can count—"

"I never lied—"

"Omission is another form of lying, whether you want to own up to it, or not."

Harry raised both his hands. "I never wanted any of this to happen. I had no idea the Sect still harbored the grudge—"

"They were established to protect the monarchy and preserve their version of history—and their first order of business was to kill Catherine and Alexander over the same damned issue. You think they just forgot about it?"

Harry jumped up—which for a man his size was no small feat—and paced around the room. Heather gave me a sympathetic look and held her hands up as if to say calm down.

Fat chance.

Harry circled back around and stood next to the chair by the fire, his hands grasped like in prayer. "I know this all feels and looks bad from your perspective, but that was not intended. I tried to prevent you from going to Scotland and had refused to tell you Catherine's last name—"

"But you didn't tell me why."

I now stood up, but not to pace. I walked toward the door.

"I don't know how to feel about all this, Harry, but it isn't good."

"I'm sorry the omission put you in danger. I'm sorry you were shot—"

"And stabbed in the back."

"—But I'm not sorry for Catherine's family. They treated her and me like rubbish. Aside from seeking a way to move beyond my despair, I wanted to succeed where they had failed and have power over them." Harry smashed the bottom of his fist into his other open palm. "All our lives could have been different if they hadn't rejected me and sent her into virtual exile."

I studied him for a long couple of seconds. My gut said his revenge on her family was an even greater reward than finding Robert the Bruce's cache, and by my finding the canister and threatening them with exposing the near-millennium-long conspiracy, was another turn of the knife in his feud with the Campbells.

And that made my skin crawl.

In three long strides I made it to the door, took the handle and turned back toward Harry. "Don't call me, Harry. I'm done."

I pulled the door open, and stormed out of the room, down the hall, through the immense foyer and out the main entrance. My feet stomped through the gravel, and I arrived at the Range Rover, but the doors were locked.

Heather had the key.

I stood awkwardly and waited for her to appear.

And when she didn't, I tried the car door again.

No luck.

Dammit!

I walked to the foot of the lake and peered into the brown depths of despair. The breeze made my reflection surreal, like I was staring into a carnival mirror.

I heard a sound behind me and turned to see Heather approach, so I rushed back to the Rover and waited for her to unlock the doors. Once inside, I held my hands up.

"What the hell were you doing?"

"I needed to use the restroom." She paused, her eyes focused on mine. "You're awfully hard on Harry. He did lose his wife and his son over all this, plus was tortured and has lived in fear for decades."

My earlier recognition that I had indeed been hard on Harry was tempered by his decision to selectively share information while the rest of us struggled for our lives. I pressed my lips together, too drained to discuss it any further. Harry may have lived this for decades, but I'd had to absorb it all, confront and outwit my biological grandparents and find the damned canister all in the last week, so was totally spent.

Heather started the Rover. "We need to get moving. It's a long trip back to London, and Lenny's and my flight leaves in a few hours."

Ugh, I groaned. It would take three days for Ray and me to fly Big Mama home.

But right now I just wanted to get out of here, away from the United Kingdom, the Council, the Sect, the Campbells, and even Harry Greenbaum.

Key West was my beacon for hope, solace, and solitude.

Once again.

"Let's go," I said.

EPILOGUE

A MONTH HAD PASSED SINCE RAY AND I RETURNED TO KEY WEST. I'd never appreciated my island home more but given that my long-term deal at the La Concha Hotel had been arranged by Harry, who was a minority partner in the ownership syndicate, I'd resolved that it was time to find a new home on the island. I'd been looking, had some good prospects, but still hadn't pulled the trigger.

As I'd requested, Harry had not called, and my sentiments hadn't softened, especially after filling Ray and Lenny in on the danger we'd suffered having been partially the result of Harry's manipulations and lust for revenge against his former in-laws.

The vacuum of our relationship had left an empty feeling inside me that rivaled the loss of my parents who had raised me, and I'd not been very good company since getting home. Heather, while empathetic, had been busy with modeling assignments in New York City, so I hadn't seen her since we parted ways at Heathrow Airport in London. As a result, I'd wallowed in self-pity for most of the last month and had lost myself flying charters aboard the different planes in our fleet of antique Grumman amphibians.

They say time heals all wounds, but time moves slowly, so I'd been accelerating it with Pilar rum. The good news was that the Sect had also been quiet. For weeks I expected to see Roger around every corner, but my threats held them at bay. At least for now.

I checked my ancient Rolex Submariner and saw that it was 5:30 p.m. It was Thursday, so I was going to grab a quick bite and then head to "open-mic, no-mic" at Andy's Cabana to see some of my favorite local musicians play when my cell phone rang.

The screen lit up with Ray Floyd's name.

"Hey, what's up?" I said.

"Something strange," Ray said. "Can you get over here, ASAP?"

I grabbed the keys to my old Land Rover off the table as I headed for the door.

"On my way."

Tourist season hadn't kicked in yet, so traffic was mild. Ray's ambiguous statement had me curious and I wished I'd asked him for details, but even though my shoulder had healed, it was hard to drive the ancient four-speed vehicle with no power brakes or power steering and talk on the phone, so I concentrated on the road. The top was off, and the rush of wind, blur of palm trees and bougainvillea led me past Smather's Beach and up the newly proclaimed Jimmy Buffett Memorial Highway, or A1A, past Fort East Martello Museum to the airport.

The construction of the new terminal was almost complete, and the result would be even more flights and people coming to enjoy the Conch Republic, but who was I to complain. I'd relocated here a decade ago, and the change I'd seen in that time was noteworthy, but that's what happens to popular destinations. You just had to look a little harder to find the soul of the island that brought you there in the first place.

I parked and hurried through the private aviation terminal, out onto the tarmac and a few hangars down until I reached the Last Resort Charter and Salvage sign that marked ours. I pulled the door open, and Ray was on his cell phone, but hung up when I entered.

"What's going on?" I said.

"It's one of our planes," he said. "Come see."

I followed Ray outside, who moved at a far faster pace than usual. Each step increased my trepidation as I feared the worst. Our cash reserves were low, and charters alone would not keep us afloat for much longer, so the pressure was mounting to get back to more lucrative pursuits. If one of our planes had developed serious problems, that would be a major issue.

Betty, our Widgeon, was ahead, and she looked fine. The Beast, our Goose, was next to her, and she was buttoned up tight, so no visible issues there. Big Mama, the Albatross, towered over them both, and we'd just flown her over 5,000 miles back from Europe without problem, so I couldn't imagine anything was wrong with her.

Ray walked past all of them and then glanced over his shoulder with a goofy smile on his face.

"Where are you going?"

He stopped next to an older Gulfstream jet, a G450, and raised his eyebrows.

"What, Ray?"

I then noticed the logo for Last Resort on the tail of the plane, along with the same blue and orange stripes that Big Mama had on her fuselage.

My jaw dropped open.

"It's Harry's old plane," Ray said. "I remember admiring it at Cotswold Airport."

His eyes were wider than those of a child's on Christmas morning. My mind rewound to my last meeting with Harry at Hampshire Manor when I stormed outside vowing to never speak with him again. I thought harder and remembered having to wait by the lake because I couldn't get in the Rover since Heather had to go to the ...

"Heather, dammit."

THE END

ABOUT THE AUTHOR

John H. Cunningham is the USA Today bestselling author of the twelve book, Buck Reilly adventure series, which includes Red Right Return, Green to Go, Crystal Blue, Second Chance Gold, Maroon Rising, Free Fall to Black, Silver Goodbye, White Knight, Indigo Abyss, Purple Deceiver, Buried in Orange and Under the Charcoal Sky, along with the alternative ending fiction novel, The Last Raft, and co-author of Graceless and Timeless.

John has either lived in or visited the many locations that populate his novels, and he mixes fact with fiction and often includes real people in the cast of characters. Adhering to the old maxim, "write what you know," John's books have an authenticity and immediacy that have earned loyal followers and strong reviews. John writes stories that concern themselves with the same tensions and issues that affect all of our lives, and his choices for the places and plots that populate his stories include many settings that he loves. John splits his time between New York, Virginia and Key West.

ACKNOWLEDGEMENTS

All books are personal to the author who penned them, and hopefully become personal to readers who connect with the characters and story. Under the Charcoal Sky has been percolating since the beginning of the series when Buck Reilly first learned he was adopted at birth, which is a topic near and dear to my own existence. I too was adopted at birth, and like Buck, became part of a wonderful family along with two siblings and caring parents who provided me with a loving home, education, a strong work ethic and clear convictions of right and wrong. I may not have always "stayed between those lines," but even when I didn't, I recognized the risks I was taking and the ramifications that my actions could result in.

Buck learned who his birth father was quite by accident in Buried in Orange, but in Under the Charcoal Sky, he deliberately set out to learn about his birth mother. While this story was highly dramatized, the nerve wracking, gut wrenching and soul challenging questions that an adoptee is often faced with when making the decision to seek out their birth parents doesn't always produce a "happy ending." Believe me, I know, and now, so does Buck. Frankly, though, I'd say we are in the minority, as many other adoptees I know found satisfactory results to their searches, and I do think it is a worthwhile effort, provided you're sensitive to the feelings of all those involved.

The opportunity to dig deep into the wonderful history of Scotland and create a unique story for Buck was great fun to research and hopefully to read. Combining history with fictional drama and adventure is a staple of literature, and I use that term loosely, because everyone, adopted or not, questions their past, their family history and how we all fit into the world. And, as Buck found out, some stones are better left unturned.

Buried in Orange took place primarily in Italy, but finished in the United Kingdom, and Under the Charcoal Sky picked up literally minutes after

246

the conclusion of that preceding story. That being the case, Buck remained in the UK, and the story took him to other parts of Europe as well, but in the end, he returned to Key West. The series has always been meant to take readers to distant lands, whether in the Caribbean, South America, the Bahamas, Europe or beyond, because like us, Buck is always searching for something, whether in his heart, a lost soul or hidden treasure.

I acknowledge that some readers prefer Caribbean treasure hunts with non-stop action, and I too love to write those stories for Buck, but in a series, or at least this series, the arc of the main characters is spread out over a long period of time. People, circumstances, relationships and story-drivers evolve to hopefully make the entire series experience a journey that takes you, the reader, along for an unpredictable ride. That's my goal, and the last thing I want to do is make every book a swashbuckling formula that is predictable from the first chapter.

As for specifics to the story, most of the history was accurate, aside from the original Catherine Campbell's relationship with Robert I, or the existence of the Sect or Council, which were total figments of my imagination. Clan Campbell has indeed been an important family in Scotland back to Bannockburn and before, and while there is a Duke of Argyll and Inveraray Castle is a real place, their depictions in this story are entirely fictitious. There are 30 dukes in the United Kingdom, not including King Charles, but there is no Duke of Oxford, which again, was a completely fictitious character for the story.

Most of the locations are accurate, including Dunfermline Abbey, Inveraray Castle, and Waddesdon Manor, Longyearbyen, the Seven Islands and the Global Seed Vault, but others, like Hampshire Manor, are fictitious. My intent is always to combine truth with fiction to make the experience as real as possible.

Thank you to many people who contributed to this story, not the least of which include Bill and Linda Klipp who invited my wife, Holly and I to join them on their trip to Amsterdam, Svalbard and the High Arctic, which was an incredible journey that I sought to partially reproduce herein. The Klipps are great friends that we get to spend time with them in Key West, Virginia, Maine and locations to be determined, and we are grateful to have them in our lives.

Terra Incognita Ecotours is a real tour operator who run incredible trips to amazing, remote locations around the world, and the owners, Ged and Teresa Caddick led our tour in Svalbard aboard the *M/S Sjoveien*, which also appeared in this story. Important note, however, none of Terra Incognita's guests have ever been attacked by Polar Bears and their guest's safety is always paramount, so the incidents that took place herein were purely fictional. Other guests noted on the *Sjoveien*, included Ralph (Lee Hopkins) and Ann (Cope), both of whom are renowned wildlife photographers, Nat Geo tour leaders and real people who are extremely knowledgeable, highly accomplished and great fun to be with. Australian Michael (Bancroft) is a real journalist, radio and television personality who was on our trip to the High Arctic, along with his sister, Danielle Loya, both of whom were a pleasure to travel with, as well as being experienced adventure seekers.

Thank you to Carl Grooms for spot-checking aviation details. When I first met Carl, he was the original rum maker for Pilar at the Key West Distillery, but his passion for flying, which started aboard A6's for the US Navy, pulled him away to becoming a seaplane pilot for Tropic Ocean Airways. Aside from flying the Bahamian and Caribbean islands daily, he was racking up hours to achieve his next goal. Carl now flies 747s for Atlas Air, and travels around the world multiple times per month. Carl also suggested the Pilatus PC-6 Turbo Porter as the ideal plane to fly on skids in the Arctic.

Another pilot and beta reader who has been very helpful on the last several books is Dana Vihlen. Thanks for your keen eye and expertise, Dana. Other beta readers included Bill and Linda Klipp, Mary Jones and Fritz Kloepfel, all of whom I greatly appreciate. Thanks also to my friend and fellow author, Nick Harvey, or Brit Nick, as my other Tropical Author friends and I refer to him. Nick is from the United Kingdom, so his input here was greatly appreciated.

Thank you to my friend, Roger Bartlett, the first Coral Reefer Band member, highly accomplished musician and avid reader for also beta reading Charcoal. I'm also working with Roger and several other former and existing Coral Reefer Band members on a documentary that I'm producing and directing called *Occupational Hazard, The Coral Reefers of the 70's*. We are targeting Summer 2025 for the film to be available, and

Roger has been great to work with on that as well. We also co-wrote a song, *Ghosts of Paris*, which he recorded on his latest album, *The Spice of Life*, which is available wherever music is sold.

David Berens once again provided an appropriate and exciting cover. David has done a vast amount of covers, and they're so good you'd think design was all David does, but no, he's another fantastic Tropical Author, and the incoming president of NINC as well.

Thank you to my friends at The Editorial Department, including Ross Browne, Sean Fletcher and David Argabright for keeping the story sharp, and free of mistakes, which is more than I can say for Buck Reilly. Thank you also to Donna Rich for doing a final proof-read before the book was published.

Thank you to Ann-Marie Nieves at GetRed PR, who is both a great friend and one of the best publicists in the business. It is truly an honor to work with you, and I always appreciate your advice and efforts to get exposure for Buck and company.

To my friends and colleagues at Tropical Authors, whom I greatly admire, learn from, aspire to replicate and enjoy swapping ideas and stories with, thanks for all you do for the genre, and for me personally. To access nearly forty other tropical authors, visit www.tropicalauthors.com and see links to their books.

Finally, and most importantly, thank you to my family, including my brother Jim and his wife Mary, my brother Jay and his wife Beth, Ron and Linda Weiner, and most of all to my wife, Holly and my daughters Bailey and Cortney, along with my son-in-law's, Will Prendergast and Scott Powers for their patience, encouragement, support and love. Both of my daughters got married in the past eighteen months, and they wasted no time to expand the brood, so we are extremely excited to welcome multiple granddaughters to the family as well.

If you enjoyed Under the Charcoal Sky, please take a minute to leave a review wherever you bought it. Remember, life is a journey for all of us, including Buck and crew, so who knows where their adventures will go next. Thank you for going along for the ride!

BOOK and MUSIC LINKS: www.jhcunningham.com